Dre...

Dream Lover

KATRINA VINCENZI

BLACK
lace

Black Lace novels are sexual fantasies.
In real life, make sure you practise safe sex.

First published in 1995 by
Black Lace
332 Ladbroke Grove
London
W10 5AH

Copyright © Katrina Vincenzi 1995

Typeset by CentraCet Limited, Cambridge
Printed and bound by Cox & Wyman Ltd, Reading,
Berks

ISBN 0 352 32956 4

Chapter One

Gem, darling, brilliant news! Alexei Racine is directing Vampire Tales! A bolt from the blue as Megalith decided Bob Ryder didn't have enough depth . . . pre-production early Jan as planned! We're off to Barbados . . . have a brilliant holiday in your cosy little hideaway in Brittany! Felice Navidad and all that jazz! Love Sy!

Gemma de la Mare sat at her desk and, incredulously, read the memo for the third time.

Briefly, but unsuccessfully, she tried to divert herself by focusing on petty, irritating details. Sy's annoying habit of addressing her as Gem instead of Gemma; his characteristic mis-use and repetition of the word 'brilliant'; the proliferation of exclamation marks; the coyly outdated holiday greeting – for God's sake, didn't people say Merry Christmas anymore? It was almost as bad as *ciao* . . . and after six months of planning Sy couldn't even get the title of the damn film right. It was 'Tales of the Vampire' not 'Vampire Tales' . . .

It was no use. Disbelief heated to anger, anger swelled to outrage, and outrage boiled to fury. Unthinkingly, she actually gnawed on a perfect

1

fingernail, chipping the impeccable red varnish that complimented her shoes, and raged inwardly.

Alexei Racine was going to direct.

She fiddled nervously with a huge baroque pearl earring and kept chewing on her fingernail, reducing the glistening red surface to a cratered disaster.

Alexei Racine.

They had never met. He was one of the few people she was happy to detest by reputation alone. In the incestuously small world of European film production, he was notorious. A legend. He was an insatiable womaniser. He was gay. He was a sadistic genius. He was strung out on booze and cocaine. He was tyrannically puritan. He was French. He was Russian. He was filthy rich. He lived from film to film.

Only one fact emerged consistently from the gossip.

He was hell to work with.

She had been looking forward to producing for Bob Ryder, a mild, gentle man of unshakeable calm, looking forward to 'Tales of the Vampire', a darkly erotic re-working of an old classic: suddenly, all that loomed ahead was six months of pure torture.

Automatically she began to tidy her desk, align the already rigidly aligned stacks of papers in right angles to the pristine blotter unnecessarily protecting the finish of the ultra-modern hardwood desk.

Alexei Racine.

Merry bloody Christmas, she thought to herself. On auto-pilot, she riffled through the rest of her messages, made three unimportant phone calls and signed various documents, unintentionally authorising three weeks holiday for Jane, her production assistant, and increasing the canteen budget. She only woke from the daze of her fury when she found herself agreeing to an absolutely absurd request from the film crew for a new and utterly unnecessary piece of equipment.

'Shit!' she said aloud, thoroughly unnerved.

Briefly she entertained the notion of calling Sy or Zippo, the studio heads, and just as quickly discarded it. Theoretically, as producer, she held a powerful position, responsible to executives, investors, script-writers and the cast. Theoretically, hers should have been the deciding vote for director. But the power base had been subtly shifting since Megalith, an American investment company, had become involved in Horror, Inc. and was starting to flex its management muscles.

On the verge of shouldering open the door, Jane, paused, eyes round with surprise. For a moment she could have sworn that she heard Gemma, well, swear. An instant later she knew she was mistaken; her boss was, as usual, calm and poised, a vision of chic serenity in a classic navy Chanel suit that matched her eyes, not a hair of that amazing mass of silvery blonde out of place.

'Gemma, hi! I wasn't expecting you in today. Almost everyone's left,' Jane greeted her. 'Coffee, tea or me?'

Gemma smiled briefly at the longstanding joke. Jane was joyously, irrepressibly gay, possibly bi, and a veritable vision of louche sensuality in punk-style black leather and silver, her black hair gelled into spikes, her amazingly long earrings shaped like scimitars.

'Nothing, Jane, thanks. I just came in to tidy my desk and look over a few things.' She looked down at the papers on her desk and noticed the chipped varnish of the fingernail she had been chewing on. She discretely slid it under the memo from Sy.

'So, you got Sy's little bombshell?' said Jane, coming to perch on the edge of the desk. 'What do

3

you think? Alexei Racine! I mean, wow! Did you hear about that French actress in his last film? They say – '

'He's a brilliant director,' Gemma said calmly. 'And I'm sure we'll all find it a challenge working for him.'

'Challenge! Is that what you call understatement? I heard that she'll never – '

'That sort of gossip is meaningless, destructive, and utterly unprofessional,' said Gemma repressively, privately wondering about the fate of the French actress.

'And what about Megalith?' continued Jane, unabashed. 'Who's calling the shots around here anyway now? Don't you think it's kind of weird – '

'No,' said Gemma, glancing at her watch.

'Okay, okay,' said Jane, conceding defeat. She hadn't really expected to get anything out of Gemma, but it was worth a try. 'You're off to Brittany, right? When do you leave?'

'The flight's at noon,' Gemma replied. 'So I'll be off shortly. There's nothing here that can't wait until after the holidays.'

'Speaking of which – ' Jane began, thinking of her memo.

'No,' said Gemma again. 'Sorry, Jane.'

'Oh, well, it was worth a try,' shrugged Jane philosophically. 'Have a great time and *Buon Natale!*'

Gemma sighed. 'Right. *Felice Navidad*, Jane.'

In Paris, Alexei Racine strolled through the Place Pigalle, enjoying the crisp December air, the soft, prim grey light and the contrasting lurid and lewd spectacle of the sex clubs spewing along the boulevard towards the Moulin Rouge gradually rousing themselves for business. If he had been a man who whistled, or hummed, or jocularly fingered the coins in his pocket expressing his pleasure in life, he might

4

well have done all three. Only the faintest trace of a smile hovered on his lips as he savoured his thoughts and the steamy atmosphere of Pigalle.

By day, Pigalle was much like any other square in Paris: shops, cafés, bistros, fast-food joints, even one surprisingly good restaurant on the corner.

With dusk, it changed. Neon lights in pink and green flickered to life, florid, flamboyant signs screaming sex for sale. Dark-skinned men emerged from shadowy entrances, inviting, enticing, hectoring the tourists and passers-by. Life-size illuminated posters of nude men and women in every conceivable combination and position, and a few less likely ones as well, assaulted the senses with a strident insistency.

Racine, an elegant but faintly sinister looking figure in a black wool coat that reached almost to the ground and a soft black hat with a wide brim that shadowed his features, neither blended in nor looked incongruous.

He paused before one of the displays, his attention caught for some unfathomable reason. Before him, a nude woman with black hair stood with her legs spread wide, her pubic hair a thin dark stripe on impossibly white skin. Her breasts were large and round, the nipples brown and jutting. A slender woman with flowing silvery blonde hair was kneeling before her, face buried between her thighs.

Clever photography, he acknowledged, a cut above the usual. There was a sense of motion and rhythm, as though the dark haired woman was almost rocking her hips, clenching her muscles, straining for release. He could almost see the blonde woman's tongue flickering against the slick pink folds.

'You can have them, if you like, after the show,'

5

ventured the Arab standing in the doorway tentatively. 'Costs extra.'

It was the hair, Racine realised, oblivious of the Arab, the flowing stream of silvery blonde hair that caressed the woman's back, came almost to her waist . . . it reminded him of Gemma's hair. For a moment he saw her naked, hair loose, kneeling to another woman at his direction, exploring the soft folds of a woman's flesh with her tongue. It was such an absurdly incongruous image of the icily controlled Gemma de la Mare that he was almost tempted to laugh; instead, he found himself hardening.

Impulsively he thrust a handful of francs at the Arab and pushed aside the swaying dark curtain concealing the entrance. As his eyes adjusted to the light he found himself alone in a small room, the two women sprawled languorously behind a pane of glass. Briefly he wondered if they could see him: some women, he knew, preferred the illusory anonymity of one-way glass, while others enjoyed watching the men who paid to watch them.

As his eyes met those of the woman with dark hair, he knew instinctively that she had seen him. The blonde had her back to him; some unseen gesture prompted her to kneel before the other woman, who had risen to her feet.

Silvery blonde hair brushed the floor as she bent her head to the dark woman's sex and licked aside the thin swathe of dark pubic hair.

He had, he realised, been expecting something different, some bored and mechanical foreplay, some ritualised prelude. This was swift and sure and greedy, almost shocking.

He concentrated on the kneeling woman. In the harsh light her skin seemed impossibly white and her hair was a dazzling stream, catching the light as her head moved back and forth, her tongue, unseen,

6

rhythmically caressing the other woman's flesh. He thought of Gemma and his arousal deepened. He was hard and throbbing now.

And then she moved her head, and for an instant he glimpsed her profile. A tiny snub nose, faintly upturned. Not the clean, pure lines of Gemma's profile. His excitement subsided, and he turned away, faintly disgusted with himself and with Paris. He would leave tonight, he decided.

Quickly he made his way outside, ignoring the Arab's surprised protests.

In her luxurious white and gold flat in Paris' exclusive 16th *arrondissement* Gabrielle de Sevigny sighed with pleasure as she felt her lover's mouth close on her breast. Leo had been late this afternoon, claiming an unexpected business meeting, combined with the ever-present, abominable traffic, but she could never be sure with him. Slowly she was beginning to understand how much her frustration excited him.

She had been wet and ready for him for hours, her body fired by memories of their last night together, hungry for more. And Leo, cool, urbane, exquisitely courteous, had not noticed or had pretended not to notice, had accepted the drink she had unwillingly offered, had chatted amusingly about the latest scandal in government, about mutual acquaintances, about the latest gossip, until she was ready to scream with vexation.

He was the most exciting lover she had ever known.

From the first time he had taken her, roughly, carelessly, urgently, barely concealed by leafy shrubbery at one of her own exclusive garden parties, she had been lost. No other man had so surely, so swiftly, so inevitably understood her body, her cravings, filled and fulfilled her so utterly.

7

Sometimes he was rough, almost brutal, thrusting into her before she was ready, as careless of her pleasure as he would be of a whore's, driving her to a quick frenzy with the sheer violent intensity of his need. Yet he could be gentle, tender, as solicitous as a bridegroom initiating a beloved virgin, endlessly patient, needlessly coaxing a response that had flared at his first touch, making her want to scratch and claw and beg.

Gradually she began dimly to perceive the subtle mastery he had gained over her, began too to understand that his loving tenderness was in its own way as brutal as his savagery, but by then it was too late.

Far, far, too late. Because Gabrielle de Sevigny, pampered, indolent, aristocratic wife of a prominent government Minister, was obsessed.

He was nipping at her flesh now, teeth just grazing the sensitive skin of her areolae, avoiding the jutting peaks of her nipples that had hardened in anticipation of his mouth. Tingling heat was arcing from her breasts to her groin, warming her skin. She was slippery with want, longing for the massive bludgeoning length of him inside her, pounding the pleasure into her, but she knew better than to urge him.

He moved slowly, leisurely, exploring her breasts with his tongue and teeth and hands, still avoiding her nipples, as if he had to accustom her to his touch before daring some act of intimacy. Her breasts were swollen, almost unbearably sensitive, and her labia were swelling in response. She wanted nothing more than his mouth, rough and hungry on her nipples, his prick, swift and hard, thrusting into her, and because he knew it also, he was unspeakably, unbearably gentle.

At long last he let his tongue curl around one

nipple and involuntarily she gasped as the white-hot pleasure snaked through her.

He drew back his head at once. 'Darling, I didn't hurt you, did I?' His black eyes were soft with concern.

She wanted to spit, to scream, drag his head to her breast, claw him to her centre, make him ignite the slow heat that was consuming her into the cleansing fire of orgasm. Wanted to rake her nails down his back, thrust wildly against him, grind herself into him.

'No,' she said, her voice almost level. 'You didn't hurt me.'

His eyes were shining as he bent his head to her other breast.

In the beginning he had been the perfect lover, understanding her needs, her desires, even before she did herself. He had been swift and rough with her before she recognised the want of it, tender and gentle when that was all she craved. Now he was becoming perverse, deliberately denying her, loving her sweetly and slowly while she longed for a rough and frenzied tumbling, or taking her urgently and without finesse when she ached to be caressed for hours.

Perversely, her body quickly learned to relish the paradox, became more responsive, more finely tuned to his, even as she learned to confront a deeper fear.

He was becoming bored with her.

She lay passive and quiescent, her body aflame as he licked her nipple gently, almost tentatively, running his tongue over the hot red point that begged for his teeth. His skilled fingers tormented her other breast, barely grazing the swollen flesh, gently caressing her until a million flickering points of light gathered under her skin.

Slowly, all too slowly, he let one hand drift down

her belly, admire the curve of her hips, pause at her navel uncertainly as though he had never touched her so intimately before. He might have been gentling a nervous horse, not caressing a lover.

Inside she was hot and wet, a throbbing void desperate to be filled, and her groin felt thick and heavy, turgid with want. The merest touch of his fingers against her centre would ignite the flickering heat, make her body spiral out of control. And because he knew it as well as she, he would prolong the pleasure until it was almost painful, prolong the pain until it became ecstasy.

She bit her lip to keep from begging as his fingers brushed through her pubic hair but couldn't stop the instinctive arching of her hips. And then his teeth were hard on her nipple, plucking at the swollen, sensitive flesh, sucking with a hard, insistent pressure close to pain, while his fingers, slow and leisured, sifted through the dense bush of her pubic hair.

She felt the muscles of her belly clench in a sudden spasm of liquid desire as his finger brushed against her clitoris, a touch too light, too fleeting to release the coiling, curling pleasure pooling in her groin. The rough friction of his tongue and teeth against her breast made her ache for the same rhythm against her sex, his mouth harsh and greedy, fingers swift and probing inside her, but his hand had dropped away to idly caress the curve of her hip.

As he shifted against her, she felt the thick heat of his erection against her thigh, and her whole body quivered.

She felt the fluttering begin deep in the pit of her belly, like the frantic beating of thousands of tiny butterfly wings, and knew she was starting to dance on the edge of climax as he fingered her delicately. Her blood turned to lava, molten and fiery, flowing and pooling in her groin and his fingers left a moist, burning trail.

Her inner muscles began to clench, the first small ripples aching for the hard, convulsing length of him.

Finally, sensing that she could wait no longer, he thrust three fingers deep inside her, while another probed the taut skin of her other entrance, and sucked the pulsing bud of pleasure hard between his teeth.

She came at once, her body convulsing as the tingling, electric waves of orgasm rippled through her, consuming her body in a hot flood of release. She arched away from him, wanting nothing more than to lose herself in the mindless bliss of climax, but he kept sucking hard on her, rhythmically palpating her inner walls and twisting his finger in the tight, forbidden channel, over-stimulating her at the height of orgasm so relentlessly that she climaxed again almost immediately.

She screamed aloud as a third, shuddering orgasm thundered through her with the force of a blow and writhed like a wild creature caught in a trap, utterly lost in the searing heat that electrified her body.

He stopped then and lay still, watching her as the spasms of pleasure racked her, and waited until her trembling body subsided, lax and spent, then kissed her softly and rose from the bed.

Her eyes fluttered open. 'Leo, darling, please . . . you haven't come.' Eyes fixed on the hard column of his erection, she held out her arms to him. 'Anywhere, my love, anyway you please.'

Knotting a towel casually around his waist, he looked down and laughed briefly at the sight of his penis jutting out from the soft white folds. 'It's getting late, Gabrielle,' he replied, glancing at the gold Rolex watch on his wrist, and moving toward the bathroom.

'No, no, it's not, Pierre won't be home for hours yet,' she said hastily, trying to keep the pleading from her voice. 'We have all the time in the world.' But her words were drowned in the gush of water from the tub, and she knew he hadn't heard her.

She lay back on the pillows, the languor of afterglow now threaded through with anxiety.

A few minutes later he returned, briskly towelling himself dry. Despite herself, despite the fact that her body was utterly sated, she felt a tingle of desire at his naked body. He was simply the most beautiful man she had ever seen, powerful shoulders tapering to an elegant waist, long, well-muscled legs . . . her gaze shifted to his torso.

He laughed again, seeing the path of her eyes. 'Regretfully, my dear, I was not thinking of Pierre. It's a long drive, and I wanted to be home before dark.'

'A long drive?' she repeated, confused. Leo had a charming town house not far away. 'But, surely – '

'I always spend Christmas at the chateau,' he explained, dressing quickly. 'A family tradition, like the masked ball on New Year's Eve . . . where did I put my socks?'

'Oh,' she replied, a little faintly. She had never been to the ancient Marais family chateau, unfashionably located on the south coast of Brittany rather than deep in the Loire valley. 'A masked ball?'

'A tradition to welcome the New Year,' he said, buttoning up his shirt.

With a start of surprise she realised that she had managed to push the holiday season to the back of her mind, her attention solely focused on their next meeting.

'You can come, if you like,' he added casually. 'Although I imagine it won't be Pierre's sort of party.' He chuckled then, as if at some private joke.

'Of course we'll come, darling,' she replied, wondering what engagements they were already committed to, wondering how to convince or coerce Pierre to go with her. Or, better yet, let her go alone. 'Of course we'll come.'

In one of the soaring skyscrapers that grace Manhattan's skyline, Jay Stone, head of Megalith, was dictating last minute instructions to his secretary. His furious pace didn't seem to perturb her; her pen flew across the short-hand pad like lightning.

'Just a few more things, Annie, while I think of them . . . cancel Donald, but send something nice to his wife, Fabergé, Tiffany's, you decide . . . re-confirm the chalet in Gstaad . . . I need this faxed off to Toyko and make sure you get a reply from Yoshi by noon tomorrow . . . tell John to finalise the takeover bid for Horror, Inc.'

A slight frown crossed her face. She continued recording his instructions with flawless precision but looked over at him, puzzled. He was running his hands through his thick, dark hair, his habit when dictating, and his brown eyes were narrowed in concentration. His passionate intensity, his meticulous attention to detail never failed to impress her; he was almost as exciting in the boardroom as he was in the bedroom and she seldom looked at him without a brief pang of regret for their short-lived affair.

'And I'll want the afternoon Concorde to Paris on the 27th.'

'I thought you were staying in Gstaad,' she interrupted in surprise.

'Leo's New Year's Eve party,' he said, lifting his eyebrows. 'Too tempting to pass up . . . everything else clear?'

She put down her pen and eyed him thoughtfully. 'Everything except your sudden interest in Horror,

13

Inc. The British film industry's dead, Jay, all the action's here.'

'Ah, that's where you're wrong, Annie, haven't you heard about the new renaissance in film in England?' He was smiling now, one eyebrow cocked interrogatively.

'Doomed, and you know it,' Annie replied bluntly. 'Besides, the company's too small to be of much interest to Megalith, or even to you. It just doesn't figure.'

He leaned back in his chair, locking his hands behind his head and gave her a sharp look. 'Perhaps you're right.'

'Why then?'

'A whim?' he offered.

'You don't know the meaning of the word,' she pointed out.

'Well, then let's just say it's a favour for a friend.'

Jean-Paul Forget was standing by the bed in his cottage on the outskirts of Carnac with a whip in his hand. He looked down at his wife Pascaline and smiled. She was lying on her belly spread-eagled before him, wrists and ankles snared to the bedposts, face buried in the pillows, her luxurious red hair streaming over her back.

Her buttocks were taut, milky globes, and he could see the muscles of the inside of her thighs trembling as he let the whip lightly snake over her flesh. Her body arched in response and she moaned deep in her throat.

'Again, Jean-Paul,' she murmured throatily. 'Again.' She squirmed against the bedclothes, finding the delicious, warming friction against her clitoris, loving the blushing ache of the lash against her buttocks. The two sensations seemed to mingle together, spreading the heat throughout her body until it consumed her.

But Jean-Paul was always careful to make her wait, prolonging the exquisite torture with cunning little tricks. Often he would pause and drink a glass of wine as she lay waiting, depriving her of any stimulation except, perhaps, a stray drop or two of Muscadet trickling down her back to the crease of her buttocks. He'd drive her nearly mindless with anticipation as she waited for him to lick her clean and then lash her again.

'There's a light on next door,' he said casually, going over to the window.

'Once more, Jean-Paul, once more,' she ground out, half-hoping that he would deny her.

'Soon, darling, soon,' he promised, drawing the curtain aside. 'Our new neighbour, the English woman. I don't remember her name . . . would you like a glass of wine, my love?'

Pascaline breathed deeply. She was learning to savour the frustration, relish the pain, the thwarted ache in her groin. 'Yes, please. Amethyst, Jade, something ridiculous and English, I think. I never understood why Leo decided to sell to her, did you?'

'Leo must have his reasons,' he shrugged, privately thinking that perhaps it was a little strange. Only a few choice friends had been allowed the privilege of purchasing the neglected old farm buildings that skirted the Chateau Marais. Several miles of forest and grassy meadow lay between the converted cottages and the chateau, dotted with the dolmens characteristic of the area.

'How strange,' Jean-Paul continued, pouring wine and still looking out the window. 'She's gone outside, I can see the torchlight. It looks as though she's making for the forest. I wonder why?'

'I remember now,' said Pascaline, raising her head

15

and sipping wine from the glass he held for her. 'I spoke to her briefly in the summer before we left and she couldn't stop talking about the tumulus, how mysterious and awesome it was, how astonishing that it was private land. She went on and on about the carving in the tomb, the image of the hunter. Perhaps that is why she wanted the cottage . . . but it still doesn't explain why Leo sold to her.'

'Ah, the tomb.' Jean-Paul nodded his understanding. The great, sepulchral mound on the Marais estate was less well known than other prehistoric tumuli in the area, St Michel or le Moustoir, a deliberate policy of Leo's, but unique in that there was a human figure carved on one wall. It was a curious thing, similar to a child's stick figure, an oblique, jutting line extending out from the torso that might have been a spear or a grotesquely enlarged male organ.

It was, perhaps, one of the earliest depictions of the human form in prehistoric art; either that or a Victorian fake. Locals called him 'The Hunter' and folklore endowed him with strange powers . . . not entirely without foundation, thought Jean-Paul, remembering the last visit they had made to the tomb. 'Do you remember, Pascaline, the night we – '

'I remember very well,' she replied, her eyes hot. 'It makes me wet to even think of it . . . Again, Jean-Paul.'

He was hardening himself at the memories. He set down his glass and fingered the whip.

Gemma moved slowly and cautiously through the deep grass of her garden at the back of the cottage which blended almost imperceptibly into the meadow she shared with the other cottages and led to the forest.

Her nervous tension was finally beginning to ease,

and she was starting to lose herself in the haunting stillness of the countryside at night. The sky was a deep, velvetly blue-black and the stars seemed at once closer and brighter. She suddenly felt a deep sense of relief, knowing now how right she had been to impulsively purchase the aged stone cottage.

It freed her in some way she was content not to define. Here she was unknown, anonymous, indeed, could barely speak the language: she could abandon the shackles of her professional life as easily as she had shed Chanel for jeans and the yellowing cashmere pullover she was now wearing.

She had felt elated yet still anxious on the long drive down, and had driven skilfully but far too fast, only enjoying the powerfully responsive engine of the rented black BMW. It had seemed to devour the road effortlessly and for a time she had diverted herself by deliberately speeding, weaving her way through the thick traffic, flashing past the slower moving cars and vans with an almost reckless abandon.

She always drove better when she was speeding, with all of her concentration focused on the road, the shifting pattern of the traffic becoming more a game of control and expertise, rather like chess on the road.

A near miss with an oncoming Citroen had recalled her, but left her mind free to wander. Back to work, back to Alexei Racine. Back to the encroaching presence of Megalith and her future with Horror, Inc.

Now, at last, car unpacked and cottage inspected, all the routine, boring tasks of homecoming accomplished, half a bottle of good Muscadet downed in celebration, she could wander and explore, indulge herself and her strange attraction to this place.

* * *

From a distance he saw the torchlight moving through the meadow and then into the forest, the light weaving through the trees like a maenad's torch, and smiled.

The tomb loomed ahead. She let the torchlight play over it for a moment, then walked slowly down the long, dromos-style tunnel, breathing in the cool, mysterious scent of packed earth and old stone, waiting for her eyes to adjust to the dark. She felt the last of her tension dissipate in the ancient embrace of the tomb, and become replaced by a sense of awe and wonder.

Her steps made no sound on the hard soil of the floor. It was utterly silent, a thick, black, enveloping stillness.

The dim light from the entranceway faded as she reached the vaulted cavern of the inner chamber and she stopped for a moment, reaching out a hand to touch the rough stone wall. It was dry and cool, faintly gritty to the touch.

She lifted the torch and traced the outlines of the primitive carving engraved on the opposite wall, and felt again the strange fascination that had gripped her the first time she had seen it. The figure was stark, almost harsh, yet seemed to emanate a raw power, a vital, vibrant force.

She edged her way inside and leaned back against the wall, breathing deeply and closing her eyes as if she could inhale the atmosphere. She clicked the torch off and let her mind wander back through time, back to the days of the long-dead warrior prince whose image was before her and in whose tomb she was now standing.

Later she was never sure if she had slept or not; the whole encounter was so steeped in the enfolding, mysterious air of the tumulus.

A match flared.

Startled, she turned but had only a brief, confused impression of a man, tall with deep-set eyes, before the flame was extinguished. The acrid smell of sulphur mingled with the rich aroma of tobacco.

'I thought I was alone,' Gemma said, unaccountably dazed and blinking her eyes.

'No,' he replied. His voice seemed strangely distorted by the echoing cavern, somehow rich and metallic at the same time. She felt attracted yet faintly repelled by the sound.

She waited for him to speak again, but he was silent. And as the silence grew and lengthened, she became aware of him as a physical presence more strongly than if he had spoken. A faint tremor of excitement, as shocking as it was unexpected, stirred her. Alone with a stranger, beneath the massive weight of rock and stone, in the thick, dark stillness, before the carved image of the hunter, she felt the first, small glimmerings of arousal. Even as her mind tried to analyse her body's reaction, he spoke again.

'Do you wish to be?' he asked.

'Wish to be?' she repeated, confused.

'Alone.'

In the darkness she could sense his body like a magnet. Her heart began to thud erratically and despite the coolness of the chamber she could feel a faint beading of sweat along her upper lip. When she spoke, her voice sounded strange to her ears.

'No' she said at last.

'Good.'

The silence and the distance between them seemed like some living thing, an almost palpable third presence. She felt at once languorous and aroused, a strange, excited lethargy weighting her limbs and dulling her mind. Vaguely she realised she ought to say something, make some conventional, banal conversational remark such as strangers make on meeting, but somehow there was no need for words.

The excitement between them was unmistakable.

Incredibly her body was already singing in anticipation as he moved closer, every nerve-end alive and tingling. Somehow she knew that he would take her here, on the roughly packed earth floor, in silence and in the darkness, and the very thought was incredibly arousing.

His hands found her unerringly, lightly traced the curves of her body, and then tilted her head to his.

It was a fierce kiss, deep and tonguing, of such annihilating eroticism that her body leapt in response. His tongue washed over her teeth, teasing, tasting, then stabbed the sensitive spot just below her palate with a bruising pressure that fired every nerve and brought tears to her eyes.

She was drowning in him, the feel of his lips, his tongue against hers. Her bones began to melt and her skin to heat as he mastered her mouth, a bruising, ravishing sensual assault that drove every thought from her mind. His mouth was hard but his hands were tantalisingly gentle as they moved over her body, finding the sensitive curves and hollows, pausing to rouse a nipple, testing the curve of her hips.

She clung to him as her knees weakened and trembled, feeling like some fragile creature caught in the force of a gale. Dizzy, lightheaded, almost faint with desire, she wanted the plunging force of his tongue against her sex, the smooth wash of his hands against her bare skin. She needed to feel the vital warmth of his body next to hers even as she relished the heated anticipation his hands and mouth evoked.

The kiss was endless, more passionate, more driving, more intensely exciting than anything she had ever known. He made her mouth come alive, become as sensitively responsive as her clitoris, as ragingly erogenous as her nipples.

It seemed to last forever.

When he finally raised his head, she was breathless.

He stripped the clothes from her body effortlessly. There was no awkwardness, no fumbling; it seemed to her that they fell away at his touch like autumn leaves in a strong wind.

And there were no words.

Perhaps he, as much as she, wanted the silence, the erotic anonymity.

There was something primitively, primally stirring, standing naked in the dark before a stranger, deep in the heart of the tomb where the only true reality was the touch of his mouth, the touch of his hands.

He caressed her gently, large, powerful hands lingering over the column of her throat, slipping down to her shoulders, just grazing the tops of her breasts before sliding down her arms, finding and fingering the sensitive skin of her inner elbow. All her senses were focused on the path of his hands, the rippling warmth they left in their wake.

She could feel her nipples puckering and hardening, the moist heat between her thighs swelling as his hands moved to her waist and traced the curve of her hips, then slid down her legs, discovering the trembling muscles of her inner thighs, the swell of her calves. She knew he was on his knees before her as a warm breath stirred the thick curls between her thighs.

Never an aggressive lover, she was seized by the sudden impulse to tangle her fingers in his hair, draw him to the centre of her body, make him lick, and suck and tongue her to climax; as if he sensed it his hands tightened on her ankles. His grasp was almost painful and she felt a tiny frisson of fear ice

21

her spine. She could sense he was taller than she, and the clasp of his hands made it clear that he was much, much stronger; he could force her, hurt her, perhaps, and she was powerless to prevent it.

And then she felt his mouth move against her belly leaving a trail of soft and delicate kisses, so light and gentle that it seemed he barely touched her skin. If she was prisoner to his hands, she was slave to his mouth, to the unerring skill of his tongue as it danced lightly through her pubic hair and found the swollen pink lips of her sex.

With anyone else, anywhere else, she might have been embarrassed by how wet she was, flooding like a river, but here in the darkness, with a stranger, she discovered a sensual freedom she had never felt before. The bruising grip on her ankles contrasted with the subtle delicacy of his tongue on her vulva, heightening her arousal, mixing a faint pain with the waves of pleasure coursing through her.

He coaxed her clitoris free from its protective flesh with his teeth and she could feel it swelling and engorging, an echoing pulse quivering and rippling through her inner walls. And then he was licking the sensitive nub, from the tiny stem to the trembling head, a rhythmic wash back and forth, back and forth, back and forth until she moaned aloud, feeling the flickering intensity of impending orgasm pool in her groin.

The flesh between her legs was swollen, almost unbearably sensitive. She wanted the burning heat to ignite in the flames of climax; she wanted to stay poised on the edge forever with his tongue on her clitoris, steadily licking and sucking. Her body began to tense, recognising that the next firm wash of his tongue would unleash the flooding heat; it was then that she felt him move to her entrance.

The heat ebbed and she would have cried aloud in

frustration had she not become aware of a new tide of sensation as his tongue probed her, then slipped inside. He kissed her there, the same plunging, driving rhythm he had used on her mouth, and found a spot so achingly, deliciously, wildly sensitive that she was engulfed in a tingling warmth that spread through her body.

And then she did cry aloud, as he flicked his tongue against it again and again and the warmth turned to heat and the heat blazed like wildfire. She was trembling uncontrollably and his hands moved to her waist, one hand holding her hard against his mouth, the other slipping between her buttocks.

She felt his finger slide lower into the slick folds of her labia and then return lingeringly to her other entrance, exploring the vulnerable flesh between the channels of her body. When at last his finger, wet with the musk of her arousal, probed at her secret place, her muscle yielded, she relaxed, and he pushed inside.

His tongue was still thrusting rhythmically inside her, and he used the same twisting stroke in her other entrance. It was as though some mighty, galvanic shock was shuddering through her, electrifying her body, melting her bones. The climax claimed her like a storm, thundering and throbbing through her veins.

Racked with spasms, she sank to the floor, and found his arms around her, easing her to the ground, holding her tightly against the warmth of his body.

'You,' she murmured wonderingly, reaching a hand out to touch his face in the dark. She felt both utterly spent and strangely exalted as the aftershocks of her climax diminished.

He caught her hand and brought her fingers to his mouth, kissing each finger in turn and then sucking harder with a more insistent pressure. Incredibly she felt her body begin to reawaken; her nipples were beginning to peak and the damp flesh between her thighs was growing moist again.

He sucked greedily at each finger, swirling his tongue and nipping at her nails with his teeth, and her breasts swelled in response, begging for the same rough warmth. She was moaning helplessly when he finally found her breasts with his teeth and tongue.

He lipped and nipped and sucked at one breast while pinching the other with his fingers until her nipples were engorged and aching, over-sensitised, stimulated to a point just beyond pain and her whole body was feverish and fervid with want. And still he sucked and sucked, drawing all her body's pleasure into her nipples until she almost screamed . . . until the electric tingling spread from her nipples to her groin and suffused her in a blinding flash.

This time he let the climax claim her utterly, caressing her gently as she writhed in abandon, soothing her heated skin as she throbbed her last and the hot red waves slackened and subsided.

When at last she turned to him, drowsy with pleasure and wanting to explore him in turn, he moved swiftly, pinning her arms above her head and driving into her with sudden force.

Gemma caught her breath at the sudden, numbing thrust. Although she was still wet, her delicate tissues were stretched by the mass of his hard rod. It was as though he filled her utterly and when he began to move she could feel him everywhere, as if he had overpowered the rhythms of her body with his own.

He thrust deep and then withdrew, guiding his penis through the tender pink folds to the curve of her belly and between her breasts, then re-tracing the path with agonising slowness, making the pulse between her legs beat even faster. Again and again he repeated the move, until the silky iron length of him was imprinted on her skin, until her inner muscles were clenching and spasming and she was whimpering in an agony of need.

Still, slowly, relentlessly, he moved himself over her body, kissing her nipples with the tip of his penis, gently probing her belly-button before guiding himself down to the swollen aching flesh between her legs.

When she finally climaxed again, it was so searingly intense, so primitively earthy, so fundamental that she flew from release to sleep in an unbroken flow.

When she woke, she was alone.

Chapter Two

*S*he woke late the next morning, limbs and eyelids heavy.The impulse to snuggle down under the covers, drift with the hazy, drowsily pervasive feeling of well-being was almost overwhelming. She felt like a thick, white cloud or a sea anemone, gently stroked by loving waves, and lazily she stirred beneath the covers . . . but it was no use. The warm, yellow sunlight was playing against her closed lids, coaxing her awake.

As she opened her eyes she experienced a momentary feeling of dislocation at finding herself in a strange place, the low slung eaves of a beamed wooden roof, the rough, whitewashed walls and the small window with painted shutters unaccountably unfamiliar. Then, as consciousness and memory began to return, she smiled to herself. Not her sleek, ultra-modern flat, but a rustic farmhouse; not London, but Brittany.

She stretched sleepily and yawned wonderingly at how stiff she was, puzzled at the unaccustomed ache between her thighs.

And then she remembered.

She had gone for a walk last night . . . gone to the tumulus . . . rediscovered the carved image of the hunter on the wall of the tomb . . . and then . . . her mind snapped shut on the memory. She couldn't recall leaving the tomb and making her way back to the cottage – surely, if it were real, she must have woken and dressed, must have retrieved the torch and found the twisting path that led through the forest to the meadow . . . it was all a blur. She couldn't remember. It was as if she had been sleep-walking. Daydreaming.

Her thoughts writhed and snaked, increasingly convoluted tangles, heated memories of a lover who had taken her to the edge of ecstasy and beyond mixing with the blank, triangular face of the hunter carved on the wall, and his thrusting spear.

Perhaps it was all merely a dream. A dream.

Of course, a dream.

Jane, her production assistant back in London, used to claim nocturnal orgasms in a barely veiled attempt to either discover Gemma's own preferences, or a more blatant sexual come-on, which she had naturally ignored. And when Jane had described in excruciatingly precise detail how she had climaxed in the throes of an erotic dream, she had vaguely envied her. Not necessarily the sensation, but the sheer efficiency of the act.

'Yes, a dream lover,' she said aloud.

That way it all made sense: she had been tired, overworking, upset by the spectre of Alexei Racine. It had been a long drive, and she had drunk some wine as she unpacked. She must have gone up to bed exhausted, and her subconscious had obligingly supplied the perfect female fantasy: wild, wonderful, frenzied, fulfilling sex with a stranger. No words, no commitments, no faked orgasms, just great sex.

'The ultimate zipless fuck,' she giggled aloud,

thinking of Erica Jong. Jane would be shocked; Jane would never know.

Pulling the sheet around her, she got out of bed and went into the small en suite bathroom, where lack of space had forced the plumbers to install the toilet, sink, bidet and bath in the same room, contrary to the perverse French custom. The water ran rusty for a few minutes, but soon a boiling hot stream was pouring forth, and she dropped the sheet and slipped into the tub.

Soaping herself luxuriously with lemon-scented glycerine soap, she glanced down casually at her breasts.

And saw the imprint of his teeth, a perfect red half-moon marring the pale skin.

The visceral, physical memory of his mouth and teeth on her nipple sent a surge of lust snaking through her veins so vivid that she almost fainted.

In his private, luxurious apartments in the east wing of the chateau, Leo Marais was taking breakfast. The table, an aggressively modern sculpture of tortured glass, was covered with Irish linen and heavy silver; five-colour Imari dishes uneasily jostled Sèvres and Wedgewood.

Like the rest of the Chateau Marais, the room was a mélange of tastes and styles, a testament to the whims and impulses of every ancestor since the sixteenth century. Prints by Durer stared disapprovingly at the lush excesses of Titian and the romanticism of Fragonard; Japonnaise marquetry vied with the severe geometry of Mies van der Rohe, in turn at odds with Biedermeier. Masses of fresh-cut flowers, most of them out of season, flowed from classic famille rose jars and Art Nouveau cut-glass. Priceless nineteenth century boxwood and ivory netsuke jostled Fabergé, and Andy Warhol screamed at Renoir.

Unbelievably, every bizarrely incongruous contradiction seemed utterly right; the privileged few admitted into Leo's private apartments never went away without a sense of bewildered wonder at how perfectly a Hockney looked beneath a Stubbs.

Leo sipped thick, pungent coffee from a delicate Sèvres cup and eyed his friend with some amusement.

'I like it,' said Alexei Racine at last, without turning around. Before him on a simple onyx pedestal was a sculpture in white marble about a foot high of a man and a woman locked in an embrace. There was a powerfully erotic sense of movement in the modelled muscles of the male back and legs, the thrusting buttocks, the sinewy tendons of the neck standing out in high relief. It captured man on the brink of orgasm. The woman, however, was obscure, her body almost completely covered by the man with only one perfect breast visible, the nipple a taut peak. Her head was flung back, and her long flowing hair disappeared into the foundation of the sculpture, reappearing to form the man's legs.

'I am so pleased,' returned Leo suavely, lavishly spreading butter on a croissant. 'Your opinion, as ever, reassures me.'

'Rodin, of course,' continued Alexei, moving to one side for a better look.

'Of course,' agreed Leo, placidly reaching for the wild strawberry jam distilled from the chateau's own crop.

'Uncatalogued, I would guess,' Alexei observed, reaching out to caress the pointed nipple. The marble wasn't purely white. He could almost see a pink vein throbbing in the gentle underswell of her breast.

'Mmm.' A tacit admission that the piece had never seen the inside of a reputable auction house and was of dubious provenance.

'I'd give a lot to know how you managed to acquire it . . . and how much you paid,' said Racine, his hand moving to caress the woman's hair.

'Really, my friend.' Leo lifted one eyebrow.

It was an old game between old friends. Both were collectors and connoisseurs; both had the money to indulge their exquisite taste and even their whims. Fortunately their interests were different. Alexei confined his collection mainly to painting and especially Picasso, while Leo was devoted to sculpture. It was the basis of a solid friendship, one that had never been threatened by something both desired equally. But Alexei was behaving strangely this morning.

'Yes, I like it very much,' repeated Racine, still fingering the flowing locks of the woman's hair.

'It complements an early version of "The Kiss" which I was fortunate enough to acquire,' Leo said gently, surprised at his friend's subtle insistence.

'An overrated piece,' said Racine dismissively, reluctantly letting his hand fall to his side. 'Too prim, too repressed. Yet here there is something deeper, more sensual. I like it,' he said for the third time.

'More coffee?' countered Leo.

'Yes, why not?' Finally Racine turned away from the sculpture. The early morning sun highlighted the shadows beneath his dark eyes. In a black silk dressing gown that reached to the floor but gaped at the chest, revealing a richly muscled torso furred with long, silky hair, he looked faintly dissipated, faintly decadent. His long dark hair was rumpled.

In contrast, Leo himself was dressed impeccably, if ambiguously, in finely tailored jeans and a black polo neck sweater.

'I'm glad you came early,' said Leo at last, breaking the faintly unsettling silence that had grown between them. 'Your company is welcome.'

'Paris annoyed me,' responded Racine, drinking

his coffee and ignoring the tempting basket of freshly-baked croissants, disdaining the steaming silver chafing dishes. 'Sometimes I crave the simple pleasures.'

'Ah, yes,' nodded Leo, 'I know exactly what you mean.'

'Perhaps we should invite her over for a drink later,' said Jean-Paul idly, pouring water into pastis and admiring the milky hue.

'The English woman?' queried Pascaline, turning away from the sink. She was wearing nothing but an apron and a pair of high-heeled shoes. Camp, yes; corny, yes; and she knew it excited him unbearably. 'I thought the whole reason for this rustic retreat was to be alone. Not so much water in mine, Jean-Paul, you'll drown it as always.'

Obligingly he added more pastis to her drink, smiling inwardly at her notion of 'rustic'. The cottage was structurally simple, consisting of one large room on the ground floor, a combination of living and dining space, and an upstairs loft that served as a bedroom. But the streamlined kitchen was equipped with every conceivable labour-saving device, the plumbing and heating were state of the art, and their sophisticated sound system occupied an entire wall.

The furniture was classic Bauhaus with a judicious mixture of Le Corbusier, clean, geometric shapes in tubular steel and black leather, with only one large armchair cushioned in black leather as a concession to comfort, An early Mondrian was displayed to advantage above it.

Pascaline 'rusticating' was a little like Marie Antoinette playing dairymaid, he mused.

'It seems the neighbourly thing to do,' he shrugged. 'Perhaps in a few days, after Christmas.'

'As you like,' said Pascaline indifferently. 'But

31

what if she's dull, what if she's boring? She seemed so . . . so . . . English,' she added with Parisian disdain.

'Mmm.' Jean-Paul was noncommittal, thinking of the amazing cascade of silvery blonde hair, the dark, navy blue eyes, the taut slim body, such a contrast to Pascaline's lush curves and luxurious red hair.

'Then she'll invite us around, and we'll be obliged to see her again,' pursued Pascaline. 'One of those dreary acquaintances one can't simply stop.'

'If that's the case,' Jean-Paul said smoothly, 'we'll disentangle ourselves gracefully. Now put down your drink and come here.'

The next few days passed strangely but sweetly for Gemma. For her, the paradox was too profound to be readily accepted. She was a competent, controlled, professional woman; she had given herself mindlessly, like an animal in heat, to a stranger on a packed earth floor. Sex, or the lack of it had never greatly moved or troubled her; he had unlocked a sensual maelstrom she never dreamed existed.

He was a man, of course, flesh and blood, but it was far, far too disturbing to think of him as such. And she had never seen his face. Images of the night became inextricably mingled with the hunter carved on the wall of the tomb; in a curious state of half-believing half-disbelieving the shocking, erotic acts they had shared, she tricked herself into thinking of him as an incarnation of the hunter, a dream lover, a fantasy fulfilled that belonged to the shadowy half-world beneath the ground.

But her body was not deluded.

She had intended to pass the time quietly, reading Trollope and listening to chamber music. More often the book lay unopened as she slipped into a delicious, dreamy haze, remembering her body's bliss, the peaks of pleasure she had found, the exquisite sensations she had experienced.

She had exchanged greetings with Jean-Paul and Pascaline and made tentative plans to have a drink together sometime, but it seemed that they, like she herself, were content to be alone. The supermarket in Carnac had provided fruit and cheese, bread and wine, some coarse pâté; there was no need to leave the cottage and, strangely, she felt no desire to explore the country.

Desire, freshly awakened, simmered beneath her skin, at first so faintly that she was unaware of it. Only gradually did she realise how she was beginning to relish the pleasurable friction of her nipples against soft wool or rough cotton, the soft thrum between her thighs against the harsh denim of her jeans.

And then one afternoon she found herself touching her breasts almost unconsciously, remembering the feel of his mouth and teeth on her nipples, the raging heat he had conjured.

She was clumsy at first, and inexperienced, but her nipples hardened to her tentative fingers, and her body led her swiftly to evoke the sensations she had, unknowingly, learned to crave; the glowing flush that spread between her legs and moistened her, the rippling warmth that heated her skin.

She kept her hands on her breasts, thinking of the frenzied rapture he had driven her to by confining his touch to her nipples, and caressed them gently through the soft wool of her sweater. But the burgeoning excitement in the pit of her belly soon led her to slip her hands beneath, find the silky skin of her breasts, press harder on her nipples, pinch them between her fingers and arouse the tingling, electric thrills that seemed to arc straight to her groin.

She could feel her lower lips begin to swell and

throb, aching for friction, for stimulation, and remembered the searing heat of his mouth as he found her, the delicious fever that consumed her.

Almost of its own volition she felt her hand slide to the zipper of her jeans and then beneath the silk of her underwear, part the plump leaves of her sex and find the centre of her pleasure. She explored herself gently, fingering the taut bud of her clitoris, amazed to find it so responsive, astonished to feel the clamouring heat pool in her groin and the sweat spring to her brow. She felt plump and slick, sensitive and quivering, and she moved her finger faster and faster until the warmth spread in a rosy flush, encapsulating her entire body. Her blood frothed into millions of tingling, tiny bubbles, sparkling and bursting as she climaxed.

She gave a low cry as her body contracted and then went lax.

'Our new neighbour may not be quite as dull as you fear,' said Jean-Paul, who had gone over to invite Gemma for a drink and happened to look through the window.

'Wine? Pastis? We also have whiskey, if you like,' offered Pascaline, gesturing to an array of bottles on a low-slung table.

'Wine, thank you,' said Gemma, settling into a plump, black leather armchair and gazing around the room. She was pleased that Jean-Paul and Pascaline had asked her over; the dream-like torpor that had enveloped her was becoming coloured with a hint of restlessness, a sneaking desire to re-visit the tumulus and a strange reluctance to do so. A bit of company was a welcome distraction.

They chatted idly for a while, Gemma winning a

smile from Jean-Paul with her feigned admiration for the Rietveld chair he was sitting on.

'Of course, they never really caught on,' he commented, standing to freshen their drinks and gesturing at the uncompromising angled slats of the chair. 'And because of that, they weren't made in large quantities. This one was a bit of a find.'

'Too uncomfortable, I imagine,' suggested Gemma, lifting her glass for more wine, and missing the glance that passed between Jean-Paul and his wife.

'Very uncomfortable,' agreed Pascaline with a smile. 'And you, Gemma, what do you like?'

'I suppose I have rather eclectic tastes,' she replied slowly. 'My flat in London is all modern, but I haven't given much thought to the cottage here.'

Pascaline and Jean-Paul exchanged looks. It was he who broke the silence before it became awkward, deftly turning the subject to the advantages of a quiet retreat in the country, local customs and curiosities, the rich, neolithic history of the area.

'Ah, but Gemma knows this,' Pascaline commented, as Jean-Paul began talking about dolmens and tumuli. 'It was, after all, Leo's hunter who entranced her here, was it not?'

'What?' exclaimed Gemma, feeling her face flush.

'The carving of the hunter in the tomb, I remember you talking about it in the summer,' explained Pascaline, a bit surprised at Gemma's reaction. For a moment the Englishwoman seemed to exude a sort of sexual flash, a heat that flared and then was just as quickly extinguished. Jean-Paul was right; she was either inexperienced or very subtle, but not dreary.

'Leo's hunter?' echoed Gemma.

Jean-Paul took over. 'It's Leo Marais who owns the land, and the tomb is thought, rather fancifully, to belong to one of his ancestors. Impossible, of course, since the family only settled here in the sixteenth

35

century, and the tomb is prehistoric, but it's a local legend . . . rather like Leo himself. You'll be going to the masquerade tomorrow night, of course, and perhaps you'll meet him then.'

'The masquerade?' asked Gemma, perplexed. Something was digging into the small of her back. Unthinkingly she slipped a hand behind her and felt between the cushions. Her look of blank surprise when she withdrew a small, black leather whip was almost comical.

'Oh, I – ' she began, then floundered.

'I wondered where that had got to,' said Pascaline, looking pleased.

Gemma was looking flustered. 'It's the costume,' interjected Jean-Paul. 'You see?'

Coming to stand beside her he plucked a long length of black leather from the top of her chair. It was a cat-suit, long and supple, bisected with a thick silver zipper that ran from neck to crotch and then split down both legs. A tiny hood was attached to the neck.

'A costume?' Gemma repeated. Unthinkingly she reached out and stroked the smooth leather. 'I see, of course, for your masquerade. Michelle Pfeiffer, right?'

Pascaline looked blank.

'Catwoman, I mean,' explained Gemma.

'*Comment?*'

'Yes, of course you're right,' Jean-Paul smiled, intrigued by Gemma's interest. 'And you, you weren't expecting a masked ball – why don't you borrow it? Pascaline and I have other . . . costumes.'

'I haven't been invited,' Gemma demurred, still stroking the leather sleeve.

'That is nothing,' said Pascaline dismissively. 'We are all expected. In other days we would have been tenants or vassals of the chateau as we live on the land. This is the old tradition of opening it to all on New Year's Eve. You will come?'

Refusal hovered on her lips, but despite herself she was tempted. There was something darkly compelling about the costume, something exciting.

'We will pick you up tomorrow at eight, then,' said Jean-Paul, smiling over at his wife. 'I'm sure you will find it an interesting experience.'

The costume fascinated her. The sleek, supple leather was warm to the touch, the heavy mesh of the silver zipper cool and lifeless and the contrast was strangely stirring. It had a mysterious allure that both attracted and faintly repelled her, an odd sensation that was familiar yet elusive.

The afternoon of the party she spent soaking for hours in a hot bath scented with her favourite perfume, luxuriating in the steamy warmth, letting herself drift. She washed her hair and towelled it dry, letting it fall in loose waves and then massaged a rich, almond-scented cream all over her body. Looking in the mirror, she examined herself thoughtfully. Her skin was flushed a rosy pink from the bath, and her nipples were firm, jutting peaks, aroused by the touch of her hands. She let her fingers drift down the flat plane of her belly and tangle in the silvery blonde thatch of her pubic hair.

She knew then that she would wear nothing beneath the slick black leather.

It fitted perfectly, like a caressing second skin, cupping her breasts and moulding itself to her body. She spared a moment's thought for Pascaline, whose plump curves would have been unbearably crushed by the clinging cat-suit and decided vaguely that she must have put on some weight recently.

The mesh of the zipper embraced her sex in a cool, metallic kiss that parted her inner lips and rubbed gently at her clitoris. In the mirror she saw a stranger, a ferally, fatally seductive black leather creature who had her own familiar silvery blonde hair and dark blue eyes.

Beneath the hood, only her eyes and lips would be visible. Deliberately she exaggerated her make-up, using thick black liner and masses of mascara, and painted her lips a deep, deep red. And when the hood was in place, her hair concealed by the black leather, she was truly transformed into the stranger she had seen in the mirror.

It was a strange sensation, she reflected, as they drove to the chateau, as though by donning the disguise she had acquired something of the sleek sensuality it embodied. Unbearably conscious of her naked body beneath the supple black leather, feeling secretly decadent and faintly excited, she paid scant attention to Jean-Paul and Pascaline, her attention only roused by the looming facade of the chateau. It was a soaringly elegant, impeccable Renaissance-style building with the remains of a discordantly crumbling tower to one side.

'What is that?' asked Gemma in surprise as the headlights of the car briefly illuminated the tower.

'Part of the old keep, an affectation of Leo's,' replied Jean-Paul as he brought the car to a halt and tossed the keys to a waiting servant. 'The graveyard as well . . . he's refused to restore it, strange, really . . .'

But as they walked up the massive stone stairs leading to the immense double doors, she forgot the tower in the new awareness of her body moving against leather and steel and knew that even her walk was slightly different, looser, faintly provocative, the gentle sway of her hips more pronounced, her body undulating under the pervasive, persuasive caress of the costume.

Pascaline and Jean-Paul, also dressed in black leather, were conversing, saying something that eluded her as the massive doors opened and then she forgot them and herself in the breathtaking spectacle before her eyes.

They were in a huge entrance hall that soared the height of the building, illuminated by a massive chandelier that shed light like tiny diamonds, drawing the fire of the brightly coloured silks and velvets, refracting the emeralds and diamonds and rubies.It was decadently opulent, a brilliant kaleidoscope of shifting shades and scents and images. A bejewelled Marie Antoinette in a dazzling confection of aquamarine silk playfully rapped Lucifer across the knuckles with her fan; an olive-skinned houri in floating gauze with a huge emerald in her belly button leaned closer to Cardinal Richelieu; an exuberant Dionysus with a laurel wreath slipping from his temples and carrying aloft a bunch of grapes was blatantly rubbing against a nun.

A string quartet was playing from a minstrel's gallery, the stately and decorous Albinoni almost drowned by the excited chatter of hundreds of voices. She recognised the distinctive cosmopolitan cacophony of French, Italian, English, Spanish and some unusual tongue she couldn't identify . . . Russian, perhaps, or some strange dialect. It was a scene both bizarre and exotic: harlequins, clowns, devils, pirates, whores and angels all captured in the shifting strobe of the chandelier.

A cloud of richly evocative Joy enveloped her as she was lavishly embraced by a Cleopatra who had no doubt mistaken her for someone else, and she quickly lost Jean-Paul and Pascaline to the shifting crowd. A waiter in formal attire offered a flute of champagne from a silver tray; she took it gingerly, brought back to earth by the expectation of the over-sweet, fizzy liquid she had learned to detest from a hundred wrap parties.

It was a cloud of sensation, a cool frothing caress that melted in her mouth, a delicious tingling so far removed from the ordinary experience of swallowing that her senses reeled in surprise. Taittinger, perhaps, or Cristal; a wickedly expensive explosion of pure delight against the palate, a heady, bubbly swirl that left her elated yet icily sober, every sense clear and somehow sharpened. Entranced, she plucked another glass from a passing waiter and in her new, anonymous persona decided to explore.

She moved through the crowd, ostensibly looking for Jean-Paul and Pascaline, secretly rather thrilled to be alone.

Incongruous in their strict black and white formality, waiters circulated, offering champagne and an array of tempting hors d'oeuvres; mounds of caviare, glistening like grey pearls on a bed of shaved ice, surrounded by toast points, chopped eggs and spring onions arranged in the form of some exotic flower; oysters on the half-shell cushioned by pungently green sea-weed and adorned with slices of lemon; delicate, tissue-thin slices of smoked salmon arranged in the scales of a leaping fish and garnished with succulent capers and black olives; prawns with a deliciously spicy dip, scallops wrapped in bacon and mussels in vinaigrette vied with more exotic confections. The mouth-watering aromas melded with the scent of exotic and expensive perfumes on hot and excited bodies.

She sipped champagne and let herslef drift with the crowd toward the end of the room, eavesdropping shamelessly, secure in her disguise.

'But no-one, simply no-one goes to Monte Carlo anymore, it's so, so, so – '

'Utterly devastated to lose the Matisse, but at least

we'd insured it for double the market value – you simply can't keep anything safe on the Riviera these days – '

'Well, one look at the Nikkei and I knew we'd made a killing – '

'So sweet of you, but they're paste, of course, the little man at the bank goes positively wild when I try to take the diamonds out of the vault, and then these boring insurance clauses – '

The conversation was almost as surreal as the surroundings, Gemma decided, as she found herself entering a huge black and white room. The floor was black, veined marble, the walls starkly white. Recessed niches held priceless Benin bronzes and the stately chords of Albinoni dissolved in the throaty smoke of slow jazz issuing from hidden speakers. In the centre of the room, on a huge block of white marble, two ebony figures, a man and woman, were posed in the act of love, their bodies highlighted by concealed spotlights.

The man seemed to glow under the hot glare of the lights, black and glistening. He was resting on one elbow, mouth poised over a dusky nipple, and his erection, a huge, dark rod, was clearly visible against the woman's thigh. The woman lay in a pose of utter abandon, legs parted and arms outstretched, a rippling mass of ebony hair snaking across the white marble surface.

It was a few moments before she realised they were real.

It was shocking, yet strangely exciting and she felt a slow pulse begin to beat between her legs as the man moved, touching the woman's thigh, urging her legs further apart. The woman's sex was fully revealed, the dusky pink leaves of her labia swollen and glistening, the bud of her pleasure protruding like a stamen of some exotic flower.

'Performance art, darling, passé, simply ages ago,' she heard a voice murmur behind her, and then the dry response: 'Not so passé. Look carefully.'

He was touching her now, testing her arousal, one finger disappearing into the channel of her body and Gemma felt her inner walls contract sharply, a shiver of lust spiralling straight to her groin. He inserted a second finger, and then a third, and thrust them in and out of the woman's body until he was satisfied. When he withdrew them, glistening with her body's musk, he touched them first to her lips and then to his own.

Gemma caught her breath. It was bizarrely erotic, standing alone in the press of strangers, enveloped in a perverse and anonymous prurience, a sweetly salacious complicity. They had all fallen silent now, and the atmosphere was thick and expectant. She couldn't take her eyes away from the rippling muscles of his back as the man prepared to mount the woman, mesmerised by the huge distended length of his erection as he positioned himself between her thighs.

She felt a hot tremor of excitement as he moved, sensing she would be too small to take him, and then, just as he plunged into her body there was a cool moan that might have been a woman's cry or the voice of the sax, and the room went dark. She felt the sharp intake of breath around her, as if they had all been holding their breath, rapt in the black and white carnality before their eyes.

Lights flowered over a huge, arched doorway at the far end of the room, and as if by common consent the crowd moved slowly toward it, leaving the ebony lovers in darkness. As Gemma drew nearer she realised that the low moan of the jazz and the woman were becoming overshadowed by the haunting, discordant lilt of a sitar.

The room was softly lit, pale light spilling from hundreds of intricately carved ivory balls suspended from the ceiling by chains. Crimson silk shot through with gold flowed from the walls and beneath her feet was the soft touch of an exuberantly patterned Chinese carpet in Imperial yellow. Even as she struggled to take in the huge and ornately gilded Satsuma vases, the flowing poetry of Tang horses and the milky blue and white perfection of Ming scattered in recessed niches, her eyes were drawn to the centre of the room.

On a raised dais, two women were moving languorously to the sound of the sitar. They belonged to the Orient, golden skin and jet-black hair, their nude, hairless, almost childlike bodies fluid and graceful. The hot tremor of excitement that had gripped her whilst watching the man and woman flushed into a rosy glow as Gemma succumbed to the more diffuse, somehow more pervasive and sensual aura of the dance.

They touched each other delicately, moving to the harsh, lyrical strains of the sitar, and Gemma felt her mouth grow dry as she watched them twine and untwine together, wreathe and separate. She drained her glass and instantly a waiter appeared at her side with a fresh flute of champagne.

There was something strangely stirring in the spectacle of two women moving together, sensual rather than sexual, more enticing than exciting.The haunting strains of the sitar lent an air of dim unreality to the scene.

And then the music and lights began to fade as the two women fastened together, belly to belly, thigh to thigh, fingers weaving between their thighs in a different dance.

Gemma felt her nipples tighten and her groin grow heavy, even as they were beckoned to a further room

43

by the low roll of drums to a shadowy space perfumed with incense.

A woman was moving through the crowd, stamping her feet in time to the drum. She was darkly exotic, dressed in gauzy, rose-coloured trousers with a ruby fixed to her navel, long dark hair free and her breasts bare. Automatically the throng parted, and soon she was alone, in the centre of the room. She jerked her hips slowly, in the rhythm of sex, thrusting and retreating, grinding and shivering, and when her arms began to tremble Gemma could feel the same hypnotic, erotic heat begin to envelop her.

The dancer's shoulders moved; her breasts shook; the muscles of her belly rippled as if in response to a probing shaft, and the rhythm of the music quickened. And then she writhed, faster and faster, and Gemma felt her own hips move unconsciously in imitation, in thrall to the music, swayed by the dancer's spell.

Watching her, the unknowing, tiny undulations of her body responding to the music, imagining her silvery blonde hair free and flowing like the Egyptian woman's, he was pleased.

'I like it,' he murmured quietly to his friend. 'I like it very much.'

'I am so pleased,' was the suave rejoinder.

It seemed as though she was being driven to climax by the voluptuous frenzy of her own body and when the music ended on a final, throbbing drum beat the dancer uttered a sharp cry and collapsed on the floor. The tension among the crowd was almost palpable as they shifted to the next sensation. It was clear now to Gemma that they were being moved from room to room, drawn by the lights and the music into a sensual labyrinth, and she found her own arousal becoming so intense as to be almost unbearable.

Senses reeling, she lost track of her surroundings and had only a vague impression of a glass-panelled room with a steaming pool. She was dimly aware of the mounds of exotic greenery where the shrill cry of brilliantly coloured parrots blended with the jungle writhing of slick and naked bodies, but before long they spilled into a narrow corridor lined with Archaic Greek sculptures of nude kouros figures.

Hot, sweaty, aroused and bemused, Gemma knew only the impulse to escape; the over-blown, lush decadence was overwhelming, and when she saw a doorway leading outside she slipped from the crowd.

The cool night air was a relief, and she took deep, shuddering breaths, drawing the freshness into her lungs as if it could cool the heat of her arousal. She stumbled forward, found herself at the base of the crumbling tower she had seen earlier as they arrived and dimly realised that she must have traversed only one wing of the chateau.

She felt at once both over-stimulated and exhausted and couldn't even begin to imagine the bizarre tableaux that must be taking place as the party progressed. She had the strange urge to stroke herself to climax; to find Jean-Paul and Pascaline and leave the chateau; to escape this elegant, contrived, perverse eroticism and find her way back to the tomb, back to the carved image of the hunter with his grossly enlarged phallus/spear, back to the hard packed earth floor where fantasy had become reality.

She was in a turmoil that had stripped away the comforting illusion of her disguise and knew she was far, far out of her depth.

And when the strong hands closed on her shoulders, and the harsh, faintly metallic voice reached her ears, she almost fainted in fear and relief and disbelief.

'I know what you want,' he said.

A sudden clap of thunder almost drowned his words, but she was sure she recognised the voice, the clipped consonants, the liquid vowels. Lightning flashed before them, illuminating the tower, and she wondered a little wildly if nature herself was conspiring in this strange drama.

And then she forgot to think as his hands reached between her thighs and unfastened the zipper, releasing her heated sex. She twisted, tried to turn to face him, to escape him, but his hand was heavy on the back of her neck, forcing her to her knees.

She felt the tip of his penis at the base of her spine, nudging between the cleft of her buttocks, tracing the path to her secret places. He paused at the taut mouth of her anus and she shivered as a frisson of dark pleasure shot through her. And then he eased forward, parting the plump folds of her labia with slick ease and she felt her flesh curl around him. He stopped at the entrance, just circling it with the engorged tip of his organ.

She felt the responsive quiver deep inside her, her inner muscles tensing and almost convulsing in anticipation of the pounding thrust, but he withdrew, guiding the hot length of his penis back through her engorged and aching flesh, back to the tender, secret passage, back to the base of her spine.

Again and again he repeated the stroke, sometimes slowly, sometimes fast and furious, sometimes pressing just inside, sometimes thrusting against the taut bud of her clitoris, varying the rhythm, keeping her poised on the very edge. He left a trail of burning moisture in his wake, a searing hunger, every sensation of her body centred on the lascivious stroke of his penis against her flesh.

The thunder pounding in her ears could have been the flow of her blood; when her climax finally struck, it was as though the lightning snaking across the sky had entered her body, so jarringly electric was the sensation of his full length finally thrusting home.

Her body writhed with the force of the stabbing pleasure arcing through her, stinging every nerve-ending from the tips of her fingers to her toes in thrilling awareness. She could have wept in sheer ecstasy had she not been screaming in release.

Dazed, she barely felt him withdraw. Moments later, when she finally gathered the strength to lift her head, he had gone.

Chapter Three

*I*t was almost midnight. Inside the chateau, the guests were gathered in the huge ballroom that was the heart of the building, a magnificently opulent Regency style room of gilt and white marble and mirrored walls illuminated by massive chandeliers. There was no music; only an expectant hush as they absorbed the spectacular tableau in the centre of the room.

It was a huge primitivo-cubist sculpture, discordant and arresting, at least ten feet high, of a man and a woman embracing. The figures were solid marble, geometric shapes differentiated only by the heavy, triangular breasts of the female and the massive, oblong rod of the male. Both figures were white, except for the male penis, which was a shaft of distended red-veined marble, disappearing between the white thighs of the woman. It was the essence of penetration, blunt and primal, the first moment of male flesh meeting female. And despite, or perhaps because, the figures were only raw shapes, cuboid symbols, it embodied the fundamental core of sex, purely, crudely, blatantly.

Around the base of the sculpture were twelve couples, nude men and women arranged in the same pose, their bodies almost locked together. The men, poised on the brink of penetration, were all fully erect, their organs as red and distended as the massive red marble shaft of the sculpture. The women stood, thighs parted, waiting to receive them. They were motionless; but for the sheen of sweat on their brows they might almost have been mistaken for stone.

The guests, too, were still, an uneasy stillness fraught with curling anticipation as they waited for the scene to unfold. Impassive waiters moved through the crowd, silently offering flutes of champagne, pressing them into unresisting hands.

They had all passed through the sensual odyssey Leo had created, passed from room to room, titillated and aroused by the scents, the colours, the music, the erotic scenes enacted before them. This was the culmination. The climax. All were moved, and some a little shocked, by the stark, uncompromising sexuality of the sculpture and its human counterparts.

'Clever,' murmured Alexei to Leo, who was standing beside him, a faint smile on his face. 'Brancusi?' he asked, referring to the sculpture.

'School of,' returned Leo softly. 'Ah. Now it begins.'

A massive gong struck, the first stroke of midnight. At its command, the men thrust, thick, engorged rods disappearing between the women's thighs, echoing the pure, brutal symmetry of the sculpture.

There was a strangled gasp from the crowd, as if each of them had been penetrated, pierced by the primal stab of the male organ, searched by the swollen, unthinking, driven red marble rod.

And then the men withdrew in perfect synchronicity, revealing glistening penises, rock-hard and pulsing, before they thrust again as the gong struck a second time. And though they measured time by each thrust, embodied the raw and rhythmic stroke of seconds with each thrust, the moment seemed endless.

Only the slick kiss of flesh on flesh filled the room between the resonant strokes of the clock. And the players were no longer stiff, impersonal representations; they were men and women clawing for release, dancing the primal dance to the command of the gong. When, on the stroke of twelve, they climaxed, the room seemed flooded with release, a euphoric swell of fulfillment.

A mild explosion of a hundred champagne corks popping heralded the New Year. Amidst frantic embraces and excited and exuberant cries the twelve naked couples slipped from the room.

'No balloons? No streamers? No party hats?' commented Jay Stone, who had joined Alexei and Leo on the fringes of the room. He had meant to sound sardonic, but even to his own ears his voice sounded forced and he was breathing too rapidly.

'And I was forgetting you Americans had such sophisticated tastes,' smiled Leo.

Across the room, Gabrielle de Sevigny observed her lover, her arousal tempered with unease. Resplendent in evening dress, he was standing with two tall, dark men she didn't recognise, one dressed as Satan, the other ambiguous in black with a long, velvet cape.

Her body was hot and aroused, almost unbearably excited by the bizarre and erotic images Leo had created and conjured, but her mind was reeling. It was a side of him she had barely acknowledged, hardly dared to suspect; an ice-cold, calculating, sensual connoisseur whose dark depths had barely been exposed by the blatant tableaux.

This was, for Leo, she sensed, a mere bagatelle, a pretty device to amuse and entertain, no more.

And if the thought frightened her, it aroused her even more.

She looked down at her dress, suddenly dissatisfied with her costume. She had wanted something erotically suggestive, something sexy. Briefly she had toyed with the notion of appearing as the Marquise de Pompadour, mistress of Louis XV, or even Catharine the Great, the notoriously whorish monarch, but discarded them both as cliché. And the costumes were too voluminous, too concealing. Finally, after much deliberation, she had decided to dress as a twenties style flapper, hoping to lure him with the irresistible, irrepressible, flirtatiously light-hearted decadence of the period.

She was wearing a shimmering knee-length silver tube of iridescent beads that caught the light, saucily slit to the waist on one side where a black garter-belt could be glimpsed whenever she moved. Her stockings were sheer black silk, her heels high, stilleto points. Diamonds dripped from her ears, flashed on her wrists and glittered on the twenties style headband adorning her brow.

She knew she looked beautiful, sexy, desirable; and she knew now that it wasn't enough. Perhaps it never had been.

Still, she made her way over to Leo with an expression of cool boredom on her face, even though her heart was pounding.

'Gabrielle, my dear,' Leo welcomed her, kissing both her cheeks. It was no more than a traditional, polite greeting between acquaintances; yet the mere brush of his lips against her skin made her blood heat and thicken.

'Let me present my friends, Alexei Racine, Jay Stone.' Conventional murmurs, then, 'What did you think of my little divertissement?' he asked, eyes glowing like coals.

'It was,' she shrugged elegantly, 'amusing. Yes, very amusing. I had no idea you were so interested in . . . sculpture.'

'One of my ruling passions,' he replied easily. 'Would you like to see more?'

The heat was still in his eyes. She recognised the look with relief. 'Yes, yes, I would,' she said, barely managing to conceal a frisson of pleasure as he ran his hand down the naked skin of her arm and cupped her elbow.

'Jay? Alexei? You'll excuse me? This way, my dear.'

He led her out of the ballroom, past a series of retiring rooms sumptuously decorated in blue, white and gold in the manner of Louis XV, then through a long mirrored hallway of gilt and crystal chandeliers into a series of interconnecting rooms so lavish and opulent that she found herself holding her breath.

They passed through a small door concealed by a Gobelins tapestry and she found herself on a dimly lit, narrow stone staircase. Leo led the way silently until they emerged into a long, low-ceilinged room with a faintly sloping floor. A massive forest of huge stone columns supported the roof. It was cool and faintly sinister and Gabrielle shivered.

'What is this place?' she asked Leo, her voice echoing.

'Part of the old keep,' he replied, moving toward a large wooden door reinforced with metal bands. 'I thought about converting it to a wine cellar, but the servants are superstitious.' He made a vague gesture to his left.

Narrowing her eyes, she saw, between the interstices of the columns, a series of rusting metal grilles.

'The dungeons,' he explained casually. 'And this,' he said, opening the heavy wooden door, 'was the torture chamber.'

He urged her into the room with a palm on the small of her back. It was dark, and she could see nothing. And then a match scraped and a torch on the wall beside her flared into life.

It was a scene from some surreal hell. Contorted, writhing black metal forms, tortured and tortuous, swarmed along the walls, some vaguely human, others simply menacing shapes.

'Modern, of course,' Leo said. 'One of the few pieces I've commissioned.'

Her eyes were fixed on a human face, eyes closed and head flung back, the mouth a contorted rictus that might have been agony, might even have been ecstasy.

'But it captures the spirit, I think.'

There were knives and manacles, whips and chains, strange and bizarre looking shapes she couldn't name. Her eyes were drawn to a female nude, the nipples pierced with tiny darts.

'A rather playful little piece in some ways. I feel sure he was influenced by Tinguely and Saint-Phalle.'

The torchlight flickered and it seemed to her as though the figures began to shift slightly, to move, to redefine themselves. What she had first perceived as a spear thrusting into the distorted flesh of some grotesque belly became an enormous, distended male organ rutting through the folds of female flesh. Pincers clawing at a woman's breast transformed themselves into clutching fingers. The tortured savagery of the piece became somehow subtly infused with a deep, dark eroticism.

'Well, what do you think? Do you like it?'

'I think,' said Gabrielle softly, 'I think it frightens me.' She had intended to lie, but it was impossible to dissemble in the face of such a powerfully brutal work.

'Excellent,' murmured Leo. 'Excellent.'

He placed his hands on her shoulders and turned her face to him. She relaxed slightly, relieved to turn her back on the writhing, metal mass, and anticipated his kiss, the warming touch of his lips on hers.

Instead, he tugged on the glittering band on her brow, dragging it down to cover her eyes. Instinctively she stiffened and tried to reach up, but he captured both her wrists in one hand.

'As you may have guessed,' he said smoothly, 'I am particularly intrigued by the physical aspect of sculpture, the translation of flesh to stone or bronze, the contrast . . . which is always enhanced, I think, by . . .'

The words washed over her, meaning nothing. Deprived of sight, deprived of movement by the iron clasp of his hand, it seemed as though all her senses had suddenly sharpened in response. The acrid smell of smoke from the torch seemed stronger, the expensive perfume of his aftershave more pungent. She could feel her skin prickling as he found the zipper at the back of her dress and the sound of it slithering to the floor was unnaturally loud.

With one hand around her waist he lifted her free of the shimmering silver folds and carried her a few steps until she felt the cool, twisted metal at her back. His erection was hard against her thigh; any moment now, she knew, she would feel the hot length of him probing her sex.

Instead, he lifted her higher and there was a harsh, metallic click as something closed over one wrist and then the other. He let her go and, as she felt for the floor, she became aware of the harsh brush of metal on the inside of her thighs.

He stood back to admire the effect. Her arms were

54

stretched above her head, one wrist clasped by a black manacle, the other trapped in the fanged jaw of a skull. Against the rough black metal her skin shone a warm, pearly white, the milky flow of flesh interrupted by the dark plume of her pubic hair, the massive black penis-spear between her legs and the black garters and stockings.

It was more than lewd, he decided. There was something almost obscene in the pose. Perhaps it was the glittering band that obscured her eyes. If only her hair were a different colour . . . Gabrielle's raven black hair dissolved too readily against the dark metal . . . a blonde would be better, masses of silvery blonde . . .

'Leo, what is this?' asked Gabrielle, a faint tremor in her voice.

'This, Gabrielle? It's called "The Torment",' he replied. 'Let me show you.'

She felt his finger slip between the lips of her sex. She was tight and dry, any arousal chilled by the menacing sculpture, and his touch was intrusive, almost painful. The quick thrum of his fingers chafed her clitoris, a rapid stroke from the stem to the tip repeated again and again until the first burning irritation began to dissolve as she heated and moistened. She felt her lower lips begin to swell in response, grow plump and slick.

His touch was hard, almost too hard, a thick, stabbing pressure that quickly roused the pulsating between her legs. She felt the delicate tissues swell and suffuse as the heat of arousal enveloped her sex, a fiery heat that followed the path of his finger.

All sensation spiralled to the hungry flesh between her legs, the quick stab of his fingers. She forgot the twisted black mass behind her, the unseen points digging into her shoulders and back, the cool metal at the top of her thighs; she forgot even to breathe as the flickering heat pooled and swelled.

She felt the first incandescent ripple deep in her belly, the first singing surge as her body gathered itself for climax, and the muscles in her legs began to tremble.

Immediately he changed the rhythm, moving his finger gently, exploring the swollen pink flesh around her clitoris, denying her the final rough, orgasmic stroke. She felt it throb and pulse as he skirted it delicately, swirling his finger around its protective flesh, a cunning, subtle stimulation.

Even as she began to flow with his new rhythm, relax to the rosy flush that replaced the burning heat, find the dreamy, languorous warmth, he changed his stroke, flicking his finger rapidly against the tip of her clitoris in a quick staccato beat.

Cleverly, mercilessly, repeatedly he brought her to the edge of orgasm and then denied her the final, cleansing explosion until the pleasure changed to a deep, physical ache and the sweet humid heaviness became a clawing need.

He made her body heat, then cooled it, startled and then soothed it, conjured the sweeping red mist that suffused her senses and then banished it before it could envelop her. And he did it again and again and again, moving to her breasts when she was about to climax from his hand against her sex, sucking them and biting them into hard, aching points, drawing all her body's focus to her nipples and then moving back to thrust his tongue deep inside her.

Even as her body succumbed to madness, she realised, finally, the purpose of his paradoxical love-making, how surely and cleverly he had led her to this dark, demonic dissolution where nothing mattered but release.

Her whole body was swollen, nipples and labia

inflamed and engorged, the hot, flickering tide swelling and subsiding and then rising again as he used his mouth, his hands and his cock to drive her to frenzy and then refuse her climax.

His penis searched for her, circling the wet, aching void, then pushed inside, just the tip, reminding the melting inner tissues of his hot, hard length before withdrawing, circling, then nudging in again, never to full length, never pulsing against the rippling muscles that ached for friction.

Writhing helplessly, she felt the harsh, metal, impaling sting against her back, her shoulders, her buttocks, and knew that she was grinding against the tortured metal hell of the sculpture on the wall. The sensation was almost a relief, a counterpoint to the excruciating, excoriating, agonising need that consumed her.

She was burningly distended; her inner lips were tumid and swollen, her nipples hard points, aching with need, a shivering, raw, animal need for release, an overpowering, atavistic need that transcended any known sensation. She felt the thick length of his penis enter her again, then withdraw quickly.

She screamed then, a primal cry of fury and frustration that echoed through the room and blended incongruously with the low sound of Leo's laughter.

'Excellent, Gabrielle, excellent. You begin to understand the essence of the piece.'

Outside, another fork of lightning hissed through the sky, illuminating the looming tower of the old keep. Gemma watched with dazed eyes. It was unreal, surreal, this eerie play of dazzling light and deep black shadow, revealing a landscape at once starkly beautiful yet mysteriously, hauntingly threatening, a scene that belonged more to the world of film or fiction, to the world of the demon lover in 'Tales of the Vampire'.

She closed her mind on the thought. Her movements slow and clumsy, she lifted her hands and removed the hood of her costume. She ran her fingers through her hair, releasing the tumbling waves of silver-blonde, combing it with her fingers, obscurely comforted by the familiar act.

Without letting herself think too much about what she was doing, she readjusted her clothing, fumbling with the heavy mesh of the zipper, barely acknowledging the sticky warmth between her thighs, and rose unsteadily to her feet.

She kept her mind determinedly, utterly blank as she walked away from the crumbling remains of the old keep, back toward the blazing lights of the chateau. But with every step she took, her body spoke to her, reminding her of the heavy ache between her thighs, the piercingly bitter-sweet ache of fulfillment.

He watched her as she entered the ballroom. The mass of silvery blonde hair that so entranced him was flowing freely down her shoulders, tumbling down her back in abandoned waves. But her eyes intrigued him more; they were shuttered, guarded, impenetrable, and she was moving like a sleep-walker, inwardly focused, unaware.

He felt the heat in his groin rise, knew the absurd impulse to take her then, take her again, rip the guarded veil from her eyes and the black leather from her body, see the lapis blue of her eyes drown in tears as he plunged into her, forced her body to recognise its master, its impresario.

He smiled a little wryly and drank more champagne.

Timing, he reminded himself, is everything.

But he kept his eyes on her as she moved, dream-like, through the crowds, mindlessly accepting a glass from a passing waiter, circling the knots of chattering guests and then disappearing through the magnificent archway that led to the hall.

Idly he wondered who or what she thought she was looking for. And what she would do when he finally let her find it.

The masked ball at the Chateau Marais never degenerated into what might be called an orgy. The setting, while opulent, indulgent and even perverse, was too elegant; the guests, self-indulgent and equally perverse, were too sophisticated. But there were discrete, shadowy spaces, barely concealed nooks and alcoves where couples, if they were so inclined, could meet and slake appetites sharpened by Leo's tableaux.

In the long, dimly lit corridor lined with Archaic Greek kouros figures, huge, blunt male nudes with blank eyes and delicately sculpted, swirling pubic hair, Pascaline shivered as she felt the stranger's hands reach for her breasts. Behind her, her husband Jean-Paul dropped a light, reassuring kiss on her shoulder as he kneaded her buttocks.

She was naked between them, as proudly, unashamedly nude as the immense sculpture beside them. Both men were fully clothed. Somehow that added to her excitement, made her feel more voluptuously, wickedly daring.

The stranger had been Jean-Paul's idea. He had made the offer in veiled terms, startling both Pascaline herself and the man dressed as Satan as they sipped champagne together around the base of the magnificent cubist sculpture in the ballroom.

And now he was standing before her, gloved hands cupping her breasts, rhythmically stroking the swollen white flesh as Jean-Paul cupped and stroked her buttocks. She felt her nipples engorge with blood, tighten into aching points even as the base of her spine tingled and the sweet, potent heaviness thickened her groin.

He was clever this stranger, falling easily into the rhythms Jean-Paul established, long, sure strokes that barely grazed the darkened nimbus of her areolae, mimicking the deft, delicious sweep of Jean-Paul's hands that opened the globes of her buttocks but merely brushed the taut aperture of her anus.

She felt herself moisten and her hidden lips swell and engorge in arousal, opening like the leaves of some exotic flower. Suddenly avid, she drew the stranger to her breast, greedy for the hard, pulling pressure of his mouth on her nipple, anticipating the hot suction against her sex, and felt Jean-Paul's finger probe her anus and then slip inside.

Moistened by the liquid of her arousal, there was no pain, only a sharp frisson of dark excitement, a stabbing pleasure. She closed her eyes and surrendered to sensation as the stranger sucked harder on her nipples, moving from one to another in desperate fury, as Jean-Paul moved inside her faster and faster.

She could feel the rolling, roiling tide of orgasm coiling in her groin, waiting to surge through her in billowing waves. It was the most delicious moment, the scant seconds before climax, knowing, recognising and welcoming the onslaught, the dissolution. Pascaline opened her eyes.

The Englishwoman, Gemma, was standing before her, dark blue eyes wide but strangely noncommittal. Almost, but not quite, on the verge of losing control, Pascaline smiled at her, a wild, feral smile that seemed to invite her to join them, find her place in this carnal triangle.

For a moment it seemed to Pascaline that she

hesitated, made the tiniest movement towards them, but then she shook her head slightly and moved away.

And then her climax flowered, and again she closed her eyes.

Gemma walked down the chateau's magnificent stone staircase, her mind ablaze with disjointed, dazzling, fragmented images. The massive, primitive sculpture in the ballroom. The huge, red marble shaft angled between the sculpted white thighs of the marble woman. The wild heat in Pascaline's eyes, the man's head bent to her breast. The blunt, uncompromising nudity of the archaic kouros figure beside them.

She hardly hesitated before turning away from the long, sweeping drive and cutting across the lawns which she was sure must lead to the forest. A short cut through the grounds of the estate would take her past the tumulus, through the meadow, back to her tiny cottage in something less than twenty minutes.

She would not stop at the tomb. She would not even acknowledge the looming mound, the home of her fantasy lover who had, inexplicably, impossibly, appeared to her tonight in the shadows of the old keep of the Chateau Marais.

She would go back home, back to the cottage. And when she finally reached it, she would lock the door, pour herself a huge brandy, shed the black leather that was clinging now like an unwelcome second skin, and have a bath. Or perhaps simply wrap herself in her ancient terry bathrobe and climb into bed. Or listen to music and drink tea. Or have a bath and listen to music and drink tea and brandy.

It seemed suddenly, crucially important to decide whether she would drink tea or brandy or tea and brandy, whether to have a bath or simply sit on the over-stuffed sofa and let some music wash over her, Mahler, perhaps, or Beethoven.

Not Albinoni, not the stately, elegant, deceptively familiar chords that had welcomed her to the Chateau Marais.

Not jazz, the low, smoky purr that had linked the black man and woman in cool carnality before her own, avid eyes. No, definitely not jazz.

And nothing exotic, like Ravel, that might recall the lilt of the sitar or the roll of the drums, the perfumed eroticism of the two women who had moved together or the hypnotically seductive movements of the belly dancer.

Perhaps she wouldn't listen to music at all, she decided, moving through the long, cool grass of the meadow, inexplicably relieved by the decision. And no brandy. When she reached the cottage she would brew a pot of tea, drink it sweet and strong, with buttered toast. Cut into strips for dunking, a comforting treat from childhood.

Then, only then, in the peace and security of the cottage, of solitude, would she allow herself to think. To remember.

Dawn was edging the night sky as, inside the Chateau Marais, waiters moved almost imperceptibly, ushering the dwindling number of guests to a smaller room off the ballroom. The musicians were still playing softly, but the guests, tired, tipsy, wearied by the night's revelry, were no longer dancing, and were willingly led to the cosy intimacy of the adjoining room.

In contrast to the glittering gilt and crystal opulence of the ballroom, the room they entered was rosily alluring, a blush-pink, warming, soothing bower. Shades of budding rose and primrose yellow beckoned, from the silken draperies concealing the windows to the linen tablecloths adorning the tables scattered between tempting armchairs and chaise longues.

Masses of roses, all in bud, in every shade from salmon to seashell pink to fuschia, from creamy white to yellow to saffron, flowered from crystal vases on every table and every surface.

Before the window, on a rose-silk chaise longue, lay a young man, apparently asleep. He was nude. Slim, blonde, well-muscled, he was as oblivious of the guests as they were of him. They all but ignored him, dismissing him, perhaps, as a fellow reveller overtaken by drink. Gratefully they sank into embracing chairs, conversations muted, nostrils teased by the enticing scent of brewing coffee issuing from some anonymous source, the mouth-watering aroma of fresh oranges, warm bread and sizzling bacon.

Sated and deliciously weary, glutted and saturated with the exotic richness of the night, they were content to loll, exchange complicit looks and await the reviving morning feast.

Almost unnoticed, the girl threaded her way through the room. She too was nude, a fact barely concealed by flowing strawberry blonde hair. She was slim, with pale, pale skin, long legs and high, lush breasts with large, pink nipples. She moved gracefully to the window and parted the heavy rose silk draperies, revealing the first flush of dawn colouring the sky.

Their attention caught by the light, the guests fell silent as she moved to the sleeping figure on the chaise longue. He barely stirred as, with long, elegant fingers she coaxed his penis awake, gently stroking the thickening length until he reached full arousal.

Languidly she reached between her thighs, parted her inner lips and then draped herself over his body. Still he slept, even as she began gently to rock her hips, her hands at her breasts, teasing the large pink nipples that swelled and distended. Almost imperceptibly she began to move faster, and her pale skin became flushed with arousal.

Perhaps because the man was still asleep, there was something strangely innocent about her movements, an unspoiled freshness that was more warming than arousing.

'Rosy-fingered dawn?' commented Alexei, eyeing the large pink nipples. 'A trifle theatrical, Leo.'

'Dawn who rolls away the night of stars, where clandestine lovers lie, entangled in sweet passion,' quoted Leo poetically, rather drunkenly and only slightly inaccurately. More prosaically, he added, 'I thought it would appeal to you, the theatrical element.'

'Too predictable,' replied Alexei, his eyes never moving from the entwined figures. 'He awakes and she climaxes, I assume, as morning breaks and the sun rises, the old fool, the unruly sun who tears lovers apart . . . a cliché from Ovid to Donne. I detest allegory. And I prefer more of a twist in my endings.'

'No-one who has seen your films could doubt that, my friend,' said Leo.

And as the sun rose, spilling golden light into the room and illuminating the two lovers, the man opened his eyes, gave a sudden powerful thrust of his hips that interrupted the smooth rhythm of the woman astride him, and she came with a low cry of sheer, surprised pleasure.

Gemma, wrapped in her ancient bathrobe, watched the same sunrise, hands curled around a cup of tea that had long grown cold. On the table before her were the uneaten strips of buttered toast she had promised herself, an unopened bottle of brandy she was still deliberating about, and her calfskin filofax, open at the section for notes and reminders. The margin was full of random doodlings, meaningless patterns, swirls and curls that led nowhere.

She had showered as soon as she reached the cottage, a long, steaming shower that both soothed and refreshed her, eradicated the memory of the insidiously seductive black leather costume she had borrowed from Pascaline. Some impulse had led her to bring it back downstairs with her, and she eyed it curiously.

She had to try and force herself to come to terms with the strange and bizarre events of the past few days. The dreamlike torpor she had shielded herself with after the night in the tumulus had been shattered; she could no longer delude herself with the false and comforting image of a dream lover, a fantasy.

Well, she could, of course, she thought, sipping her tea and grimacing at the nasty taste of cold tannin. She pushed the cup away and resumed doodling. She could ignore it. Forget it ever happened. Pretend it never happened. Pretend that she had never given herself to a stranger who had roused and then slaked a hunger she had never known. Pretend that he had not returned to her, taken her in the looming shadow of the old keep, made the lightning blaze through her body as it had blazed through the sky.

She was acting out of character, she mused, absolutely and utterly out of character. In a film script it would be unconvincing; in real life it was more than unnerving. It was impossible. Impossible to reconcile the determined professionalism of a successful female film producer making it, still against the odds, in a male-dominated world, with the flagrant, reckless, wanton abandon of a woman who would give herself to a stranger. Recklessly. Wantonly.

She doodled some more, moving from the margins of the page to the centre. She was aware of the two sides of her nature, the authoritative professional persona, always flawlessly groomed and impeccably, rigidly controlled, and the more lazily relaxed self that preferred to dream and dawdle in blue jeans and bare feet. The cottage in Brittany had been a gift to that second self, a place where she could shed the constraints of her professional life, her professional self.

She looked across at the black leather costume and shivered. The woman who had worn it last night, screamed in heated ecstasy as the faceless stranger had taken her in the shadow of the old keep, was a stranger to her.

She shook her head. Looking down at the page in front of her she saw that she had drawn a stick figure with a huge phallus jutting from the groin. It was the image of the stone carving from the tomb. What was it, she wondered, that so fascinated her, that made the carving so compelling? He was faceless, like her anonymous dream lover, defined only by the massive length of the male organ.

No, not a dream lover, she reminded herself. Idly she thought back to previous lovers. There were not many, not few; ten or so, perhaps one or two she had forgotten.

A respectable number for a woman of thirty.

Not one had moved her deeply, seared her sexually. In the past, if she thought about it all, she had concluded a bit vaguely that perhaps she was rather cold. Not frigid, but not easily moved.

She shivered again, and belted her bathrobe more tightly.

For a long time she sat at the table lost in thought, and when she heard a knock at the door she started in surprise, suddenly frozen, her heart thudding erratically. Realising how foolishly she was acting she forced herself to get to her feet and opened the door.

Pascaline was waiting outside, wearing jeans and a bulky white cable knit sweater, her cheeks pink from the crisp fresh air and her long red hair flowing free. She was carrying a bottle of champagne.

'I thought I would come to you,' said Pascaline, entering the cottage and looking around with undisguised curiosity. 'We looked for you later last night at the chateau, but I did not see you.'

She had a sudden, vivid memory of her last glimpse of Pascaline, her nude body only partially concealed between two men, the fiercely exultant expression in her eyes.

'I left early,' Gemma explained a little awkwardly, following her into the room.

'But you enjoyed yourself, no?' asked Pascaline, setting the champagne on the table and then curling up on the over-stuffed sofa.

'No. I mean yes, yes, of course,' replied Gemma automatically.

'You are lying, I think,' observed Pascaline, cocking her head. 'Why don't you open the champagne? It is very good to drink a little after such a night, some chemical in the body. And why don't you say what you mean? The English, they never say what they feel.'

'No, I suppose we don't,' agreed Gemma with a slight, reluctant smile, plucking at the gold foil of the champagne bottle. 'We call it good manners.'

'Manners,' repeated Pascaline thoughtfully. 'It is mere pretence, I think, and that we understand very well. That is why I am so much enjoying being in the country.'

'I'm sorry?' asked Gemma confusedly, and then

laughed at the ironic expression on Pascaline's face. 'I mean, I don't understand.'

'In Paris, where we are known, of course we are obliged to be respectable for my work, and for that of Jean-Paul,' said Pascaline, accepting a flute of champagne. 'Like all Frenchmen, he aspires to the politics, and I am Caesar's wife.'

'Of course,' Gemma said, privately thinking that there could be no less likely Calpurnia than the lush redhead she had last seen naked in the hall of the Chateau Marais. 'Of course.'

'Yes,' said Pascaline a little sharply. 'It is true, I assure you. In Paris, I am above reproach. Here it is permissible to be myself . . . or even not be myself, which is sometimes more interesting. Much more interesting.'

'That, I think I understand,' replied Gemma slowly, recalling her disjointed thoughts of the morning.

'Drink some champagne, then, and come and sit beside me,' said Pascaline, patting the sofa.

Gemma moved over towards her, setting her glass on the low table in front of the sofa. As she bent forward, her robe parted revealing the swell of her breasts, and she quickly tugged it together.

Pascaline's laughter rang out, fresh and joyous. 'So, you are thinking then I am also a daughter of Sappho?'

'No, no,' apologised Gemma, flustered, remembering the feral smile Pascaline had given her last night. Hastily she sat beside her, trying to conceal her embarrassment, and reached for her glass.

'You are sweet,' smiled Pascaline. She reached out and gently touched Gemma's hair. 'And would it be such a terrible thing if I were?'

Gemma looked at Pascaline, saw the light, flirtatious laughter in her eyes, the daring impudence, and had to smile herself. 'No, no it would not.'

'I am glad for that,' said Pascaline. Leaning over, she kissed Gemma softly, just at the corner of her mouth, a delicate brush of a kiss, neither invitation nor promise, yet somehow sensually eloquent.

Strangely, at the touch of her lips, Gemma felt herself relax, almost as if the crushing, bewildering confusion of the morning was seeping away, dispelled by Pascaline's kiss.

'Yes, you are like me,' pronounced Pascaline, draining her champagne and pouring herself another glass. 'We are both of us two women, perhaps. Maybe more. You saw me last night?' she asked Gemma with a sidelong glance. 'In the hall?'

'Yes, I saw you,' nodded Gemma, surprised to discover that for some reason she felt no awkwardness between them.

'It was the first time for me,' confided Pascaline, almost shyly, a little proudly, a devilish sparkle in her eyes. 'I have never been with two men before.'

'What was it like?' asked Gemma before she could stop herself.

Pascaline paused before replying, a thoughtful frown on her face. 'It was good,' she said at last. 'Different, and a bit strange, but good. I shall think of this when I am back in Paris with my boss who is a pig, and I will smile.'

Gemma's expression of confusion was so comical that Pascaline burst out laughing. 'No, no, what are you thinking? That I sleep with him, my boss? He has fat fingers and smells and I detest him. Besides, I could never be unfaithful to Jean-Paul,' she declared seriously.

Even as Gemma was trying to work out the convoluted morality of her last statement, Pascaline continued. 'But he wants me. And he treats me like his servant. French men can be pigs. And so now when I look at him when I am back in Paris, I can think to myself, I have done things you will never even dream of, and I will feel good. You see?'

'No. At least, I am not sure,' said Gemma, finally taking a sip of champagne.

'It gives me power,' explained Pascaline. 'Power in my mind. Like wearing the black leather in my imagination,' she added, nodding at the costume Gemma had worn the night before. 'You felt it too, no?'

'I felt . . .' Gemma hesitated. What had she felt? Liberated in some strange way, abandoned, darker yet lighter . . .

'Ah, yes, for you too,' said Pascaline, accepting Gemma's silence. 'So, tell me, your boss? Is he a pig like mine?' she asked, changing tack.

'He might be,' Gemma said evasively, relieved to avoid the subject of the black leather costume, thinking of the looming spectre of Alexei Racine. Not that he would be her boss, of course, but . . .

'Well, you think of the party, and you think of what you have seen and, perhaps, even done, and you will see,' assured Pascaline, a deviously infectious glint in her eyes.

'Tell me more about the party, then,' said Gemma, succumbing to her charm and taking another sip of champagne. Pascaline was right; it was fresh and refreshing, and she could feel her spirits reviving at the taste.

And she laughed at Pascaline's description of some of the guests, fell silent as she described the sunrise, exclaimed at the lavish banquet offered for breakfast and the array of limousines assembled to carry guests back to Paris. Pascaline was an amusing and vivid story teller, with a wicked sense of humour and a sly grasp of innuendo, and Gemma enjoyed listening to her as they finished the champagne together.

'But one thing was strange,' said Pascaline with a small frown as she got up to leave.

'One thing?' exclaimed Gemma, laughing. 'Only one thing!'

'Yes,' said Pascaline seriously. 'Very strange. When we are leaving, we kiss each other farewell, so and so, on both cheeks, the French way, you understand?' Standing at the doorway, she kissed Gemma on both cheeks, an impersonal salute utterly unlike the soft kiss she had given her earlier.

'Yes, I understand,' said Gemma.

'Well, I was waiting to say farewell to Leo, Leo Marais, our host, you know? And a woman in a silver dress was before me. She, she knelt down and kissed his feet. Very strange, I thought.'

Over the next few days, fragments of Pascaline's conversation kept returning to Gemma's mind. The thought of being two women, or perhaps more. Pascaline's strange notion of fidelity, and power in the mind. Curiously, it was all very reassuring. Gemma felt more at peace, more at ease with herself, a peace she did not try and disturb by visiting the tomb with its carved image of the hunter, its memory of her dream lover.

Instead she read the Trollope she had brought, and began leisurely to pack her belongings. The black leather costume, which Pascaline had insisted she keep as a gift, she folded carefully at the bottom of her case. She listened to American rock and roll on a French radio station, cleaned the cottage and, with increasing confidence, began to look forward to returning to work.

Perhaps it wouldn't be so bad, working with Racine, she decided. He was, after all, a gifted director; she was an extremely competent producer. She polished the old, thick glass cottage windows pensively, looking for her reflection. She loved the old movie of 'Tales of the Vampire', the new film script was sound, almost verging on inspired . . . she had stretched the budget to the utmost possible limit and casting was secure.

Everything was in place and nothing could be faulted. Surely, she mused, his reputation as bastard extraordinaire was exaggerated; it was probably nothing more than envy, odium, jealousy, the nasty backbiting, backstabbing response to success. Yes, she thought, finally seeing her face in the window and smiling, things would work out. And if they got rough, she could always think of Pascaline's power of the mind. Wearing black leather in her imagination.

It wouldn't be bad at all.

Chapter Four

*I*t wasn't bad.

It was worse.

It was hate at first sight.

It was as though some malignant electric current passed between them, vivid, vibrant, almost shocking.

Racine had been an hour late for the first meeting. The cast and crew, for the most part in jeans and sweatshirts, were sprawled comfortably around the boardroom table, smoking, drinking coffee, exchanging gossip and, surreptitiously, a bottle of brandy. Her assistant Jane, spectacular in a shiny black leather dress that surely cost every penny of her Christmas bonus and reminded Gemma of Pascaline's costume, was flirting with the male lead, a dissipated looking character with a vampiric smile that had won him the part.

Gemma, in serene Chanel winter white with navy blue braid, looked over her notes and tried to curb her irritation. Eventually Sy and Zippo joined them, secretary in tow, shrugged at Gemma and took their accustomed places at the head of the table, where they immediately began to confer in low voices. At the other end of the table, Gemma had almost decided to join them and find out what was going on, when the door opened.

Racine swept into the room trailed by a crowd of pale faced, androgynous looking acolytes all wearing black, and suddenly the very air seemed charged with his presence. Gemma watched, bemused, as Sy leapt from his chair to greet him, as the normally placid Zippo rose hastily, brushing imaginary dust from his jacket. Even the film crew, jaded, blasé, world-weary and impossible to impress, straightened in their seats. Half-smoked cigarettes miraculously disappeared and the brandy bottle vanished behind a flip-chart. Sy's secretary, who had always reminded Gemma of an elderly ghoul, actually blushed and fiddled with the cameo at her throat, a sure sign of almost unbearable excitement.

Appropriately enough, Sy introduced him first to Zippo and then to her. The first touch of his eyes, a strange, pale grey, the colour of old stone under running water, eyes that raked her body and then flicked away dismissively, set her teeth on edge. The first touch of his hand, brief and impersonal, sent a shudder down the back of her spine.

The antagonism that flowed between them was so fierce, so hot, so thick, so shocking that Gemma actually caught her breath. The hairs at the base of her nape prickled, and it seemed to her as though every nerve-end in her body bristled. She felt her nipples tighten and the blood drum in her ears.

Never had she experienced such a sudden, purely visceral reaction to any man. The muscles in the pit of her belly clenched and she could feel her heart racing.

Mouth dry, she swallowed and withdrew her hand. Rocked, she raised her eyes to his, but he had already turned away. Legs inexplicably weak she sank down into her chair and watched as Sy and Zippo completed the introductions, fawning obsequiously like puppies.

If they had tails, Gemma thought furiously, swiftly recovering herself, they would be wagging . . . even Jane was quivering like a bitch in heat.

Alexei Racine looked, Gemma decided angrily, like a refugee from film *noir*, dressed in tight black trousers, a black polo neck sweater and a flowing black cape. He had a nose like a hawk and pale skin . . . a little white make-up base, a few fangs and he could easily play the demon lover in 'Tales of the Vampire', she decided nastily.

The thought drew her eyes to his mouth, the upper lip thin and cruel looking, the lower lip full and sensual. She had a sudden, vivid mental picture of his mouth covering her own and had to suppress a shiver of revulsion.

But his voice was beautiful, a rich, deep baritone flavoured with the trace of an indistinguishable accent, and unexpectedly mellifluous. For some reason, that annoyed her even more.

His entourage seemed to have melted into the background. Casting her eyes about, Gemma saw them standing silently some distance behind Sy's chair at the opposite end of the table, except for one man who had perched on the window ledge and was leisurely lighting a cigarette. He looked vaguely familiar, and she was just trying to place him when her eyes were caught by Racine.

He strolled back to the head of the table and tossed his cape to one of his followers who caught it and smoothed the folds with reverent hands. Outraged, Gemma watched Racine settle himself in Sy's chair and waited with a certain amount of malicious pleasure for Sy's explosion.

It never came. Instead, incredibly, Sy bustled over to the side of the table, dragging his secretary and Zippo in his wake, dislodging not only the first camera man but his own hair piece, and making windmilling gestures with his arms that seemed to indicate some kind of benevolent enthusiasm.

Unmoved, Racine lounged back in his chair, steepled his fingers, silenced the room with a glance, and began to speak.

Astounded by his arrogance, expecting the usual, peppy, exaggerated mix of hype, lies and promises, Gemma at first listened with half an ear. Gradually, as the sense of his comments filtered through, she felt her temper kindle.

He flicked a casual, dismissive finger at her detailed prospectus as he disparaged her carefully planned schedule, raised an ironic eyebrow at the budget, then curled a sarcastic lip at the script and the suggested location shots. He didn't take the trouble to damn with faint praise; he simply, bluntly excoriated every aspect of the entire project under her control in that implacably harsh and beautiful voice.

'Act three,' he was saying, flipping through the script and then tossing it aside, 'might work. Might just possibly work. Might even be regarded as inventive. Innovative. Even daring. In a spaghetti western. Not in Gothic horror.' He ignored the nervous laughter and continued. 'The costumes, of course, are perfect.'

It seemed as though everyone relaxed infinitesimally. Racine paused and poured himself a glass of water.

'Yes. The white nightgown. The Edwardian dinner jacket, cummerbund and black velvet cloak. Perfect. Perfect for a Gothic parody. Perfect for a comedy sketch, perhaps, for BBC 2. Not for this film.'

Across the table Gemma saw Maggie the wardrobe mistress, veteran of thirty years costume work on stage, screen and television, whiten as if she were about to faint. Her own temper finally snapped. Just as she opened her mouth to interrupt Racine's blistering, unprofessional tirade, she was distracted by Sy, who was desperately trying to catch her eye. His bushy eyebrows were wriggling frantically, like two caterpillars trying to mate across his forehead, a signal he fondly imagined was subtle. She knew what it meant. Keep your mouth shut.

Incredulous, Gemma gritted her teeth. One more barbed comment, one more sarcastic jibe, just one more, and she was going to cut loose and damn the consequences. Not only was Racine demoralising the crew, interfering in her sphere of authority, fulfilling his reputation as a complete and utter bastard, but he actually seemed to be enjoying himself. His mouth was faintly twisted in some expression that suggested a lurking smile . . .

It was the last straw. And just as she steeled herself to avoid Sy's eyes as she let rip, Racine decided to finish.

'So. A challenging project for us all. My assistants will no doubt prove invaluable,' he said, waving a careless hand at the pale, androgynous knot of people behind him. 'And I must make known to you Nicholas Frere, who will be joining us for a few days.'

Gemma's heart sank as she heard the name of Britain's most famous – or infamous – film critic. The slender man who had been perching on the window ledge smoking slid to the floor and nodded at the room in general. Nicholas Frere.

Impossible to speak now, under Frere's watchful eyes. The merest hint of discord would no doubt find its way into his next column and the last thing 'Tales of the Vampire' needed at this point was bad pub-licity. It made investors nervous. It made them anxious. It often caused them to withdraw the much needed funds that the studio fed on like . . . like . . . vampires.

Still, she had to say something. Something that would reassert her own authority. Something to reassure the crew. Something to let Racine know that, as far as she was concerned, he could fuck off and die.

Slowly she rose to her feet, and because she couldn't think of a single thing to say, began to applaud. For a moment or two, it was the only sound in the room, but when she swept her eyes over the crew, a withering blue glare they were well familiar with, slowly others joined in, and soon everyone was clapping. Gemma shot a quick look at Racine, whose expression remained unreadable, and then signalled for silence.

'Ladies and gentleman,' she began. 'And of course, Sy and Zippo,' a sally that caused a small ripple of laughter, 'I am sure you are as astonished, and as delighted as I am, that we will be working with a director whose sense of humour is only exceeded by his acting ability.'

Inspiration was flowing. There was a puzzled murmur as Gemma paused for effect, then turned directly to Racine. 'Indeed, I'm truly tempted to convince you to join the cast . . . but, as you rightly point out, this is not a comedy.' She laughed, a warm, spontaneous sounding laugh that had the crew laughing in turn, hardly knowing why.

'As we all know, the business is cruel, uncaring, riddled with gossip and every kind of malice. Even our director, Alexei Racine, has been smeared with poisonous rumours. That he's hell to work for.' Shrugging, she briefly turned to Racine and for a split second let the blue anger blaze from her eyes. 'That he's an unfeeling tyrant. That he's a sarcastic and sadistic bastard.' She smiled at him warmly, hoping he could see the hatred in her eyes, then looked around the table.

'Well, we have just seen a brilliant parody of his reputation, delivered by the man himself, an impersonation acted with such depth, such conviction that I don't hesitate to admit that even I was fooled at first.'

Heart pounding, she turned back to Racine.

'Let me welcome you to "Vampire Tales" and I know I speak for us all when I say how much we are looking forward to working with you. There's food, wine and champagne waiting in Studio Three for a welcome party where we can toast our new director!'

A burst of spontaneous applause greeted her words, occasioned, no doubt, by the promise of free booze, and an eager shuffle to the doors ensued. Smiling, laughing, herding them out of the room, only pausing to hiss a few quick words in Jane's ear, Gemma waited until everyone had left before collapsing onto the nearest chair and reaching for the phone.

'Catering? I need a buffet, wine, champagne and spirits in Studio Three for thirty people in five minutes. No. Food for thirty, booze for sixty. I want them pissed, drunk as newts, I need a party, and I need it now! Don't tell me it's impossible, just do it. Start with the spirits and champagne, we can wait for the food!'

She slammed down the receiver and raked her fingers through her hair, disarranging the elegant coils of her chignon. Her eyes lighted on a pack of cigarettes someone had left on the table, and impulsively she grabbed the pack and extracted a cigarette with shaking fingers, even though she didn't smoke. She puffed at it furiously.

She was so shaken, so dazed, so angry, that she didn't even flinch when the lighter clicked before her.

'You'll find it works better when it's lit,' said an unseen voice which obviously belonged to the thin brown fingers holding the elegant black and gold lighter.

She watched the flame of the lighter meet her cigarette and inhaled. The harsh curl of smoke at the back of her throat made her cough in protest. Eyes and throat smarting she inhaled again and, still coughing, swivelled in her chair to face him.

'Impressive,' commented Nicholas Frere dryly, lighting his own cigarette.

She let out a cloud of smoke, and eyed him through it. He was of medium height, slight but well-built, a pleasant, anonymous face that could blend into any crowd and must have served him well as self-appointed film executioner. His green eyes were alert.

'I don't smoke,' she replied with a smile, referring to her coughing fit, deliberately misunderstanding him.

'You simmer instead, I take it,' replied Frere. 'Quite a treat, watching you and Alexei lock horns for the first time.'

'Wasn't he wonderful?' gushed Gemma, mind working furiously. 'So subtle, such a diabolical sense of humour, such an imaginative way to break the ice with a new crew, and so convincing, such – '

'Alexei and I are old friends,' he said calmly, dropping his cigarette into the water glass Racine had left half-full.

'Oh,' said Gemma, her mind suddenly blank. The look in his eyes, admiring, sardonic, complicit, was more than enough to let her know that he hadn't been taken in at all by her bluff. Any more than the crew would be, unless she managed to get them tight and create an atmosphere of false bonhomie, head Racine off, grab Sy and Zippo and find out what the hell was going on . . .

'You only made one slip,' Frere continued.

'Oh? And what was that?' asked Gemma blandly.

'You got the name of the film wrong . . . it is "Tales of the Vampire" isn't it?'

'Shit!' she exclaimed, running a distracted hand through her hair. 'Damn Sy!'

'Never mind,' he said soothingly, 'I doubt anyone noticed . . . another cigarette?'

'No. Thank you. Mr Frere, it's been – '

'Nicholas,' he corrected, smiling at her, a little hopefully, she thought. 'And I'll call you Gemma. Please?'

'Of course,' she said, mind racing. She had to get to the studio, had to find Sy and Zippo . . . but first, she had to disarm Frere.

'It's a beautiful name,' he said, green eyes warm. 'Very beautiful.' Unspoken was the thought that he found her beautiful as well.

'Thank you, I – '

'And you were just as sharp with Alexei as your name . . . quite glittering, just like a gem.'

'Do you know him well, then?' said Gemma, glancing quickly at her watch. 'You're with him for . . .?'

'One of those dreary "day in the lives of" sort of thing,' replied Frere offhandedly, naming one of the most prestigious Sunday magazines. 'I've been toying with a biography, unauthorised or authorised. I've known Alexei a long time. But perhaps,' he added, 'we should make our way to the studio and make sure the crew are dulling any sensibilities by getting well and truly drunk? That was your plan, I take it?'

81

'Yes,' said Gemma, quickly and expertly recoiling her hair. 'You're right, we really should join the party.'

'And perhaps when this, umm, welcoming party is over, you'd let me buy you a drink?'

Gemma hesitated, and eyed him briefly. He was that most dangerous animal, a critic; a self-professed friend of Racine, which surely made him some kind of lunatic; all in all, a useful source. And she was feeling dangerous, defiant, still on a skittering adrenalin high from her first confrontation with Racine.

'Only,' she said at last, 'if it's a very large one.'

The impromptu party was already in full swing by the time Gemma and Nicholas Frere reached Studio Three. The promise of free drink was as irresistible to the crew as the scent of fresh blood to a pack of sharks and any ice or awkwardness had quickly dissolved in a sea of gin and tonic.

Frere quickly melted away into the crowd, leaving Gemma to circulate. Grabbing a glass of Perrier she fixed a smile on her face and systematically worked the room, testing the atmosphere and looking for Sy and Zippo, who seemed to have vanished into thin air. Nor was there any sign of Racine and his assistants.

Frustrated, she made sure Jane was keeping an eye on the refreshments and exchanged a few words with the wardrobe mistress, Maggie, who was still white-faced and knocking back gin and tonic as if she'd never heard the word 'hangover'. Apart from Maggie, everyone seemed perfectly at ease; the few muttered remarks about the director from hell she quelled with a glare. For the moment, at least, her bluff had worked.

She had all but given up on Sy and Zippo and was

even starting to relax a little when she turned to find herself face to face with Alexei Racine.

'So,' he said softly, 'we have things to discuss, you and I.'

His voice sent a slow shiver down her spine, a tingling frisson that quickened her pulse and she felt her mouth grow dry.

'We do indeed,' she said coolly, meeting his pale grey, predatory eyes. Her whole body seemed to tighten under the force of his stare. Suddenly she felt small and defenceless, like something small and furry caught in the glare of headlights, impaled by the stare of a cobra.

Think of Pascaline, she told herself wildly, the power of the mind, the black leather of the imagination. Look at him and think that you have done things, seen things that he has never dreamed of.

His eyes were almost colourless, ancient eyes that had seen and scorned, eyes older than time and colder than ice.

'My hotel, then, tomorrow at noon. And there is something for you to reflect upon, Gemma de la Mare.'

'Oh?' she said, voice deceptively cool, heart beating erratically.

'I have absolutely no sense of humour.'

It was a relief to escape when the party finally began to wind down and could safely be left in Jane's hands, a relief to wait outside the building, away from the menacing, compelling, hypnotic pale grey eyes of Alexei Racine, even a relief to shiver in the crisp air as Nicholas Frere flagged a taxi . . . and a huge relief to finally relax in the bar of his hotel and sip an ice-cold martini.

To her surprise, he made no mention of 'Tales of the Vampire' or Racine and seemed to deliberately avoid anything to do with the world of film. If, in one small part of her mind, Gemma was aware she ought to be on guard, pumping him for information, selling the film and studio to him, she was too relieved that the day was over, so relieved to be free of Racine that she pushed the thought from her mind.

He was a good conversationalist, witty but not malicious, well-informed but not opinionated, with a wide range of interests and eclectic tastes. He diverted her with his views on Georgian architecture as they drove to his hotel, amused her with his account of a concert he had recently attended, a recent best-seller he had read.

And he was attentive without being patronising, concerned that her martini was just right, that she wasn't in a draught from the door. After the strains of the day, it was like relaxing in a hot bath, like warm balm on a fresh bruise and she was grateful for his company.

It seemed natural to continue their conversation over dinner, utterly right to find herself seated next to him on a plush velvet banquette, thigh to thigh as they discussed the menu.

And over dinner, he let her know in a thousand, small, subtle ways that he wanted her. His eyes were warm and openly admiring, the fleeting brush of his hands too intimate to be accidental, the pressure of his thigh against hers too pronounced . . . and, unaccountably, very, very welcome.

They drunk a sprightly young Chardonnay with fresh oysters, a lush, plush Barolo with fillet steak and a sweetly perfumed Barsac with meringue and fresh strawberries. By the end of the meal Gemma was feeling pleasantly relaxed, like a cat whose fur had been stroked and stroked in exactly the right way, and she agreed rather lazily to a brandy.

'A rather poor selection,' commented Nicholas, frowning at the wine list. 'I have a much better bottle upstairs.'

Their eyes met. It was more than an invitation for a nightcap; the warmth in his green eyes made that obvious. He smiled slightly, a smile at once shy and faintly mischievous, a smile that invited her to join him yet promised no ill will if she refused.

But it was the warmth in his eyes that decided her. It seemed suddenly a very, very long time since she had seen such frank and open desire in a man's eyes, looked into eyes that were warm with wanting, observed a mobile, witty, expressive mouth that assured her of pleasures shared. Pushing aside the memory of her faceless, anonymous dream lover, she smiled back at him.

'It would be a shame to drink poor brandy after such lovely wines,' she agreed.

He touched her hand lightly and signalled for the bill.

His lovemaking was as smooth and as subtle as the brandy they sipped when they reached his room, as lighthearted as the smile that played across his lips.

He kissed her gently as she sat beside him, a light brush of his lips against hers, no questing, plunging tongue, not a hint of teeth, just the warm, gentle pressure of his mouth tasting her, learning her, teasing her.

He took the pins from her hair and ran his fingers through the silky, silvery blonde mass until it was in tumbling disarray. His eyes were half-closed and his mouth had hardened in passion but his hands were gentle as he smoothed her hair around her shoulders, separating two long strands to fall across her breasts.

And still he kissed her, light, teasing kisses, sweet and tantalising, outlining the curves of her mouth, tracing the arc of her eyebrows, the firm line of her jaw. Playful kisses that nibbled at her ears, danced across her throat, flirted with her mouth until Gemma at last slid her hand to the back of his head and pressed his lips more fully against her own.

Their tongues met and tangled. Yet still he teased her, delicately licking her teeth with the tip of his tongue, slipping between them and then darting back. She was warming to his kisses, growing lax and languid, suffused with a blush of pleasure that banished any lingering trace of tension.

His hands moved to the large gold buttons of her suit jacket and he undid them deftly, drawing aside the winter white wool to reveal the navy silk camisole she wore beneath. He made no attempt to free her arms from the sleeves, and when she shifted beneath him, tried to slip out of her jacket, he restrained her with a firm kiss.

She opened her eyes in surprise, but then he moved his mouth to her eyelashes, touched them gently with the tip of his tongue, coaxing them shut, and she understood that he wanted her to lie passive, eyes closed.

His hands were at her breasts now, stroking her through the navy silk camisole, just skirting the nipples that had already hardened to taut peaks. With clever fingers he caressed the soft underswell of flesh that ripened to his touch, long, brown, clever fingers that never grazed the pointed nipples.

Her nipples were almost painfully engorged, hard as pebbles, aching for the sweet suction of his mouth, and she felt her lower lips swell in response, the warmth rise between thighs pressed too tightly together by the slim line of her skirt. He must have felt her shift, must have recognised the tensing of her thighs, because he placed one firm, restraining hand on her leg.

When he finally moved his mouth to her breasts,

sucking them through the silk, biting her gently, rolling the silk covered nipples between his teeth, urging and coaxing them, making them even harder, she moaned aloud.

His mouth was as clever as his fingers, moving from breast to breast, always leaving one nipple before it was fully stimulated, before it was fully sated, never giving her the wild, plundering suckling she craved.

Only when he felt her rub her thighs together, arch her hips in the gentle rhythm of sex, did he move his hand beneath her skirt, slowly, delicately, pausing at the soft skin behind her knee even as he increased the suction of his mouth on her breasts.

And then he pulled hard, sucking the painfully aroused points into his hot mouth, sucking with a desperate fervour that seemed to draw all the blood in her body to her nipples. The silky barrier of her camisole, now wet from his mouth and tongue, clung to her breasts, gave a tiny, delicious friction under the ravenous drag of his tongue, enhanced the hungry pull of his mouth.

She had almost surrendered to his hungry mouth, almost lost herself in the ripe, warm, wet drag of his tongue and teeth through the wet silk, when she felt his hand questing between her thighs, fluttering against her centre, fingers tentatively stroking her core through the silk of her tights, through the silk of her panties.

His mouth was hot and sure on her breasts, his fingers gentle, almost too gentle as he found the tiny stem of her clitoris and caressed it through the barrier of her clothing. She felt her lower lips swell and engorge with blood, felt the humid heat in her groin begin to pulse. The contrast between his ravaging mouth and tender fingers, between the flickering teeth that snapped at her nipples and the gentle hand that cupped her mound was deliciously exciting, feverishly stimulating, and she found herself longing for his rapacious mouth against her sex, his gentle fingers on her nipples.

He moved away and swiftly stripped off his clothes. Opening her eyes, she watched him in the soft light of the two over-sized table lamps he had not troubled to extinguish. His body was lean and slim, torso almost hairless, only a thin, long strip along his belly leading to the dense thatch of pubic hair at his groin. His penis, firmly erect, jutted forth. For a brief moment she saw the carved image of the hunter in the tomb superimposed over Frere's elegant body, the huge, distended shaft, the blank, triangular face, and then it dissolved as he coaxed her to the floor.

He arranged a cushion under her head, then touched her eyelashes gently with the tip of his tongue. Obediently she closed her eyes, willing to drift away with his lips, the feel of his hands running along her body, slipping off her shoes, removing her skirt and then her tights. He left the jacket pushed halfway down her shoulders, restraining her arms, and drew her legs slightly apart.

For a moment he simply looked at her, feasted on the long legs now naked to his eyes, the narrow scrap of dark blue silk encasing her mound, the camisole clinging wetly to her breasts, the hard nipples stiff and erect, and then he bent his mouth to her body.

He was kneeling between her thighs. She felt the brush of his mouth against the silk strip concealing her sex, a whisper of a touch, barely grazing the fabric, a subtle, teasing, playful promise. He toyed with her, browsing with his nose, nudging against the stiffened nub of her clitoris, nuzzling her, inhaling her, while his hands roamed along the smooth

88

length of her legs, admiring her inner thighs, playing with the soft and sensitive skin, teasing her by fingering the elastic edge of her panties before moving away.

He was an elegant lover, almost whimsical, interrupting his eloquent exploration of her sex to kiss the rounded swell of her hip, blow gently on her heated, silk-concealed mound, nibble at the inside of her thighs, finger the muscles of her calves. And when he stroked the sensitive arch of her foot, the sensitive, ticklish arch that made her clench and squirm and giggle reflexively, she felt the low rumble of his laughter between her legs.

And when he finally urged to her feet, licked open the corners of her eyes which she had kept determinedly, obediently shut, eased her suit jacket from her arms, the navy silk camisole from her body and led her to the bed, she was as warm and willing and playful as he, frolicking over his body with her hands and mouth, succumbing momentarily to the deep, dark erotic impulse to suck his penis hard, hard to the back of her throat, hard and deep, then tickling his nipples with her hair until he laughed and pulled her to his mouth for a kiss.

It was sheerly and utterly delightful, a playground of pleasure, a carnal carnival interspersed with laughter, fresh and unspoiled, an erotic roller-coaster of chaste kisses and deep, thrusting fingers, of open mouths and shy, timid fingers. It was the skilled and skilful lovemaking of a man who made sex the meeting of minds as well as bodies, who made laughter lie down with love, who examined and licked the lines on the palms of her hands, speculated on her life-line even as he thrust three fingers up deep inside her.

'Let me find your love line,' he said gazing intently at her palm as his thumb found her clitoris.

'Yes, I think you've found it,' said Gemma breathlessly, half-choking from laughter and the swell of heat that rippled through her. His fingers were moving faster inside her, his thumb slow and sensuous on her clitoris.

'No, it's a bit to the right . . . no, to the left,' he answered, swirling his thumb around the slick protective flesh.

'No, wait, ah, yes,' she murmured, laughter dissolving in anticipation as his thumb returned. She could feel her climax hovering, waiting for the next slow glide of his thumb over her clitoris, waiting for the soft exploding friction.

'Are you sure? It's important to get it absolutely right.'

'Yes, yes, I'm sure, that's it . . . that's right!'

Orgasm frothed and bubbled and fizzed through her, dizzying as the finest champagne, as warming as sunshine, delightful as laughter. It was reaching a plateau after a long, hard climb, an exultant, joyous joyful relief.

As her body arched in pleasure, he entered her, prolonging the pulsing waves with the measured thrust of his body and she heard herself laughing.

Later they showered together, playful as seals under the cascading torrents of water, dried each other and returned to bed. Her last thought, as she drifted off to sleep wrapped in his arms, was how incredibly, astonishingly nice it had been.

She woke to find him cuddled against her spoon fashion. Stretching luxuriously, she caught a glimpse of the digital clock at the side of the bed. Ten o'clock. Thank god for Saturdays, she thought lazily, content, replete and utterly starving, and then remembered her meeting with Racine at noon.

Her first impulse was to dive for the shower, dress

and grab a taxi back to her flat, but even as she impetuously thrust both legs out of bed she began to change her mind.

She showered slowly, taking the time to appreciate the sweet, tender ache between her thighs, and when she finally emerged from the bathroom it was to find Nicholas presiding over a lavish room-service breakfast for two.

They shared the paper and chatted desultorily over coffee and croissants, bacon and eggs and sausages and fresh fruit while Gemma tried to find some way of introducing the subject of Racine. 'So, you're an old friend of Alexei's?' was about the right note, but it was difficult to slip the question in naturally while Nicholas was muttering about the stock market, the latest plane crash, reading aloud excerpts of a book review . . . then tossing aside the paper to kiss her.

'Nicholas, really, mmm,' she began, between kisses, 'that's delicious, but I've got a meeting at noon. With Alexei Racine.'

His arms dropped to his sides and he glanced at the clock. 'Then you'd better hurry,' he pointed out. 'It's almost 11 already.'

'I don't mind being late,' said Gemma casually, reaching for her clothes. 'Punctuality doesn't seem to be one of his virtues . . . what is he like, really? You two are old friends, you said.'

His green eyes were watchful. 'Did I say that?'

'Yes, you did. You said you were considering a biography of some sort,' she prodded, slipping on her tights and fastening her skirt.

'A fascinating subject,' he replied evasively. 'The *enfant terrible* who became the angry young man and now? Who knows. He's nearly forty. I'm curious to know what he has left to say, if anything. And how he's going to say it.'

91

'Yes, why "Tales of the Vampire"?' she wondered. 'Not his sort of flick at all, and why – '

'Gemma,' he said seriously, 'I never work on weekends. I don't mix pleasure and business. OK? Call me when you're through and I'll buy you dinner. But I don't want to talk about Alexei. You understand? It's devouring, takes up too much space, too much time – I'd rather be alone with you. OK?' And he kissed her again.

'He's not ready to see you yet,' announced the tall, slender, pale faced acolyte in black leather who opened the door of Racine's suite.

'I'm sure you'll find that he is,' corrected Gemma coldly. By now she was, deliberately, rather more than an hour late, a nicely calculated riposte to his arrogance of the day before. She had taken a certain amount of satisfaction in dawdling, changing her clothes several times before settling on an arctic grey sweater dress that matched her mood, had enjoyed imagining Racine's growing irritation.

'No, he's not ready yet,' insisted the creature, nodding at the closed bedroom door.

Gemma eyed the creature thoughtfully. It had large eyes dramatically ringed with kohl, fine features, a long, hooked nose, long, shoulder-length black hair and a thin, sweet speaking voice. She couldn't tell if it was a man or a woman. 'Perhaps you would tell him I'm here,' she suggested.

The creature opened its eyes wider. 'Oh, no. I couldn't disturb him.'

'Fine,' she snapped. 'I will.' She strode across the room before it could think to stop her and flung open the door of the bedroom.

Racine was just rising from the bed as she entered. He was nude, a flagrant, blatant nudity that was beyond nakedness, and she felt the heat stain her cheeks as he returned her stare, one ironic eyebrow lifted inquiringly.

She found herself unable to look away. His body was, quite simply, beautiful, the beauty of a dark angel, a Lucifer revelling in his fall. He was force-fully, primitively male, tensile, well muscled with a thick pelt of dark silky hair covering his chest that exploded in tangles at his groin. Involuntarily her eyes fell to his penis, which was slick and tumescent, as if he had just had sex. His penis was large, as perfectly formed as the rest of his body, the very essence of male virility. And yet there was something strangely elegant about him, something pure and cold and vital and bred in the bone.

She had thought Nicholas elegant. Nicholas was a pale imitation, a shadow, insubstantial.

'Gemma de la Mare,' said Racine in the horribly beautiful voice she was learning to detest, 'I wasn't expecting you until two o'clock at the earliest. Three, perhaps, if you had any temper at all.'

She bit her tongue. Obviously in this dance of calculated insults she had made a misstep. She tore her eyes away from his body and saw behind him a vague shape huddled under the covers of the bed. 'Oh, am I early?' she exclaimed disingenuously. 'I do hope I didn't disturb you,' she added. The venom in her voice surprised her.

'Disturb me?' he repeated, moving toward her.

She found herself taking a step back, flinching from the dark, compelling, sensual aura, flinching in fascinated revulsion so powerful it was akin to arousal. He was going to touch her, she could sense it. Her skin was already crawling when he unhur-riedly reached for a black silk robe draped across the foot of the bed, and she felt herself flushing.

'No,' he said reflectively, leisurely belting his robe, 'You don't disturb me. Quite disappointing, really. I rather expected more from you, given our first meeting.'

'With all due respect, Mr Racine,' she began, mustering her nerve and letting malice drip from every syllable.

'Don't bore me, Gemma de la Mare,' he interrupted. 'Your trite, hypocritical, conventional little preambles I can barely tolerate, so don't bore me.' His tone was cool, almost affectedly languid, but his eyes were hot, an intense, boring heat that seemed to fuse her bones.

'You are insufferable,' she bit out, abandoning any semblance of civility. 'Insufferable. An arrogant, egotistical, insufferable bastard, and I'll have you off this film faster than – '

'Daahhling,' he said, his voice pure Noel Coward, 'I rather doubt it. Perhaps we should discuss this further in less, um, conducive circumstances,' he added, nodding at the apparently sleeping figure in the bed and taking her elbow to guide her to the door.

She shuddered at his touch. It was like being kissed by a cobra, caressed by a razor, an icy heat that froze her spine and melted her blood. She walked to the sitting room in a daze, watched the androgynous acolyte swarm over him, offering coffee, arranging the cushions behind his back, fluff needlessly about until a curt nod from Racine dismissed him. Her? It?

'I have already summarised the problems,' said Racine, sipping black coffee. 'I presume you are here with solutions. I am waiting.'

'I don't think you understand your position with the Horror studio,' said Gemma bitingly. 'Nor your role – '

'Yes, this is boring,' nodded Alexei, as if agreeing with her. 'Obviously the paper trail has yet to reach you.' He snapped his fingers and the acolyte produced a file from nowhere. Racine riffled through it, plucked a thick piece of paper loaded with gold seals and dense legalese, and tossed it across the table.

She tried to read and listen at the same time, but it was impossible to take in the wherefores and insomuchases that seemed to indicate Alexei Racine – impossibly! – was now a major shareholder in Horror, Inc. *The* major shareholder.

The words swam before her eyes as she listened to the strangely caressing knife edge of his voice.

'The budget, obviously . . . well, shall we say, money is no object? At my discretion, of course. The script, the wardrobe . . . the pathetic location shots, these are your concern, I think.'

If she had looked up, she would have seen that his eyes were fixed on her intently, but she was trying to focus on the page in front of her even as her mind whirled.

'My "Tales of the Vampire" will become a classic, the demon lover a role to aspire to, like Hamlet. Like Lear. A *tour de force*, a symbol of our times, of love and death and greed.' His voice was hypnotic, compelling. 'With, of course, a twist. It may be true that each man kills the thing he loves. But it is much more subtle to maim it just a little, wound it ever so slightly. Infinitely more subtle. Don't you agree, Gemma de la Mare?

'Think of something vampiric, something otherworldly, a place for lust. For bloodlust,' he prompted softly. 'Use your imagination, free and wild.'

Free. Wild. Vampiric. Otherworldly. Bloodlust. 'There is a place I know in Brittany,' she began unthinkingly, responding reflexively to that harshly satiric, seductive voice.

'In Brittany?' he mocked gently. 'How very convincing for a Transylvanian vampire. Imaginative indeed, Gemma de la Mare.'

'Near Carnac,' she said more strongly. 'There is an old keep, even a graveyard, a place . . . a place where . . .'

'Yes?'

Where I felt the bloodlust. She couldn't say the words aloud. 'And near the Chateau Marais, there is . . .'

Racine was nodding. 'As it happens, I am slightly acquainted with Leo Marais. Yes. Intriguing. Perhaps,' he concluded in his normal, chilling tones.

She felt as though she had awoken from a trance. Puzzled, angry and confused she tossed the sheaf of papers she had been holding onto the table and glared at him. 'None of this makes sense!' she exclaimed. 'We can't restructure now! You don't seem to realise! You've been hired to direct a horror flick with a modest budget and a strict schedule and you're turning it upside down! It's going to be a disaster. A complete and utter disaster! You have to understand – '

'It will be a masterpiece,' he said implacably. 'And you will help me create it.'

Suddenly his mood seemed to change, and he stretched his legs out negligently. His robe parted to reveal long legs firmly muscled, furred with the dark, silk hair that covered his chest. Inexplicably her mouth went dry.

'Or not, as you choose.' He smiled then, as if he had said something amusing. 'Speak to your friend with the beetling eyebrows and the appalling hairpiece. What is his name? Sly?'

'Sy,' she spat out, interrupting him.

He shrugged indifferently. 'Sy, then. Speak to your lawyer. Examine your contract. Consider the prospect of a dark and exciting voyage to the heart of the vampire. Look into your soul, Gemma de la Mare. And I think you will find that you have no choice.'

Chapter Five

A lone in her flat, Gemma called Sy. She listened to lies, half-truths and evasions as frantic as his manic eyebrows. She listened to 'oh darlings' and 'sweethearts' until she thought she might gag. She slammed down the phone. She read her contract and groaned. She called her lawyer and then poured a stiff drink.

She didn't call Nicholas Frere.

Racine appeared to be right. She didn't seem to have much of a choice at all.

She ignored his enigmatic, melodramatic advice to look into her soul. She scorned his invitation to . . . what was it? Explore the heart of the vampire? Rumour was right. Obviously he was an addict. Perhaps he would overdose soon. Tonight, with any luck. And then she wouldn't be faced with a penalty for breaking her contract that seemed to exceed the national debt.

She shut the curtains on the afternoon sun, undressed and scooted into bed, burrowing deeply beneath the covers, knowing she wouldn't sleep, merely craving comfort. She tried to lull the frantic turmoil of her thoughts by thinking of the night before, the warm rightness, Nicholas and his deliciously playful lovemaking, the comforting warmth of his body, tried to banish the spectre of Racine with the memory of Nicholas. She wrapped it around her like a blanket that could ward off the chill of reality, and eventually, to her vague surprise, fell asleep.

And he came for her as she slept, tore her away from the comforting embrace and enfolded her in pale arms with silky dark hair that became the wings of a black velvet cape.

And then he fed on her, fed on the flesh between her legs as if it were her heart, ripe and red and pulsing; devoured her with his greedy, ravenous, avid mouth, drank from her as if her body's moisture was his lifeblood.

The sudden heat that flooded her was dark and all consuming. She gave herself over to it, desperate to be devoured, aching to pour herself into his greedy mouth, feed him with her body. His tongue was plunging deep inside her, so deep that she could imagine it curling around her heart, pulling it down to the pit of her belly where her muscles knotted and clenched, spasming in liquid tension.

He was fierce and overpowering and she succumbed eagerly, willingly, an ardent victim to the rapacious dracula mouth that fired her as he fed on her. Swift and sure, with the clean precision of a predator, the killing grace of a striking hawk, he forced her climax, a shuddering, thudding, pulsing climax that was ecstatically annihilating.

She writhed and convulsed, the force of her climax driving her awake even as the red glow coursed through her. But in the scant few seconds before she woke, he had raised his face to hers, cruel grey eyes shining in triumph, lips stained with her blood.

It was the face of Alexei Racine.

It was a long time before her breathing slowed to normal, before the rippling aftershocks of her orgasm finally stilled, before she could forget the look in his eyes, the silvery triumph, the dark ruby drops of her blood staining his lips.

'Cut,' said Racine flatly, rising from his canvas director's chair to pace irritably. Gemma watched him move with catlike grace, avoiding the heavy cables and leads that snaked across the floor and wished fleetingly that he would trip and break his neck. She glanced across at the two actresses now waiting sullenly under the hot studio lights and read the same wish in their eyes.

Two weeks had passed in a frantic blur of revisions and re-writes, major changes and minor details. It seemed to Gemma that half of her life was now spent on the phone, making arrangements, changing arrangements, confirming, cancelling, re-confirming. She was worn out, and the cast and crew all seemed to be in that strange, exalted exhaustion that belongs to the last days of a shoot. Racine himself never seemed to tire.

Fortunately he had agreed to begin with a few simple scenes that could be filmed at the studio, which would save time and money . . . or so Gemma had hoped. But he was a merciless perfectionist, demanding take after take of the most basic scenes, and the budget was in severe danger of spiralling completely out of control, especially given his decision to move the bulk of the filming to Brittany . . .

His voice broke into her thoughts. 'This is a simple story,' he was saying with overt condescension to the two actresses who had been struggling with a single take for almost two days now. 'We encapsulate the tale of Dracula into a single night. You, Lucy, and you, Mina are old friends on a European tour with your husband and your fiancé. A sudden, brutal storm has overtaken you, driven you to seek shelter in the castle. You have been shown to your rooms to change, your clothing is wet, heavy, sodden. As you went up the stairs, you both caught a brief glimpse of the Count. No more than a glimpse, you understand?'

'But it was a powerful moment, profound, shocking. You both saw it, both felt it. It was lust, blood-lust, craving, clawing desire. It shivered through you, made you wet, made you want, yes? But you are respectable, Victorian women. You don't understand. You repress. But your bodies remember. You must use your bodies . . . show me your bodies remembering.'

He returned to his chair and nodded at the crew.

'This is a take,' called out a hidden voice. 'Quiet on the set.'

Gemma stood at his side, intently watching the two actresses resume their poses, hoping desperately that they would find some way of interpreting the scene to his liking. He seemed determined to infuse the film with a dark eroticism, even the most basic, connective passages, and she felt sorry for the two actresses now sweating under the lights. Difficult, she mused, verging on the absurd, to show the memory of repressed craving, clawing desire, when all the scene called for was Mina to help Lucy off with her cloak and tidy her hair.

'Cut! It's no good,' Racine called out, rising from his chair and striding across the set, oblivious to the collective groans. 'I will show you what I want,' he said, waving the two actresses away. 'Where's the extra for Lucy? Wait . . . no. Gemma, come here.'

'What?' she asked, startled.

'Here,' he said, pointing to the red line taped to the studio floor. 'Walk to the chalkmark, wait while I remove your cloak, then sit before the mirror.'

He didn't wait for her assent, merely walked over to the blue line that directed Mina across the set. As Gemma opened her mouth to protest, she was caught by a subtle difference in Racine's movements. He was somehow more graceful, more fluid, more feminine. She could almost hear the muffled rustle of heavy, rain-soaked skirts dragging on the flagged stones, sense the chilled weariness of pale limbs smothered by the heavy fabric . . .

'Now,' he ordered.

She blinked, startled by the momentary illusion he had conjured, then tossed her notes onto his chair and moved to the set, tugging the sodden cloak over her shoulders that Lucy had handed her.

She stood on the chalkmark, blinking a little at the heat of the lights. They were using 'in limbo' lighting, with the background blacked out and only the actors and the dressing table lit and it was almost insufferably hot. Her back was to Racine.

'Observe,' he said. She felt him behind her as his hands came to rest gently on her shoulders in a touch that was almost impersonal but strangely intimate. They lingered for a fraction too long, a brief moment that seemed like infinity, and then moved to the ties at her throat. She was amazed to feel his hand tremble slightly against her skin, an accidental, fleeting touch, so fleeting that a second later she wondered if she had imagined it.

'The subtle gesture,' said Racine. 'This is film, not stage. The camera observes with a searing, minute eye. Mina, let your hand shake a little against Lucy's throat. Just a little, as you feel the silken touch of her skin in a new way, a disturbing way, only subconsciously aware of the jugular, the lifeforce so near

101

your fingers. Let the cloak slide down slowly, tenderly, lovingly, as though your fingers sense what your mind cannot.'

She could feel the heat of his hands through the cloak as he eased it away from her shoulders, as surely as if he were touching her naked skin. There was a controlled intensity to his touch, an unseen, inarticulate longing that seemed to speak to her body, rouse her nerve ends, liven her skin.

She knew she was merely standing in for the actress who played Lucy, no more than a convenient shape; she knew the crew were watching intently; knew too that she detested the tyrannical, abrasive, arrogant man who stood behind her, sliding the cloak from her shoulders.

But somehow there was magic in his hands, an illusory magic that deceived her body, making her skin heat and pulse quicken, almost as if she were the naive, Victorian Lucy responding to the innocently erotic touch of her friend.

'Sit before the mirror.'

Only the voice jarred, that clipped, cold voice with icy vowels and harsh consonants. Strangely, though, it didn't break the spell of his hands, and she walked wordlessly to the dressing table. She sat before the mirror and closed her eyes.

'Again, observe.'

His hands were sifting through her hair. With fingers gentle as a woman's he loosened the coil of her chignon and let her hair fall around her shoulders. And then he took the heavy silver-backed brush from the dressing table and began to brush her hair in long, smooth strokes. Somehow it was soothing, yet strangely exciting, sitting motionless under the hot lights, under the watchful eyes of cast and crew, feeling the soft bristles of the brush against her scalp, the caressing touch of his fingers as they smoothed her hair.

He used firm, rhythmic strokes that echoed deep inside her with the sure ease of flesh against flesh, as though he was stroking her inner depths. She felt at once soothed and caressed, petted like a favourite child, yet deeply, wetly aroused.

It was Racine and not Racine, the delicate womanly brush against her hair belied by the sharp male musk of his body. Under the merciless lights they were both sweating and she could smell him. She swallowed, mouth suddenly dry.

He was brushing her senses alive, creating a warm, tingling awareness that suffused her entire body, from her scalp to her toes, a fluttering, melting warmth that pooled between her thighs. She felt her nipples tighten, her sex swell and moisten, and she pressed her legs together, just shifting slightly, trying to contain the feeling, obscure the thrumming arousal that was beginning to simmer just beneath her skin.

No-one could guess, she thought wildly, no-one could imagine the burgeoning, insistent heat coiling deep in the pit of her belly, the slick warmth between her thighs. It was the craving that could only be satisfied by the hard length of a man against her body, driving into her . . . involuntarily she leaned back ever so slightly, instinctively arching to the hot male presence behind her.

'Excellent,' pronounced Racine, tossing the brush onto the dressing table. The noise jarred her and her eyes flew open. In the mirror Gemma could see her face was flushed, the tell-tale rosy flush of desire and she gritted her teeth. Thank god for the lights, the hot stage lights. She glanced warily around the set, but everyone was focused on Racine.

'The subtle movement is everything,' he was saying. 'Compress. The faint, slight indication, the

103

merest hint . . . you saw Gemma press her thighs together, lean back to me almost imperceptibly? Unwilling, unwitting arousal . . . oh, very well acted,' he added, a sardonic gleam in his eye as he turned briefly to Gemma that left her in no doubt that he had sensed her body's response.

And at that moment she hated him more than she could ever have imagined.

'Now,' he said, looking at the actresses playing Lucy and Mina. 'Resume. And you, you will watch,' he said to Gemma, hand tight on the back of her neck.

She was dazed, didn't remember moving from the highlighted set, couldn't recall slumping in the canvas director's chair. But she was, and his hand was heavy on her neck. It seemed like the first time he had touched her and she was both embarrassed and revolted, disgusted and secretly, shamefully, thrilled.

She watched Lucy and Mina re-enact the simple movements, the simple gestures, and, unwillingly, felt herself succumb to the subtle sensuality of the scene, of two women intensely aware of each other, naive yet lascivious, innocently, lewdly, lubricious.

The set was absolutely still, a stillness strangely unlike the silence that usually accompanied a take. There seemed to be an awareness, a silent, complicit, avid awareness that fed on the quiet eroticism of the two women under the hot lights. Gemma felt drawn into the scene, drawn back to it, wished for a brief, wild moment that she was back under the hot lights, under the gentle, womanly hands, tasting for the first time the sweet, forbidden decadence of a perversely innocent carnality, and was vaguely shocked at herself.

'Cut and print.' Alexei Racine released his hold on the back of her neck and moved away. There was an audible sigh of relief and triumph, and then everyone was talking at once, laughing, self-congratulatory and excited, almost euphoric.

Her body still simmering, frustrated, Gemma watched as Racine nodded and gave a half smile to the two women on the set and knew, without a shadow of a doubt, he meant to have both of them. The intent in his pale silvery eyes was unmistakable.

She turned away, a faint, fastidious disgust almost masking her own excitement.

That night Gemma called Nicholas. They had spoken once or twice on the phone since the night at his hotel, friendly, inconsequential conversations in which, thankfully, the question of when to meet again had remained unspoken. He seemed to be as busy as she – with what, she wasn't exactly sure. He hadn't reappeared on the set, so if he was trailing Racine it was outside the studio. Perhaps he'd abandoned the notion of a biography. She didn't know and didn't care.

What she needed – no, what she wanted, she corrected herself – was a break. A pleasant evening in pleasant company. A decent meal, instead of the horrible microwave/boil-in-a-bag concoctions she'd been eating recently that somehow all managed to taste the same or, which was worse, taste of nothing much at all. Yes, a good meal, a good bottle of wine . . . and some good sex. Something to appease the hungry ache between her thighs, obliterate the memory of Racine's hands sifting through her hair, the sight of Lucy and Mina . . .

For a moment she paused, hand hovering undecidedly over the telephone. A month ago, two months ago, she wouldn't have thought this way, she realised in vague surprise.

If she had never believed herself particularly

passionate, she had never deluded herself that she was a romantic. The old eighties ideal of 'having it all' had vanished along with the concept of 'Superwoman'. In the ashes of too many breakdowns, divorces and broken dreams, the sex wars of the nineties smouldered. She had been, by and large, as indifferent to the issues of sexual politics as she had been to sex itself, she realised with a start of surprise.

And now, quite simply, she wanted to get laid. A good meal, a good wine, and a good fuck, preferably in that order. The thought rather stunned her. Was this, she wondered, how men thought about sex? It seemed so crude, somehow, so, so . . . unloving.

In the event, it was neither crude nor unloving. They shared a good meal, pâté followed by lemon sole and a cheese board, good wines – a Beaujolais and a Niersteiner, and some of the excellent brandy he kept in his room.

And they shared each other, a long, leisurely coupling that was alternately fierce and sweet. He kissed her everywhere, deep, tonguing kisses, light, playful kisses, open-mouthed, plunging kisses on her shoulders, her arms, her breasts and belly and between her legs, lapping and nibbling and sucking until she came in a warm rush of pleasure.

But even as she lay beside him, sated, Gemma found her thoughts returning to the wild red heat that had washed through her under the hot lights of the set, the feel of Alexei Racine's hands sifting through her hair, the lewd innocence of Lucy and Mina, and wondered idly what perverse games the three of them were playing.

Alexei Racine was sipping champagne and watching the two actresses who played Lucy and Mina undress. They seemed at once shy and unselfconscious, awkward yet adroit, and they were watching him with awed, excited eyes. They wanted him, he knew, even more than they wanted each other.

It didn't surprise him.

He had struck a performance from them that had astonished them, perhaps even shocked them a little, had forced them to find a secret, purely feminine sensuality. He was the catalyst, the conjurer, the magician . . . the director. It was he who stole their will, forced them to bare themselves to the merciless eye of the camera, strip their souls for the sake of celluloid. He was at once priest and pirate, confessor and executioner. Power. The ultimate aphrodisiac.

He enjoyed the familiar look in their eyes, enjoyed the familiar, heady rush of knowing he could do anything to them, anything at all, and they would welcome it gratefully, open themselves to him utterly.

Briefly he thought of Gemma, the look of vague contempt in her eyes as she had turned away, and smiled.

He pushed the thought aside as Lucy and Mina approached him. As they undressed him, Mina fumbling with the buttons of his shirt, Lucy expertly opening his flies, he felt himself hardening and wondered how to take them. That they would find, tentatively, covertly, ways of discovering each other, pleasuring each other, even as they devoted their bodies to his, he had no doubt. It would be amusing to feel them feeling for each other, intriguing to watch them explore the subtle delights of female flesh for the first time.

Kneeling before him, Lucy closed her mouth on his distended penis, swirling the throbbing tip with her tongue, elated to feel him swell further. Almost breathless with excitement she ran her fingers along his hard, muscled thighs, silky with dark hair, and

107

shuddered as she felt the fleeting, gentle brush of Mina's fingers against her own.

That was how she thought of her now, as Mina, just as she herself was Lucy, a shy and innocent Lucy tasting lust for the first time.

And it was lust, pure and hot, as she felt his hard length swelling between her lips, pulsing a little as she traced the great vein of his undershaft with her tongue.

She forgot that she had rather disliked the actress playing Mina, forgot that she was learning to detest Racine, forgot everything in the dark magic of surrendering to the role he had created for her. She was a lascivious innocent with a skilled and knowing tongue, a naive virgin with a heated pulse between her legs that was growing stronger, more insistent.

And when he pulled her to her feet, drawing her head to his blunt, male nipples, she knew he wanted her to lick them softly, tease them delicately, tongue them as though they were a woman's nipples, soft and sensitive, not the hard nubs that tightened only slightly to her mouth.

Slipping her tongue through the dark, curling hair, tonguing the hard points that seemed barely responsive to her flickering mouth, she imagined Mina's nipples, large, pink buds that would turn rosy, suffused with blood, tender nipples that would pucker deliciously under the shy, sly, sure suction of her mouth.

Mina was behind her now, pressing her breasts against her back, nipples rubbing deliciously against her shoulder blades. She felt a hand move between her thighs, parting her inner lips, fingers thrusting inside her, testing her arousal. Already damp, she felt herself grow wetter, muscles spasming and clenching, responding to the hard, probing length inside her.

And then she felt Mina move, felt the warm brush of her nipples down her back, pausing at the base of her spine, then lower, sweeping against the taut globes of her buttocks. The delicate, questing touch seemed somehow to heighten her awareness of the hard, male flesh beneath her lips and fingers.

There was a strange sensation between her thighs, something soft yet hard, forcing her legs further apart as the probing fingers inside her withdrew. The soft caress of Mina's hair against her heated vulva almost triggered her climax as she realised that Mina's head was between her thighs. She felt Racine's hips begin to thrust against her own, felt the echoing, rhythmic drag between her legs as Mina took him in her mouth.

Mina's head was moving back and forth, her hair brushing against her slick, secret lips, against her swollen clitoris, moving with a driving, pressing urgency. She felt the first, fluttering intimation of climax, the liquid heat between her thighs growing molten, the tingling tension gathering and knotting, deep in the pit of her belly.

And then Racine stepped back. At his gesture, she moved to the bed, drew aside the soft coverlet, intending to hide between the sheets, cool her heated skin like the tremulous virgin she half-believed herself to be.

'No.'

He arranged her body to his liking, spreading her legs wide apart so that the moist, pink leaves of her sex were fully visible, opening her fully to them. She began to lose the reassuring veil of her role, shivered a little at the harsh, intrusive edge of reality, and shifted a little. At once he was beside her, mouth hot and hungry at her throat, hands hard on her breasts, and she felt the soft touch of Mina's mouth on her body.

Her tongue was dainty, lightly skimming the sensitive, delicate folds, sipping at the moist and secretive crevices, just fluttering against her clitoris then slipping away to lick the insides of her thighs.

Under the rough clasp of Racine's fingers on her breasts, her nipples were hard and distended, swollen, aching points stimulated to the point just verging on pain. Even as she longed for the gentle wash of his tongue, his mouth descended to suck on her ferociously, avidly.

She gave a low cry and felt Mina's tongue thrust deep inside her.

Rather later that night, in Paris, Leo Marais received a telephone call. He was lounging in the small salon of his townhouse. Before him a small fire was burning merrily in the neo-modern marble fireplace. The flickering light played across the attenuated lines of a female bronze by Giacometti he had acquired that afternoon; he was admiring the gaunt beauty of the piece as he sipped an old brandy and smoked a cigar.

In front of him Gabrielle de Sevigny lay at his feet, wearing a tissue thin oyster silk peignoir. Through it he could see the dark nimbus of her areolae, the darker plume between her thighs. She was stroking his feet gently, waiting submissively.

He knew that she was freshly bathed and perfumed, anticipating his touch; knew too that she was wet inside and her anus oiled, both channels of her body ready to receive him at his whim. The merest gesture would open her to him, but she knew better now than to ask.

A few weeks ago she had complained that he was too distant, too cold. They had been lying in bed, drinking champagne, relaxing after sex.

Without a word he had taken some ice from the ice bucket, pressed it against her still heated core, thrust an ice cube deep inside her with his tongue and forbidden her to move until it melted. The fierce intensity of her climax had surprised him.

Yes, Leo, mused, she had learned well. He was pleased with her. He had trained her painstakingly and the rewards were sweet. Like the Giacometti, Gabrielle was a victory. Soon, of course, unlike the sculpture, she would begin to pall. Why was it, he wondered, that contentment – for he was indeed content – eases so gently, so imperceptibly, so inevitably into boredom?

He sighed and poured a little more brandy, rather relieved when the telephone rang.

'*Oui*? Yes, yes, my friend,' he said, impatiently removing his foot from Gabrielle's caressing hands. It caught at the hem of her peignoir, which she took as a signal to disrobe. He hadn't meant it, and rather abstractedly waved her back to the floor.

'Yes, of course, it can be arranged, it is already well in hand. But I must tell you, my friend, I fail to understand your reasons.'

There was a long pause.

'A strange fancy, my friend,' Leo commented at last with a slight frown. 'Me, I give my women away when I have done with them. You do this before you begin. Why, I ask myself?'

'A deliberate inversion. Or do I mean perversion?' said Alexei Racine, before breaking the connection.

Gabrielle watched her lover with an impassive face as his words burned into her heart. Leo? Give his woman away when he had done with them? It was a fierily chilling thought that etched her soul with acid.

She had not been living in some fool's paradise, had never lied to herself that this liaison with Leo was anything more than an exquisite meeting of the flesh. If she ever wore rose-tinted glasses they came with a designer label and matched her latest outfit.

111

But she was honest with herself. Leo was an obsession, a potent, dominating, driving obsession. She couldn't think about him now without a reflexive spasm of craving, a liquid, lubricious wanting. The merest memory could make her soaking wet. The thought of his hands, his beautifully shaped fingers. His hair, dark and thick and glossy, as he bent his head to her breast. The white teeth that closed on her nipples.

But it was not just his body.

He had a Machiavellian sensuality, a taste for power faintly edged with cruelty combined with a hedonist's appreciation of pleasure that made him, quite simply, the most spectacular lover she had ever known.

He was the first lover she had known whose sexual imagination exceeded her own. Unlike most men, he wasn't averse to aids in loving, dildoes and vibrators, beads and unguents. Perhaps it had never occurred to him that so many of them were meant to replace the male organ; perhaps he was so confident in the prowess of his tongue and hands and mouth and penis that he could use them to enhance his own performance and thus her pleasure.

With a vivid flush of desire she remembered how he had watched her arouse herself with her vibrator, leaned between her thighs as she let the pulsing rod play over her delicate tissues, thrum against her clitoris. He had let her insert it, let her revel in the whirring internal massage until she was about to come, and then torn it away. But as he drove into her himself, he had thrust a tiny vibrator he had kept concealed deep into her back passage, and the electrifying, galvanic shocks of his own powerful thrusts against the trembling vibrator had created a climax unlike any she had ever experienced.

She cast a quick look at him from beneath her

lashes. He was frowning at the fire. So, Leo Marais gave his women away when he finished with them, did he? Well, she acknowledged, he did seem that sort of man. Pride, of course, dictated that she finish the affair before he did . . . and that she was not ready to do.

Was there, she wondered, any way to keep this man, turn his sexual prowess against him, enthrall him as he had enthralled her?

'Come here, Gabrielle.'

Gracefully she draped herself beside him in the oversize white leather chair, mind and will almost dissolving in a heated rush of sensation as his clever fingers unerringly sought her clitoris, quickly rousing her with firm, rapid strokes. So well attuned was her body to his touch that she was almost immediately on the verge of climaxing.

But Leo seemed vaguely abstracted, an abstraction that showed itself in his eyes, now fixed on the Giacometti, not in the quick thrust of his fingers.

'Would you like more brandy?' she asked softly, fighting to match his distance, aware of the tightening knot of impending orgasm.

'Mmm. Thank you, my dear,' he replied.

With his free hand he held out the brandy balloon. As she lifted the decanter from the table beside her, her hand trembled slightly.

His fingers slipped inside her, testing her arousal, teasing her inner walls. She felt the first, faint throb of her climax begin. His fingers moved faster, in and out, circling the mouth of her vagina then driving deep, mimicking the pulse that was beating deep inside, driving her to the edge.

He felt her convulse around her fingers, small spasms that increased in intensity as he kept his fingers moving in and out of her, spasms that became shudders as her body contracted and convulsed again and again. He waited for her moan, the tiny, mewing sigh of surrender she invariably made as she came, but she was silent, the only sound her ragged breathing as her body stilled.

Curious, he tore his eyes away from the sculpture and looked down at her. Her cheeks were flushed and her eyes were bright. 'Gabrielle?' he said, fingers still deep inside her.

'Mmm,' she replied. 'I too would like some brandy, Leo.'

'Of course,' he said, a slight smile lightening his eyes. She really was a superb actress, he thought absently. Only the rosy blush of her cheeks and the brightness of her eyes betrayed her orgasm. 'I shall be leaving Paris at the end of the week,' he added, watching her reaction intently.

'Really, darling?' she replied, slipping away from his fingers and bending down to retrieve her peignoir. When she turned to him her expression was bland.

'Yes. I shall need to visit the chateau, make sure everything is in order.'

'Poor Leo, what a bore for you,' she said, taking another brandy balloon and pouring herself a glass.

'No, no, it won't be a bore, I'm sure of that,' he said. 'Come with me?'

He said it impulsively, as if the invitation half-surprised him. She looked at him consideringly, then responded. 'Perhaps I will.'

Gemma was in the small studio screening room watching the rushes. It was early, so early that she was alone, and for that she was grateful. Because she was absolutely astounded. They were brilliant, utterly compelling, completely enthralling. The disconnected, disjointed sequence of apparently unrelated incidents had all the force and power of a full narrative.

Racine, she admitted, was a genius. A sarcastic, egocentric, intolerable bastard, but still a genius. She froze the film on the scene between Mina and Lucy, and shook her head in wonder. After cutting it would run two minutes, perhaps less, in a total running time of an hour and a half; in itself it was a triumph of the art.

What would he do with the location shots, she wondered, the old keep and crumbling graveyard, the naked, listing trees? They had almost completed the filming in the studio; Racine had insisted that the bulk of the film be shot on location for atmosphere and had taken it upon himself to make the arrangements.

Strange, now that she thought about it. He had apparently agreed to her suggestion sight unseen, yet seemed to know the owner. She shook her head. Racine had thrown the normal, orderly, well-defined management hierarchy into chaos; her assistant, Jane, had been absorbed into the androgynous coterie surrounding Racine that collectively seemed to function as an assistant director; her own role seemed subject to change without notice – just yesterday he'd used her as a stand-in! Briefly she envied Sy and Zippo who, unsurprisingly, had turned tail and gone back to Barbados.

She sighed and returned her attention to the screen.

'It's good,' said a voice behind her.

She knew that voice. It crawled over her skin. Had it been anyone but Racine she would have told the truth, that it was absolutely, astoundingly, brilliant.

'It will do, yes,' she replied levelly, without turning around.

Strangely, he didn't seem offended. 'I think so,

too,' he replied. As she turned to face him, a match flared and she smelt the acrid smoke of his cigarette.

Her senses swam. For a moment, the darkened screening room was the tumulus deep beneath the earth, the flare of the match a prelude to the fiery, flaming assault of his mouth against hers, her dream lover, her demon lover . . .

'We'll leave for Brittany at the end of the week,' said Racine, switching on the lights.

She blinked as the strange sensation vanished, dispelled by the light and the familiar harshness of his voice. 'Impossible to arrange at such short notice,' she argued automatically. 'Transport, accommodation – '

'All arranged,' he interrupted, drawing on his cigarette. 'We need to go before the light changes, before spring. Six weeks should do it.'

Chapter Six

As the grey Jaguar shot along the road to Carnac, Gabrielle de Sevigny buried her nose in the collar of her full length ranch mink coat and eyed Leo thoughtfully. Paris was behind them now; he had barely spoken as they weaved their way through the dense traffic and she had respected his silence, assuming he was concentrating on the maddening tangle of cars and buses, vans and bicycles, Japanese tourists with cameras and an incomprehensible predilection for standing in the middle of the road.

Now the way was clear, and he still hadn't said a word. Perhaps he didn't like to talk when he was driving? She wasn't sure, couldn't tell. In truth, she knew very little about Leo, she realised.

Conversation had never figured largely in their affair; theirs was the language of bodies. She would have known every inch of his skin blindfolded, recognised his cock, his taste, amidst a hundred, a thousand others. But they rarely spoke. And when they did, it was with the explicit vocabulary of sex. Harder. Faster. Deeper. Slower. Now.

So she was curious to learn more of him, outside

the bedroom. Not, of course, that ever they confined themselves to the bedroom, she thought with an inward smile. But this long drive to the chateau was the first time they had spent together when sex was not their immediate goal, and she was eager to explore him in other ways. For a certain class of Frenchwoman – educated, politically aware – conversation is just as stimulating as sex, or very nearly so, and Gabrielle loved to talk.

'Your friend, Alexei Racine,' she began, selecting a topic at random. 'What is he like?'

Leo was silent for a long time, so long that she began to wonder if he was going to answer, or if he had ever heard her.

'He likes Picasso,' he said finally.

'Ah, yes?' prompted Gabrielle encouragingly.

'Yes.'

Miles flashed by. Just as she was about to express her own views on Picasso, how she preferred the realistic romanticism of his early work, her reservations about his Blue and Pink periods, Leo spoke again.

'He also likes Renoir and Modigliani, but he prefers Picasso.' It was said regretfully.

'I see,' replied Gabrielle. Sensing Leo wouldn't welcome a long discussion on Cubism versus Neo-Classicism, she returned to her original topic.

'He is truly gifted . . . what did you think of "Naked Under the Stars"?' she asked, referring to Racine's last film.

'I didn't see it,' he replied, eyes fixed on the road.

'No?' she asked in some surprise. The critics had gone into raptures, describing it a major *tour de force* . . .

'I dislike the cinema,' he explained briefly.

'Oh,' she said in a small voice. Not art, not film;

politesse rather excluded politics, given her husband Pierre's position; what next?

Leo's mind was elsewhere. He was thinking about a dancer by Degas that had recently come on the market. His dealer had called him that morning, quoting a ridiculous price. An absurd figure. Absurd.

Yet she was beautiful, that dancer. Just the photograph he had seen had lifted his spirits. She was young and graceful, fresh as spring, fluid and lithe, her body embracing the dance, and he wanted her.

He had two ruling passions which coalesced in the sculpted figures of women: sex and the female body. A passionate love for sculpture in all its forms allied to an intense, almost obsessive, greed for women. The tableaux he had arranged for the New Year's party at the chateau perfectly expressed, perfectly encapsulated, his twin obsessions. He fell in love with his sculpture and made love to the women who seemed to embody their essence. And he had dedicated himself to those two arts that often intertwined.

He was a clever collector.

A superb lover.

At times, an indifferent conversationalist.

He was thinking now about Gabrielle and Degas, what Degas might have made of her, and how he, Leo, could transmute that imagined inspiration into some balletic carnality that could pay tribute to their separate, complementary geniuses. Nothing so banal as a tutu and a ballet barre; he was both a lover and a connoisseur of some imagination.

Yes, he thought, hardening, he would buy her, even at the ridiculously inflated price his dealer had quoted. And he would have her. Yet in his imagination, Gabrielle didn't quite mesh with Degas, certainly bore no relation to the gaunt Giacometti he had just purchased . . . still, he remembered how she had convulsed around his fingers last night, so tightly, so strongly that he could almost feel the semen dripping from his fingertips, knew that if it had been his penis inside her he would have come in an instant, driven over the edge, milked dry of every life-giving fluid with her convulsing, pulsating, throbbing spasms.

He was hard, whether from the memory of her climaxing around his finger or the impending purchase of the Degas, it was impossible to tell.

'Gabrielle, give me your foot.'

'What?'

'Your foot . . . your calf, your thigh.'

'Leo?'

'I'm thinking of the dance, the ballet . . . give me your foot,' he repeated.

His eyes were still fixed on the road, but his right hand was waiting on the seat between them. Her body reacted instinctively to his words. She slipped off her shoe and raised one silk clad leg to his hand.

'The ballet?' she said interestedly. 'Pierre and I were at the Opera de Paris Garnier last week for Swan Lake, and I –'

'Hush, Gabrielle.'

His fingers were exploring her foot, caressing the high arch, the tendons and muscles, stroking her toes, his touch sensual yet strangely clinical, as if he needed to trace the path of every vein. Her sheer silk stockings were like gossamer under his hand.

Her body replied smoothly, softening, swelling, nipples hardening and sex tingling. Inside she was growing moist, dampening, the familiar red ache beginning between her thighs.

How could he do this to her, she wondered dazedly, senses swimming, how could he melt her bones with a single touch? It seemed his attention never faltered from the road even as his hand moved

120

higher, searching her calf, feeling the tendons at the back of her knee.

'Flex your muscles, Gabrielle, as if you were dancing.'

Automatically she tightened her leg muscles, amazed to feel an echoing, flexing cramp in her inner muscles, as though they were trying to clasp the hard length of some invisible rod.

'Harder, Gabrielle, harder.'

Swallowing, mouth suddenly dry, she obeyed. The answering throb of her inner body was becoming stronger, deeper, and she could feel the slick heat of her sex. She was soaking wet now, unbearably aroused, almost ready to climax simply from the firm, repeated clasp of his fingers on her calf.

She waited, hardly breathing, for his hand to move higher, find the curve of her thigh, press against the swollen heat of her sex, knowing she would come instantly.

'Yes, just there,' said Leo, as his fingers probed the tendons at the back of her knee.

Reflexively she tightened her muscles again. The pulse between her thighs gathered, knotted, then exploded, orgasm cascading through her in a swift, electrifying tide. She shuddered as it rippled again and again, the red heat slowly diminishing to a rosy glow.

Leo was holding tightly to her ankle, only releasing his grip when her body quietened.

'Yes,' he said, turning to face her for the first time since they had left Paris. 'There is something about the dance.'

The rest of the drive passed in silence.

She would never have believed that the memories could be so vivid, so real. It was as if time had telescoped itself, and she was the Gemma who had driven this road scant weeks before. The landscape had changed little; the land was still sleeping a grey sleep, waiting for spring, trees stark and still bare of leaves. But she had the strangest sense that she was returning without having left, as if the intervening space had been a mere dream, without substance or reality.

Dreaming, dream lover . . . she felt the heat rise to her face and glanced over at Alexei Racine. He ignored her, apparently immersed in a paperback edition of Bram Stoker's *Dracula*. In front of them, separated by a panel of smoked glass, the chauffeur seemed absorbed by the road; behind them, three huge vans carrying the cast, crew and equipment, struggled in their wake. It was an arrangement Racine himself had insisted on; having played havoc with the line of command in the studio in London, he was now establishing some strange hierarchy. She and Racine were to stay at the chateau itself, while the crew were to be quartered in Carnac. She had almost mentioned her cottage, but some strange, secretive impulse had stopped her . . .

She looked back out of the window. The countryside was becoming more familiar with each passing mile; she recognised the spire of a church set back some distance from the road, an aggressively ugly service station attached to a café.

It was, of course, his land, his country . . . the home of her anonymous dream lover, the man who had taken her twice, seared her body with his, once in the dark embrace of the tomb, and then again in the looming shadow of the old keep of the Chateau Marais. Taken her with such annihilating, devastating sensual savagery, taken her to the edge of complete carnality . . . taken her without words.

Suddenly, strangely, he seemed more real than ever before, and the gritty day to day reality of the past month seemed dreamlike, insubstantial. How could she have returned to London to work, immersed herself in her life without realising she was changed, utterly changed?

She had given little thought to him since she left Brittany, involved in her work, distracted by Racine . . . or was that really true? Her body remembered him, remembered the dark heat, the slow burn, the craving, the electrifying, cleansing explosion of climax under his mouth, his hands.

With an almost painful clarity she could recall every detail, every movement of his body, his mouth. The gentle cruelty of his tongue, softening, warming, then stabbing, plunging, deep into her mouth. The way her body had leapt to his, blood singing.

The tantalising delicacy of his hands as they explored her naked body, how they lingered on her throat, slipped to her shoulders, grazed the top of her breasts . . . the hard clasp of his hands on her ankles as he bent his mouth to her body, the gentle rasp of his tongue against her clitoris . . . the hard urgency of his tongue surging deep inside her.

Yes, she remembered every detail.

How he had fixed on her nipples, sucking and suckling one with an almost painful intensity while pinching the other until her breasts were swollen and nipples rock hard, how every sensation flowed to the sweet, hot pressure of his mouth, how the red throbbing of her nipples arced to her groin and then exploded.

How, finally, he had filled her, numbing her with his first, driving entry, overwhelming her body with the rhythm of his against the hard packed floor of the tumulus.

She remembered, too, how he had come to her again the night of the party at the Chateau Marais, how he had taken her from behind, found a path between the two entrances to her body and imprinted the hard length of his rod on her with a ceaseless, seamless carnality that stung her to a screaming climax.

And now she was returning to the scene . . . the scene of the crime? Beside her Racine chuckled, a faintly chilling sound that recalled her from her reverie, but when she turned to him he merely shrugged, still engrossed in his book.

Would he find her again? She turned the thought over in her mind. Had it been a bizarre erotic accident that he had come to her in the shadows of the old keep, or had he followed her, known where to find her? But she would have been unrecognisable, unknowable in the concealing black leather cat suit . . . was it the same man? It was a new thought, disturbing.

Improbably, for the first time, it occurred to her that it might be possible to trace him somehow, discover his identity . . . he must have been a guest at the party, must have been staying in the area to have been in the tomb that first night . . . did she really want to know?

The answer was immediate, instinctive. Yes. Not to know was suddenly unthinkable.

The vans behind them pulled away at Carnac, but Gemma barely noticed. She forgot the crew, forgot the film, forgot even Alexei Racine sitting beside her as the densely wooded forest came into view. Concealed by the trees, the tumulus waited, home of the hunter, the carved image of a warrior whose weapon was his rod, whose blank, triangular face had watched her frenzied coupling with a faceless lover.

And then the chateau came into view, the elegant Renaissance facade, the crumbling tower of the old keep, as familiar as if she had known them forever.

'And so we begin,' said Racine as the limousine

124

came to a halt before the massive stone stairs. The chauffeur was opening her door, and as she slipped out she noticed the immense double doors of the chateau were open.

A white-haired, middle-aged man in formal attire hurried down the steps to greet them. 'Monsieur Racine, welcome, welcome back. And Miss de la Mare. The Count regrets that he is not here person-ally to receive you – '

'The Count?' echoed Gemma in surprise.

'Leo, Comte Marais,' Racine explained in a quick aside.

'But he will welcome you at dinner,' continued the man, raising his voice over theirs. 'And I shall escort you to your rooms. A pleasant journey?' he asked, ushering them up the stairs into the entrance hall.

'Unremarkable,' replied Racine. 'And you, Henri, how are you faring?'

'Well, sir, very well. You are in the west wing, not your usual suite, follow me, please.'

The two men continued talking as Gemma struggled to make sense of what she had heard. Not his usual suite? Racine, then, was a frequent visitor to the chateau, knew it well – it would account for his willingness to accept her impulsive suggestion, move the location shots to Brittany . . . but hadn't he said he knew Leo Marais only slightly?

They were walking down a vast corridor that Gemma didn't recognise. The walls were intricately carved and gilded, interrupted along one side by windows that ran from the floor to the domed ceiling. Crystal wall sconces at either side of every window shed a golden light, illuminating the cosy knots of delicately carved tables and plush little settees. She had not forgotten the breathtaking opulence of the chateau, but she was still taken aback as they passed glass-fronted cabinets displaying what appeared to be a collection of Fabergé eggs, Oriental netsuke, Victorian silver, Roman glass, Staffordshire pottery . . . she shook her head.

'I trust you will find everything satisfactory,' said the man, gesturing to a set of doors. 'You have, of course, only to ring.'

He melted away as Racine opened the doors. Confused, Gemma opened her mouth to ask about her room – surely they didn't imagine she'd be sleeping with Racine? – and then caught her breath.

It was dark, almost completely dark. And then her eyes adjusted and she shivered.

Soft, eerie light seeped from black metal wall sconces, casting strange shadows on the walls. Thick black velvet draperies shot with black silk shrouded the room, a thick black carpet concealed the floor . . . everything was black, an enfolding, ominous black velvet embrace.

In the centre of the room, on a raised dais, something pale gleamed. She turned her head and saw that it was a coffin, gold handles gleaming dully in the uncertain light, lid flung back to reveal white satin lining. There was a dagger fixed to the white satin pillow.

The room seemed to tilt crazily, spin off its axis, and she barely bit back a scream.

'Ah, Leo,' chuckled Racine. 'He has what you might call a rather schoolboyish sense of humour.'

He went over to the coffin and pulled out the dagger. A piece of paper fluttered to the floor. 'He hopes we find the sitting room inspirational . . . there are adjoining suites.'

'Oh, very amusing,' snapped Gemma, unnerved.

It wasn't until much later, soaking in a huge claw-footed tub with fittings that appeared to be solid gold, that she began to laugh.

* * *

'Yes, very amusing,' said Gemma, almost sincerely, a few hours later. They were standing around the coffin, she, Alexei, Leo and Gabrielle, having a pre-dinner drink. A drinks trolley had appeared; champagne was cooling in an ice-bucket; thick black tapers in heavy silver candlesticks warmed the room with a soft yellow light.

'It was Sarah Bernhardt who used to sleep in a coffin, wasn't it?' offered Gabrielle. She looked stunning in a bronze silk cocktail dress that plunged dramatically in the front and the back, baring her spine and emphasising her high, pointed breasts. It was obvious she wore no brassière. Her black hair was coiled in a loose knot and intricately moulded long gold earrings caught the light as she moved.

She looked very chic, very sophisticated, and beside her Gemma felt distinctly underdressed in jeans and a soft navy pullover. She had packed for the shoot, warm, sensible clothing, jeans and sweaters, and right now she rather regretted it.

'A curious fancy,' remarked Leo, refreshing his drink. He and Alexei were drinking whiskey, Gemma and Gabrielle champagne.

'Rather appealing, really,' corrected Racine, letting his fingers trail over the white satin pillow.

'Brrr!' shivered Gabrielle, giving a mock frisson of horror.

They dined in a massive hall so large it almost dwarfed the long, hardwood table. It was set, Gemma was astonished to see, with gold plate and an impressive array of silverware and sparkling crystal glasses that reflected the light from the crystal prisms of the chandelier overhead. Uniformed servants presented platters of smoked salmon and pâté de foie gras. The white wine was fresh and flowery, and Gemma found herself drinking it a little too quickly, unsettled by such opulent luxury. Magnifi-

127

cent tapestries lined the walls depicting a medieval hunt. She was seated directly across from a fallen stag with a spear in its throat, ruby blood staining the leaf green grass. She looked away and caught Leo's eye.

'You don't care much for hunting scenes, then?' he asked, noting her faint distaste.

'Not at dinner, perhaps,' she admitted, taking a bite of pâté. It was rich and smooth and seemed to glide down her throat.

'A family taste, I think,' said Leo, sipping his wine. 'There are many hunting scenes of all sorts in the chateau. My ancestors, I imagine, liked to pay tribute to the spirit of the place.'

'The spirit of the place?' repeated Gemma.

'The hunter,' he explained. 'The prehistoric carving on the wall of the tomb. An impressive figure. The family rather adopted him, I think.'

'Yes, yes, I know it,' stammered Gemma.

'Of course you would,' he agreed. 'It's not far from the old stable block.'

It was the first indication he had given that he knew she had purchased the tiny cottage, but he seemed disinclined to pursue it.

'It was my favourite hiding place as a child,' he went on. 'I used to spend hours there, pretending I was the warrior prince, the hunter, and the tomb was my domain. A remarkable place, especially at night.'

He was looking directly at her as he spoke and she felt her heart thud. A remarkable place . . . especially at night . . . the words rang in her ears. A stray remark or a subtle allusion? Was it possible? Leo Marais, her dream lover?

She drank more wine and studied him across the table, trying to imagine his body against hers, searching for some sign, some clue. She watched him raise his glass to his lips. His hands were large and shapely, large enough to have clasped her ankles as he buried his face between her thighs, strong enough to have held her in that vice-like grip as her legs trembled and her body shuddered under the onslaught of his mouth.

But he was wearing a ring, a large gold signet ring on one finger. She would have remembered it digging into her skin . . . or perhaps not.

His voice was smooth and liquid, unlike the harsh, grating voice she remembered, but the echo in the chamber tomb distorted sound. And how many words had he spoken? Three? Four?

The thought drew her eyes to his mouth. It was firm, well shaped, his lips rather thin. Impossible to know if it was the mouth that had covered hers with such annihilating eroticism, moved over her body, kissed the damp, secret flesh between her thighs.

The memory of his body was seared on hers, yet she had no idea what he looked like, only an impression of strength and power, a body firm, lean and well-muscled.

She had lost the thread of the conversation. She looked up to see that Gabrielle had claimed Leo's attention, and Racine was watching her with ironic eyes.

She concentrated on acting normally, squeezing lemon over her salmon and spearing a plump caper with her fork. Smiling as her plate was removed and replaced with a passion fruit sorbet, which was then followed by venison in a wild cherry sauce. She drank the accompanying rosé and smiled and nodded, giving every impression of an interested, attentive listener, peripherally aware that Racine was not deceived. Occasionally she caught his eyes flicking over her briefly, like a stray, sarcastic remark. She avoided his gaze, relieved when Gabrielle diverted him, asking him about the symbolism of his last film.

Their conversation should have intrigued her, but she was strangely indifferent. The rosé was replaced with a perfumed Barsac accompanied by delicate meringues filled with chestnut purée and whipped cream. She toyed with dessert and drank the wine, vaguely aware she was drinking too much, vaguely surprised to feel so icily sober.

She felt a creeping tension, a coiling inner conviction that something loomed ahead, that something was about to happen, an irrational premonition that might be soothed or blurred by the comforting warmth of just one drink too many.

So she didn't refuse the port that arrived with fruit and cheese. It was thick and sharp and sweet and glowed like fresh rubies under the prismatic lights of the chandelier.

She watched Leo's hands cradling his glass, long fingers caressing the stem of the delicate Baccarat crystal, and wondered again if they were the hands that had urged her to the hard packed earth floor of the tomb, and released her heated flesh from the black leather skin the night of the party, the night of the storm.

Racine, too, was playing with his glass, twisting it this way and that, admiring the ruby wine. It seemed to Gemma as though the light was staining his fingers with blood.

'The shadow, of course, is everything, where the illusion has more substance than reality, the chiaroscuro of the psychological landscape,' he was saying to Gabrielle, who looked enrapt.

Leo yawned. 'Films bore me,' he explained unapologetically to Gemma, pouring them both more port and dismissing the servants with a languid gesture.

She smiled a little warily. She couldn't, of course, agree, but she shrugged noncommittally and then found herself smothering a yawn in turn.

'You're tired, then?' asked Leo, concerned. 'It is a tedious journey.'

'A little,' she admitted, relaxing with the effects of the wine and port.

'Let me show you to your room,' he said at once. 'Gabrielle and Alexei are still conversing and I must confess to crushing ennui whenever he starts talking about the psychological inner landscape.'

He had risen and was offering his arm. She looked over at Racine and Gabrielle, a glance which Leo intercepted.

'Gemma is weary,' he explained. 'I shall show her to her room and then return.'

It seemed to Gemma that Gabrielle froze for a moment, became utterly still. Her eyes narrowed to slits and her body stiffened. And then she relaxed and opened her eyes wide. She looked at both of them and smiled, a warm curl of red, red lips. Deliberately she held out one white hand to Gemma, and said, 'Of course, Leo. I have been selfish, but it is such a delight to meet and speak with such a genius of film. And Gemma, I hope you sleep well.'

Racine nodded, gave Gemma a brief, piercing stare from pale grey eyes, and then looked back to Gabrielle.

Her thoughts were whirling as Leo led her from the dining hall. He guided her subtly, one hand touching yet not quite touching her shoulder, the small of her back, as he led her through a different door into a smaller passageway. In contrast to the imposing, imperial elegance of gilt and crystal, it was warm and welcoming. Thick Chinese carpets muffled their footsteps and recessed lights illuminated a magnificent but jarringly discordant array of prints, silkscreens and oil paintings. She recognised a Caravaggio still life alongside a portrait unmistakably by Van Gogh, a Tintoretto canal scene next to a Warhol Campbell's soup can, and something that looked suspiciously like a Rembrandt, before letting it all wash over her, letting the colours and images dissolve in her awareness of the male body beside her.

She was intensely aware of him, the expensive perfume of his aftershave, the way he shortened his steps to hers, the maddening touching but not quite touching of his hands as he directed her towards her room.

This was the moment for disclosure, away from Racine, away from the beautiful Gabrielle who was most surely his lover. Was he toying with her, or had his remarks at dinner meant nothing?

'This way,' he said, motioning her to the right.

'It's so large it's sometimes confusing,' Gemma said, altering her direction.

'Indeed it is,' agreed Leo. 'As a child I often used to get lost in the chateau, and drive my tutors to distraction.'

'As a child?' she prompted, thinking of what he had said earlier about hiding in the tumulus.

'And even now,' he returned. 'There are many interesting ways to lose yourself in the chateau, in the grounds.'

A provocative remark, or was she simply looking for provocation? Another corridor, lined with tapestries, and then another, windowless, whitewashed and austere, where blazing canvases leapt from the walls, a sunset, a sunrise, a seascape so real she almost expected to feel the spray of water on her face, an unexpected turn and they had reached the door to her suite. She turned to face him, every sense alert.

The silence stretched between them as they shared an appraising look.

She saw a man, tall and lean, powerful shoulders tapering to an elegant waist. His white shirt was open at the throat, baring his neck and part of his chest. Leo, Comte Marais, owner of this vast and luxuriously bizarre chateau, friend of Alexei Racine, lover of Gabrielle, her host who had done her the courtesy of showing her to her room himself . . . Leo Marais, her dream lover?

He saw a woman, slim and fresh-looking, silvery blonde hair scraped back from her face, emphasising high cheek bones and navy blue eyes. In contrast to Gabrielle's studied, sophisticated sleek chic, she seemed almost unconsciously provocative, he thought, the curves of her body concealed by a long, dark blue sweater that matched her eyes. But he could sense the underlying tension in her, and wondered at it, before recalling Alexei Racine's cryptic words the night he had called from London.

They were, naturally, aware of each other, the furtive, unspoken, assessing sort of awareness that flows between male and female, presaging attraction.

He bowed over her hand, very correctly kissing the air above her skin, not even brushing his lips against the back of her hand. She felt his breath on her skin like a searing, scorching wave. The gesture was more intimate than if he had actually touched her.

If part of her mind was feverishly waiting for some sign, some signal, some betraying word or gesture, her body was responding instinctively to the implicit promise of the almost touch of his mouth.

Alone together in the opulent, hushed corridor outside her room, bathed in the warm glow of crystal light and gilded walls, anything was possible. She felt dizzy, lightheaded, a legacy of the wine and the intoxicating, whirling sensation of physical anticipation. Would he touch her? Would he kiss her? Would he reveal himself to her?

Senses heightened, she looked down at his head, the thick, glossy dark hair curling over the collar of his white shirt, the olive skin at the nape of his neck, the elegantly moulded lines of his body. She imagined him nude, bending to her, saw the play of muscles rippling along his back, the elegant, eloquent arc of his erect penis, and her breathing grew short.

A little breathless, she stood motionless as he raised his head and took a step back. Her hand fell, nerveless, to her side and she waited.

Still he did not move, and the silence thickened, grew more potent. His eyes seemed hungry, yet puzzled, as they played over her, lingering on her face, her breasts, her thighs. When he finally leaned toward her, she was ready, prepared for the driving force of his mouth, his body, ready to be taken standing there in the hallway, hard against the carved wood of the door, as hard as the packed earth floor of the tomb.

Her body had loosened, swollen, grown hot and lax in anticipation, responding to the maleness so close to her, stimulated almost reflexively. When his head, his mouth, drew near to hers, she closed her eyes.

And felt the faint brush of his lips first on one cheek, then the other. And then the faint, hollow emptiness of the air, that meant she was alone.

Leo walked back along the corridor, for once oblivious to the jewel toned canvases that blazed from the walls, and rather wished he had a cigar. A good Cuban cigar, a glass of brandy, and a good explanation.

Alexei's words rang in his ears. 'Feel free, my friend, to exercise your *droit de seigneur*, and aid me in this so very complicated seduction.'

Well, he hadn't. Not because she wasn't desirable, and not because he hadn't desired her. Few men could withstand the temptation of that primly coiled hair and those deep, navy eyes, the half-opened mouth that begged to be kissed, the trembling heat of her body that had called to his.

Yet he had hesitated, then left. And for the life of him, he didn't know why. Some vague uneasiness, some half-felt, half-understood premonition. Mentally he tried to account for it.

Was it because Alexei had been so uncharacteristically insistent, as strangely insistent as he had been over the Rodin so many weeks ago? He loved Alexei like a brother, or as Leo, an only child, imagined brothers loved each other. But he didn't trust him. No-one trusted Alexei. He was too subtle, too complex, too fundamentally perverse.

And he was alone with Gabrielle. That thought stopped him short, in front of a rather fine Seurat. Jealousy was not in Leo's nature; the circumstances of his birth had virtually eliminated the impulse to envy or possessiveness. That Alexei was the more clever, the more subtle, he freely acknowledged; these were traits his own impeccable lineage, vast wealth and enviable physique rendered unnecessary and thus even the faintest bit *déclassé*.

He turned away from the Seurat. Introspection was not one of his favourite pastimes; he abhorred it in others, and seldom indulged himself. Yet it made him walk the more softly as he approached the dining hall, and made him pause before he entered.

Alexei and Gabrielle had left the table and were standing before one of the windows, looking out to the winter garden. Leo stood motionless, his connoisseur's appreciation of the truly beautiful keeping him silent, motionless, unwilling to break the spell.

She was smaller than Alexei, and in the circle of

his arms looked fragile, delicate. Her head was thrown back and he could see the vein pulsing in her throat, the flush of wine . . . of arousal? – turning her ivory skin to rose.

And Alexei was bending to her, his hands loosely clasping her sides, palms held flat below the swell of her breasts, his mouth hovering at her throat. Even at such a great distance, Leo could hear the sound of their voices, the low ripple of Gabrielle's laughter.

Centuries of breeding, the essentially French awareness of civility, sometimes translated as *politesse*, more often untranslatable but spiritually more akin to the Japanese concept of 'face', led him into the room, apparently imperturbable and unmoved.

As was Alexei, who spoke to him without removing his hands from Gabrielle's body, without moving his mouth, which was hovering above the warm ivory of her throat. 'Ah, Leo. I was showing Gabrielle the lure of the vampire. You see?'

And then he bent his head to the pulsing vein in her throat and sank his teeth into the white skin.

It was a playful nip, hardly a touch, not strong enough to draw blood, hardly strong enough to leave a mark.

'Of course, my friend, of course,' said Leo. So, he thought, hardly understanding it, first blood has been drawn. But whose?

'Alexei has been demonstrating to me how the camera looks at bodies,' said Gabrielle, fluidly dissolving their embrace, without awkwardness, without embarrassment. 'And how to capture the psychological nuance with the pose.'

'Indeed,' said Leo, pouring more port, not blind to the hotness of her eyes, nor Alexei's brief look of ambiguous frustration. 'Indeed.'

* * *

In an Empire bed that had once belonged to the Empress Josephine, canopied and curtained in red velvet, Gemma tossed and turned. Sleep wafted, tantalising, teasing, only to be driven away by some stray thought that jolted her briefly into drowsy wakefulness. The location shots for tomorrow . . . the tumulus in the forest . . . her cottage . . . the hot, anticipatory longing she had felt as Leo Marais led her to her room. Consciousness swelled and subsided.

But the slow, secret throb of her body pulsed, waiting for stimulus, waiting for something to assuage the heatened, heightened sensual awareness that had been gradually flowing and building since she had returned to the chateau, since she had glimpsed the forest hiding the tumulus from the tinted limousine windows. She shifted irritably, and dragged one of the feather pillows close against her, cradling it like a lover.

Finally she slept, and dreamt he came to her, embraced her, held her fast in an iron grip, moulded her body to his, fused them together, his face in the shadows.

And she struggled furiously, clawed at him, clawed at the shadows obscuring his face, writhed and bit and struggled futilely as he entered her, imprinting his body into hers, making her curl and coil into the hot, primal wanting that obliterated thought.

Making her move to the demanding thrust of his loins, the implacable rhythm of his thighs, his penis, driving hard against her, into her, making her wet and wanting despite herself. He was stronger than she, harder, more forceful, subdued her in the unequal contest almost effortlessly.

She woke to the electric surge of climax firing through her, her body hot and sweaty, sheets twisted between her thighs. It was time out of mind as she lay there, feeling the shocks subside, feeling the imprint of a phantom lover, a demon lover, a dream lover who did not exist. She let the tingling waves flit through her until they slackened, became softer, duller, looser. Then, breathing deeply, she edged herself over to one side of the massive bed and, leaning on one elbow, felt for the light at the side of the bed. She groped a little uncertainly, fingers first finding the heavy gold cord that swept the draperies to the bedpost, then moving beyond to the bedside table.

She could see it in her mind, a delicate confection of gilt and crystal prisms set squarely at the centre of the intricately marquetried table. A little to the left, she decided, edging closer to the side of the bed.

Suddenly her arm was seized in a bruising grip and she was pushed roughly back into the yielding depths of the massive feather mattress. A large hand covered her mouth, cutting off her instinctive cry, there was a rustle of draperies, and she was plunged into utter darkness.

She struggled, lashed out with hands that were quickly seized in a vice-like grip, bucked and writhed against a hard body immeasurably stronger than her own. It was her dream yet not a dream; an over-whelming sense of *déjà vu* mingled with the first rippling waves of anger.

'Stop.'

She recognised the harsh, distorted whisper that had once echoed in the closed walls of the tumulus beneath the earth. It was his voice, unmistakable, unforgettable. Suddenly she was furious. She twisted and lunged, tried to bite the hand covering her mouth, but the weight of his body held her almost immobile, pressing her face down on the yielding softness of the bed. She used every ounce of energy,

138

every strength she had to fight him, and her breathing became ragged. The air inside the curtained cocoon of the bed grew thick and heavy.

The sheets tangled around her thighs and slipped, baring her lower body, and as she thrashed against him her naked buttocks pushed against his groin. She felt the hard rod of his erection against her flesh and froze.

'Not again,' she said against his hand. 'Not like this. I have to know. Leo?'

He couldn't have heard her, but he must have felt the words against the palm of his hand. He lifted his hand from her lips just fractionally, enough to allow her to speak.

She dragged air into her starved lungs, taking several deep breaths before repeating, 'Not like this. I have to know. Leo?' Her voice came out as a strangled whisper.

'Know?' he said in a harsh, tight voice. Or was it 'No?'

And then his hand returned to her mouth, more gently, pressing her lips together. Infuriated, she twisted against him, determined to see his face, but the movement brought her hard against his loins and she felt him slip between her thighs and slide inside with sure, hot ease.

She was slick and ready, still moist from her dream climax, unknowingly aroused from the silent struggle for dominance that had brought her into such fiercely intimate contact with his body.

And she struggled, struggled against it, struggled against him, bucking and writhing, the frenzied movements of her body driving him deeper and deeper inside her. She hardly knew when it changed, when fury became passion, when the lunging thrusts of her hips and buttocks against his hard male loins were driven by furious need rather than fury alone.

It was a fast and frenzied mating, and her climax struck quickly, firing through her body. He bit her neck as she came, like a stallion holding himself to a mare, and she felt him shudder.

His hand was still against her mouth. She should bite, would bite, would score him with her teeth, make a sign, recognisable, indissoluble. So that when daylight and sanity returned, he would bare her mark. Sated, she had almost summoned the energy, when his hand closed hard over her mouth again.

'Think, my little Psyche, of Cupid, and reconsider,' said the harsh whisper.

Cupid? Psyche? Her mind veered wildly, Valentine's Day images of plump cupids with bows and arrows and leering mouths, a half-remembered illustration from a school text of a winged god looking angry beside the bed of a half-naked woman holding a candle, and then she felt the achingly sweet pain of his withdrawal.

She sighed, breathed deeply, and inhaled a strange, unfamiliar, aromatic scent that tumbled her from consciousness to sleep almost instantly.

Chapter Seven

When Gemma opened her eyes the next morning, it was to the thick, black darkness of midnight. Yet she felt wide awake, refreshed. She yawned and stretched, one hand brushing against the heavy velvet draperies curtaining the bed, and then she remembered.

She frowned, then, inexplicably, smiled. Wriggling over to the side of the huge bed, she parted the curtains. Pale grey light was filtering through the windows, and she saw that the ormulu clock on the bedside table stood at eight o'clock.

A thoughtful expression on her face, she went through the morning rituals of her toilet in the sparkling white and gold bathroom, oblivious to the solid gold dolphins cavorting as fixtures, oblivious to the perfumed luxury of her surroundings.

She showered, washed her hair, and, wrapping herself in a huge, fluffy towel, cleaned her teeth and began to apply the minimum amount of make-up. Looking at herself in the mirror, she paused, then put down the tube of light foundation. Her skin looked fresh and glowing, and her eyes were bright.

She looked as if she had just risen from the arms of a lover . . . which, in a way, she had, she decided.

She smiled at herself in the mirror and her reflection smiled back conspiratorially, as if they shared a delicious, raher risqué secret. She couldn't account for her mood; she felt bubbly, lighthearted, almost elated.

She let the towel drop and surveyed her naked body in the mirror. Another morning, she remembered, the sight of the red crescent moon of his teeth on her breast had sent the lust snaking through her like a white hot flame. But now her breasts were unmarked, free of any trace of passion.

He hadn't touched her there, hadn't kissed or bitten or suckled her nipples, had barely touched her body before driving into her. She let her hand drop to her groin, idly fingered the golden floss of her mound.

He had found her, come for her, taken her. Before she could mark him, before she could fix the imprint of her teeth on the hand that had covered her mouth, smothered her cries.

Cupid and Psyche. The myth itself was obvious enough, in the cold light of day. A god who had fallen in love with a mortal, visited her under the cover of darkness lest his godly beauty blind her. And when Psyche, impatient to know her dream lover, had lit a candle to illuminate his features, a drop of wax had fallen on the god's arms, arms that became wings . . . and then he awoke.

Had Pysche perished in the blinding beauty of her immortal lover? Gemma couldn't remember. And it hardly mattered.

Automatically her hands lifted to her hair, but even as she began to braid it into a French plait she changed her mind and brushed it free, letting it tumble loose in waves that cascaded down her back.

142

In the bedroom, she dressed quickly, jeans and soft, flat suede shoes in a dull mulberry that matched her cashmere sweater, adding a long scarf patterned in blue and purple, mauve and gilt, and decided she was ready.

He would find her again . . . or perhaps she would find him.

Right now, the body that felt so glowingly, freshly alive, sated and well-used, craved food. She was starving.

A plump and smiling girl in a black uniform found her hungrily prowling the passageway and directed her to a glass conservatory. Gemma paused at the door. It seemed as though she was about to step into a tropical rainforest, lush and humid. Luxuriant, leafy green trees soared to the ceiling, trailing vines and creepers. Orchids peeped through banks of moss, and everywhere she looked there was a profusion of exotic and brilliantly coloured flowers. She heard the distant, musical splash of running water and the chittering twitter of birdsong.

The maid smilingly urged her forward, and led her to a large, round table covered in white linen and set for breakfast. Gabrielle was already there, sitting in one of the deep, white wicker chairs and sipping coffee. Dressed in a tailored scarlet tunic and slim trousers, lips and nails painted to match, her raven hair coiled in a fat braid that fell across one shoulder, she seemed to belong to the exotic setting.

'Good morning, Gemma,' Gabrielle said in her lightly accented English. 'You look . . . well rested.' For a moment her eyes were sharp, speculative. 'Come and sit down. Marie will bring you whatever you like.'

'Coffee, please, some juice, bacon and eggs if possible,' replied Gemma, settling herself in one of the deep wicker chairs. They were padded with cushions in a vividly coloured print of purple, red and green, and were astonishingly comfortable. 'Oh, and some toast.'

The maid broke into a rapid and lengthy explanation, of which Gemma understood perhaps one word in ten.

'She is offering you eggs of any sort, scrambled, fried, soft-boiled, eggs benedict, an omelette,' explained Gabrielle with a slightly superior smile. 'Crêpes, waffles, sausages, fruit, anything you wish.'

'Scrambled, please,' Gemma said to the maid, who responded with another excited stream of words.

'Filter coffee, espresso, capuccino, decaffeinated,' translated Gabrielle.

'Filter coffee, please,' said Gemma.

'And the toast, brown, white, wholegrain – '

'Brown is fine,' replied Gemma, beginning to be amused. 'What a production,' she said to Gabrielle after the maid had left.

'Not really,' shrugged Gabrielle. 'Now that she knows your tastes she will bring you what you prefer unless you tell her differently. Leo likes to make sure that every whim is catered for, and he has an excellent staff.' She sipped coffee from the large, bowl shaped cup that the French prefer to mugs and eyed Gemma over the rim.

'It's a fabulous place,' said Gemma sincerely. 'And it was generous of Leo to allow us to stay here, and to use the chateau for the location.'

'Generous?' mused Gabrielle, tearing apart a flaky croissant. 'Mmm. Perhaps.' And perhaps he had another motive. She looked at Gemma closely. She was very pretty, she conceded, almost beautiful with that long, silver-gilt hair and those deep blue eyes. She lacked the French flair that would have arranged the scarf rather differently and added a belt in a contrasting shade, lavender suede, perhaps, but she was still attractively groomed.

Leo's type? she wondered. He had not come to her bed last night, and she had lain awake for hours, staring at the plump cupids and full breasted nymphs carousing across the ornately moulded ceiling, thinking about him, wanting him, wondering if she had miscalculated.

She had flirted a little with Racine last night for two reasons, because he was intriguing in a dark, louche sort of way and because she wanted to make Leo jealous. But she hadn't expected the sharp nip of Racine's teeth on her throat, the sudden piercing thrill that shivered through her at his touch.

Perhaps, just perhaps, her obsession with Leo was weakening a little. How interesting. How intriguing. And how to find out?

'Did you make love with Leo last night?' she asked Gemma casually, pouring herself another cup of coffee.

Gemma, who had just taken a sip of water, choked.

Gabrielle watched her, an amused smile hovering at the corners of her perfectly painted mouth. She waited until Gemma's sputtering had subsided, and then continued.

'I am curious, you understand, not jealous,' she explained. 'At least, I do not think I am jealous. Ah, here is Marie with your breakfast. Leo and I have been lovers now almost six months, he is superb in bed, utterly superb. And I was so afraid that he was becoming bored with me, you know?'

Gemma murmured something inarticulate, as Gabrielle seemed to expect a response, and wondered dazedly if she would ever understand the French. Absently she picked up a heavy silver fork and toyed with the fluffy mound of scrambled eggs.

'It is a thing of the bodies, purely,' Gabrielle said.

'But it is good, so good that I can't stop myself. Difficult, no?'

No. The word echoed in her mind, in her memory. No, she had said last night, no, I have to know.

'But perhaps I am shocking you?' asked Gabrielle, leaning back in her chair and lighting a cigarette.

'No, not at all,' Gemma disclaimed. In fact, she realised, she was a little shocked, but more by the blunt honesty Gabrielle was showing to her, practically a stranger, than by her story.

'When you have a lover who makes your body burn, who finds cravings in you that you have never known . . . well, it is a special man,' mused Gabrielle. 'For me, Leo is such a one. But if he is becoming bored, ready to discard our affair, I must break it off first, myself. Or find some way of intriguing him anew, until this hold on me slackens. A dilemma, you see? And one that only a woman could appreciate.'

'I see,' said Gemma, pushing her plate away. Her appetite seemed to have vanished, killed, perhaps, by the heavy smoke of Gabrielle's cigarette.

'This is why I am curious to know if Leo made love with you last night, you see? It is a complicated affair.'

'Not as complicated as some,' said Gemma with a sigh. 'May I have a cigarette?'

And so, between sips of coffee and cigarettes, the whole, improbable tale began to unfold. Gabrielle listened attentively, eyes wide, murmuring encouragingly when Gemma faltered, only interrupting to summon Marie for more cigarettes and a bottle of champagne to mix with the freshly squeezed orange juice.

'It's hardly a drink at all,' she assured Gemma, 'and a story such as this deserves champagne.'

It did loosen her tongue a little, and she found

146

herself confiding in Gabrielle, even silly, meaningless details, until there was nothing more to tell.

'So,' said Gabrielle, squashing her cigarette and immediately lighting another, 'Our stories intertwine, at least a little. Your lover must be either Leo, or Alexei Racine.'

'Racine?' repeated Gemma, horrified. 'Impossible.'

'He was at the party that night,' insisted Gabrielle. 'I met him, and another friend of Leo's before . . . well, I met him, I'm sure of it.'

'God, no,' said Gemma, her skin crawling at the mere thought. She gulped more champagne.

'But what is interesting is why the secrecy? Why does he not reveal himself to you? It is a game of some sort, I think.'

'But for what purpose?' asked Gemma. 'Why?'

'Well, Leo has a very strange imagination,' replied Gabrielle thoughtfully. 'But Cupid and Psyche . . . I don't understand. Perhaps it is Alexei, because he knows you detest him.'

'But he *made* me detest him, Gabrielle, he worked at it! You have no idea how disgustingly arrogant he's been, how . . . oh, never mind, that doesn't matter now.'

'No,' said Gabrielle firmly, 'It doesn't. What matters is to find a plan, a ruse of some sort. We both wish to know if Leo is your lover . . . would you recognise him? Would you know him again if you had him?'

'Yes,' said Gemma. 'Yes, I'm sure of it.'

'And if I help you, you will help me?' Gabrielle stretched out her hand to cover Gemma's and stroked it gently. Their eyes met.

'We will have to be . . . imaginative,' coaxed Gabrielle, her index finger softly probing the delicate web of skin between Gemma's fingers.

'Imaginative?' echoed Gemma, conscious of a

147

sudden, sexual tension between them, etching the itimacy of shared confessions.

'Yes,' said Gabrielle. 'For me, too, you understand, the stakes are high. And I am quite prepared to be bold . . . even like this.'

She leaned forward deliberately, slowly, paused, still holding her hand, and then kissed Gemma on the mouth. Gemma was still, half-expecting the touch, half-frozen in surprise. She smelled the exotic scent of Gabrielle's perfume, felt the softness of her lips against her own, and then the delicious warmth of her tongue slipping into her mouth, swirling against her teeth and then withdrawing.

Gabrielle drew back. 'Yes?' she asked.

'Yes.' It felt as though the words were dragged from her.

'Gabrielle, my dear, and Gemma. I hadn't thought you would waken so early.' It was Leo, just entering the conservatory, and beside him a tallish, well-built man with brown hair and brown eyes. 'Jay, I am sure you remember Gabrielle? Gabrielle de Sevigny, Jay Stone.'

'Oh, yes, of course I remember,' Gabrielle said, perfectly at ease, extending her hand. 'We met New Year's Eve.'

'Jay, this is Gemma de la Mare, Alexei's producer,' Leo continued. 'Jay arrived late last night.'

Greetings were exchanged, the men seated themselves as Marie bustled up, and there was a complicated discussion as Leo questioned her about the strawberries she suggested. Were they ripe? Were they imported? Gabrielle lit another cigarette and gave Gemma a meaningful glance.

Gemma's mind was whirling. She smiled and chatted casually, trying to disguise her confusion, and, as soon as she could, excused herself and fled.

* * *

148

Propped on the white satin pillow of the open casket, clad only in a black silk dressing gown, Alexei Racine watched the flickering amber light of the two black tapers. The crew were due to arrive early afternoon; several hours would be consumed by the tedious technicalities of setting up, the mechanics of which could safely be left to others. The day was perfect, cloudy and overcast. By dusk the shadows would be lengthening.

In his mind's eye he pictured the scene. The crumbling headstones of the old graveyard, tilting towards the ground. The looming spectre of the old tower. The woman moving trancelike, sleepwalking through the eerie landscape, drawn by the mysterious lure of the count.

Naked, he pondered, or in the diaphanous white gown suggested by the wardrobe mistress? It was hackneyed, so hackneyed that it might work. The play of light through the filmy white gown, highlighting her legs, the shadow between her thighs, would be both subtle and erotic. But nude might be better, he mused, closing his eyes, the pale gleam of naked skin under a grey sky . . .

'What on earth are you doing?'

Gemma's voice, a blend of astonishment and disgust, interrupted his reverie. He opened one eye, then closed it. 'Thinking,' he replied.

'You look . . .' her voice trailed away. She had been about to say that he looked ridiculous, absurd, but the thought had caused her to look more closely.

Against the white satin his long dark hair gleamed like polished onyx. His black silk robe gaped at the chest, revealing the thick, silky pelt that grew denser along his torso. The amber light played uncertainly across his features, highlighting the aquiline nose, the deeply undercut eyes, the sensuously cruel mouth.

'Absurd,' she finished strongly.

Only the faint twitch of his lips indicated that he had heard her. 'I am considering the relative merits of naked flesh and a transparent, filmy white gown,' he said.

She felt the heat rise to her face at his words. Gabrielle's voice echoed in her mind. 'It must be Leo or Alexei . . . he was here the night of the party, I am sure of it.'

'I am inclined to nudity, I think,' he continued lazily. 'Naked flesh, pale and cool, waiting to be warmed by the annihilating red heat, devoured by the rapacious, fatal kiss of the demon lover.'

Her breathing quickened and her pulse began to beat faster. It wasn't possible –

'Of course the silly bitch will probably complain that it's too cold,' he added, opening his eyes and propping himself up on one elbow. 'There's no nudity clause in her contract, I assume?'

'What?'

'She didn't specify partial, did she?' asked Racine with a frown.

'Who?'

'Lucy, of course,' he snapped.

'Oh,' said Gemma, with dawning understanding. 'No, no, there's nothing in her contract. You mean the graveyard scene?'

'Of course I mean the graveyard scene. You may recall that we have such a thing as a shooting schedule? A thick folder bound in black, prepared by your staff? Sadly defaced by innumerable typographical errors and some improbable grammar but still bearing some faint resemblance to a schedule?'

'I seem to recall something of the sort,' retorted Gemma icily, relieved to find her momentary physical confusion dissolving under the familiar acid of Racine's tongue. His sarcasm was absurdly comforting, and she was pleased to find her mind focusing on the concrete problems of the afternoon's shoot. It was tangible, real, unlike the bizarre Satyricon that plagued her . . . Gabrielle's kiss. Leo as her lover. Or Racine. And then there was Jay, who had arrived late last night . . . with a certain amount of relief, she concentrated on Racine's words.

'It's scripted with the nightgown,' she pointed out. 'And Lucy is supposed to be virginal, Victorian . . . hardly likely to be wandering about nude.'

'True,' he agreed, swinging his legs over the casket, 'but irrelevant. Think of Polanski's witches. The film creates its own world, its own reality. She could, quite convincingly, bare herself under the hypnotic, compelling allure of the vampire lover.'

'You'll lose the ghostly effect of the transparent cloth,' she said, eyeing the long legs dangling from the dark, polished wood of the casket. His feet were bare, long, bony and perversely elegant, with a high arch and long, long toes.

'I know,' he acknowledged regretfully, 'and that saddens me. Perhaps we should shoot it both ways, discover what the camera prefers?'

She could hardly believe it. For the first time, it seemed, he was actually consulting her, actually involving her in the basic decision making . . . and all the while, a wild, insane impulse was forming in the back of her mind, the wayward impulse to kneel before him, run her tongue along the high arch of his foot, look up into those pale grey eyes and see his response.

'More efficient to make the decision now,' she responded levelly, amazed at the perverse turn of her thoughts. If it was Racine, what would she do? Would she want to know? 'I'd have to check for continuity, but as I recall it wouldn't matter much.'

It was an equivocation, and he recognized it.

'And you, the producer, Gemma de la Mare, have no artistic bias? No preference? No opinion?'

Yes. Suddenly the thought was overwhelmingly attractive, running her tongue along his naked flesh, lulling him for a moment, then biting down hard, feeling the harsh crunch of bone between her teeth, the warm, coppery gush of blood filling her mouth.

She looked at him through narrowed eyes, coldly assessing the pale elegance of his body, the black silk dressing gown that seemed to cling to him yet revealed the lean, muscled torso. 'With the gown, I think,' she said calmly. 'More alluring, more deceptive . . . better depth for the camera.' Good God, she was actually beginning to talk like Racine!

'Mmm,' mused Racine, lying back in the white silk embrace of the casket. 'I like deception.'

It was late afternoon. The sky had decided to oblige Alexei Racine, and was grey, overcast and threatening. The crew were ready, and the actress playing Lucy was shivering in a transparent white gown. Gabrielle, swathed from head to toe in mink and perched on a nearby tombstone, watched the scene before her with steadily declining interest as equipment was adjusted and re-adjusted. Making a film, she concluded sadly, seemed to consist of large numbers of people standing around, smoking, drinking coffee from styrofoam cups, and waiting for something to happen.

Amazing, she mused, that something so creative, so artistic, was actually so tedious. So dull. Idly she wondered if she had ever spent a more boring afternoon. The answer was a definitive *non*.

She watched Racine stalk around the cameras, a controlled tension obvious in his sharp, abrupt movements. Gemma was deep in conversation with a husky, pugnacious looking man wearing black leather and a pony-tail. Leo, of course, was absent. Perhaps she should go and look for him.

She shifted irritably on the tombstone, and had almost decided to return to the chateau when a voice called out 'Quiet on the set. Quiet, please.'

She watched as the actress with the long, blonde hair began to move hesitantly across the graveyard, eyes wide and blank, the white gown trailing behind her, fluttering a little with each step, revealing long, slim legs.

'Cut!' came the whipcrack of Racine's voice.

They repeated the same scene again and again. As Gabrielle watched her move, she felt the first, faint glimmerings of an idea begin to take shape.

Gemma lolled in the bath, letting the steaming, perfumed hot water ease the tension from her body. Racine had been at his sarcastic worst this afternoon, demanding take after take, and she had been too preoccupied with the shoot to spare a thought for anything else.

Now she let her mind wander, mentally re-playing the morning's conversation with Gabrielle in the conservatory. A dim air of unreality seemed to cling to her memory of every event since her arrival at the chateau. Perhaps, she mused, the chateau itself, so bizarrely luxurious, so decadently opulent, was in some measure responsible.

She could never have imagined sleeping in a bed that once belonged to the Empress Josephine, eating off gold plate . . . and now here she was, soaking in a huge tub in a bathroom the size of her London flat, feet resting on solid gold taps in the shape of dolphins, breathing in the exotic perfume of an expensively scented bath oil she had discovered on the ledge, and contemplating seduction.

She let her thoughts drift to her dream lover, to

Leo Marais, to Jay Stone, and then to Alexei Racine. She gave an involuntary shudder at the thought of Racine, but forced herself to consider the possibility. All three men were tall, around six feet or so, she guessed. All were lean and fit, well-muscled . . . All of them had attended the New Year's Party. Any of them might have arrived a few days early and prowled the grounds, found their way to the tumulus in the forest. Would she recognise him again, her mystery lover, as she had so confidently said to Gabrielle?

Idly she reached for one of the solid gold dolphins and let more hot water gush into the bath. She could, of course, try and ferret out the details, play at detective, casually inquire 'Where were you the night of?' but some deep instinct made her shy from the notion. A calculated seduction, perhaps . . .

Sighing, she lay back and heard a soft knocking at the door of her suite. 'Yes?' she called out.

'Gemma, it's me,' Gabrielle replied. 'May I enter?'

'Yes, of course, come in,' said Gemma, reluctantly preparing to get out of the bath. But even as she rose to reach for a towel, the door had opened and Gabrielle had slipped inside.

'I did not mean to disturb you,' smiled Gabrielle, running her eyes appreciatively over Gemma's naked body, 'but I thought we might have a drink together and perhaps talk a little. Shall I ring for something? What would you like?' She seated herself on the white and gilt chair before the vanity and waved Gemma back into the bath.

'Oh,' said Gemma, sinking back in the oily, perfumed water, 'I'm not sure, I – '

'A martini,' interrupted Gabrielle decisively. 'A vodka martini, ice-cold, with olives. My favourite drink for in the bath. Yes?'

'That sounds fine,' agreed Gemma, a little taken

154

aback. Gabrielle seemed so utterly assured, so perfectly at ease, as if there was nothing unusual in her sharing the room while Gemma bathed. And perhaps, in light of the conversation they had shared that morning, and the kiss, there was not.

Gabrielle spoke quickly into an intercom affixed to the vanity, then turned to Gemma with a satisfied smile. 'I have ordered a pitcher. You will enjoy it, I know. So tell me, is it always so tedious, your film work? I had not guessed it could be so excruciatingly dull!' She chatted away until a knock at the door signalled the arrival of their drinks, and it was not until she had poured two large martinis, lit a cigarette and crossed her perfect legs that she broached the subject dominating both their thoughts.

'So,' she said. 'The arrival of Jay Stone. A most fortuitous coincidence, no?'

'Fortuitous?' asked Gemma, very aware of her own naked body in the scented, oily bathwater, very aware of Gabrielle's presence.

'Perhaps that is not the word,' replied Gabrielle, wrinkling her nose. 'My English is not absolutely perfect. But you understand what I mean?'

'Yes, I think so,' said Gemma, taking a sip of her drink. It was delicious, tart and icy, a refreshing contrast to the heat of the bath.

'And what do you mean to do?'

'I don't know,' said Gemma. Impossible to believe that moments ago she had seriously been considering seducing Jay or Leo . . .

'Well, it is simple, of course,' Gabrielle said. 'You must try all three, no? Or wait until he comes to you again. But I have one idea for us both.'

'Yes?' said Gemma, unnerved and taking a gulp of her martini.

Gabrielle extinguished her cigarette and walked over to the bath. Perching on the edge, she let one hand drop into the water and swirled her fingers, making tiny ripples.

'I told you that I am wondering if Leo is bored with me?' she said, looking Gemma in the eyes. 'And I am thinking that you and I together might pique his interest.'

'You and I together?' echoed Gemma in a voice that didn't seem to belong to her. She felt Gabrielle's hand brush against the top of her breast in a soft caress. Despite the heat of the bath, her nipples hardened, puckering into taut peaks.

'Together,' coaxed Gabrielle, letting her fingers drop to the hardened point and clasping it gently. 'Leo will be intrigued with me anew, and you – you can see if he is your mysterious lover, your mystery lover. Perfect, no?'

'No. I mean, Gabrielle – '

'Think a little, Gemma, consider,' said Gabrielle.

Slowly, luxuriously, she trailed her hand through the water, lingering on her ribcage, her belly, until she came to her mound. Gemma swallowed, her mouth suddenly dry.

'This is something I have never done, you know,' Gabrielle continued in a soft voice. 'But I am thinking it could be very . . . exciting. And you are very lovely.'

Her hand was just above the lush delta between Gemma's thighs, wavering, not quite touching. 'Aren't you curious, even a little?'

It seemed to Gemma as though every sense was suddenly attuned to the path of Gabrielle's hand, the soft coaxing voice. She was curious, yes, excited too, a low, trembling, forbidden excitement that was throbbing between her legs. She felt the muscles in her belly clench and spasm. Vaguely, she was just a little frightened, frightened to say yes, frightened to say no.

Curiosity warred with cowardice. Her emotions must have been written clearly on her face, because Gabrielle smiled gently and let her hand fall. With one slim, index finger she touched Gemma on her clitoris, finding the soft, hidden nub immediately, unerringly, and pressed it lightly. A silken tremor passed through her, a delicate tingling that arced from her groin to her nipples.

'We are women, you and I,' Gabrielle was saying, 'and we can help each other. Perhaps even please each other. Yes?'

'Yes,' said Gemma. 'Yes.' She sighed, feeling as though a great weight had suddenly been lifted from her.

'Perfect,' smiled Gabrielle, and lifted her hand.

Gabrielle stayed with her as she finished bathing, chatting inconsequentially and sipping a second martini.

Strangely unselfconscious, Gemma wrapped a towel around her and combed out her hair, lulled by the sound of Gabrielle's voice, the heat of the bath, relaxed by the second martini. After Gemma had applied her make-up, together they went into the bedroom, and Gabrielle broke off in mid-stream to exclaim, 'Oh, yes! I was forgetting! I thought you might like to borrow something a little more . . .' she shrugged and lifted one bare shoulder, subtly emphasising the sleek lines of her black evening dress.

It was actually a little less. A sin of a dress in thick watered white silk that bared her arms, her back, and plunged in a deep vee at the front. Slit to mid-thigh, it clung to her sinuously, sensuously, like a second skin.

'No, no, no brassiére, my dear,' insisted Gabrielle. 'You will ruin the line. You see?'

'Yes, I think you're right,' agreed Gemma, removing the offending garment. The silk was cool and heavy against her naked breasts.

'Now, you see?' asked Gabrielle, coming up behind her so that their reflections met in the huge mirror. 'A study in contrasts, you and I, black and white. I thought of you in this dress this afternoon as I watched that poor girl wandering through the grave-yard in the white robe, and I knew that it was right for you.'

They dined in the great hall, where the brilliant, prismatic light of the massive chandelier warmed the gold plate and struck sparks off the crystal. Because the numbers were uneven, Leo sat at the head of the table with Gabrielle at his right and Gemma at his left. Beside her was Jay Stone, and directly across was Alexei Racine.

The meal was sumptuous and elegantly presented, the accompanying wines chosen with flair. A fresh, pale white was served with a mousseline of lobster decorated with Beluga caviar; a champagne sorbet prepared the palate for noisettes of lamb and a rather magnificent Bordeaux. There was a tempting array of beautifully prepared vegetables, tiny potatoes glis-tening with butter and garnished with chives and parsley, hothouse asparagus with a rich Hollandaise sauce, matchsticks of carrots and courgettes in a lightly garlic flavoured batter, spinach with raisins and pine nuts and new peas garnished with mint.

The conversation seemed stilted, thought Gemma, or was it merely her imagination? She should, of course, be paying closer attention to Jay Stone and Alexei Racine as they discussed the film, but she was strangely indifferent, even when she heard the name of Horror, Inc., bandied about. Gabrielle and Leo were talking together in French, though Gabrielle would often look over at her and smile, translating the odd remark.

It was almost like being in suspended animation, she decided, suspended, waiting. And she had merely to wait, knowing that Gabrielle would manipulate and manoeuvre events to her liking, knowing that she and Gabrielle and Leo would find themselves alone before the night was over.

And then? she wondered. For Gabrielle, this planned threesome was a piquant diversion to titillate the appetite of a lover she feared was flagging; for her, the opportunity to discover if Leo was her mysterious dream lover. Yet, if she were honest, she would have to admit that she didn't need Gabrielle's help, could confront Leo alone.

Yes, she thought, the idea itself, the three of them together, held a perverse temptation, the lure of the forbidden. What would it be like to make the beast with two backs with three, a woman and a man and a woman all intent on pleasuring each other, a tangle of limbs and needs, breasts and cock, shared, a rivalry of pleasure.

'Don't you agree, Gemma?' Gabrielle was saying.

'Yes, of course,' Gemma heard herself reply.

Champagne was served with the white chocolate mousse, thick, bitter coffee with the brandy. As the meal drew to a close, Gemma found her body tightening with anticipation, her heart beating more strongly.

In the end, it was Racine himself who offered Gabrielle her opening.

'Your study, Leo, do you mind? Jay and I have some business to discuss and I may need your fax,' he said, rising from the table.

'Of course, my friend,' nodded Leo. 'Ask Henri for whatever you like.'

Did she imagine it, or was there a brief moment

when Gabrielle's eyes met Racine's in a look of subdued complicity?

And then they were alone.

Gabrielle stretched and yawned delicately. 'Leo, will you walk me to my suite? I am a trifle fatigued . . . oh, and Gemma, you must come as well. The dress, you see,' she explained to Leo's raised eyebrows. 'Gemma borrowed it from me tonight . . . it's very lovely on her, don't you think, Leo?'

'Ravishing,' he agreed politely, offering one arm to Gabrielle, the other to Gemma.

The voyage to the bedroom is often a blur, the memory dissolving in the crucible of the journey's end.

For the rest of her life Gemma knew she would recall every step that led to Gabrielle's suite, every pause. The warmth of Leo's body as he lightly held her arm, the heavy, exotic scent of Gabrielle's perfume, the slick rustle of her white dress.

'A brandy, perhaps?' offered Gabrielle as they entered her blue and gold suite, waving Gemma and Leo to a blue velvet settee. Without waiting for a reply, she poured Leo a snifter of brandy and then sat beside him. There was hardly room for three, and Leo's eyes narrowed a little at the enforced intimacy.

'And you, Gemma? What would you like?' she asked softly. She leaned over and took Gemma's hand, guiding it to Leo's fly and pressing it gently down.

For a moment it seemed Leo stiffened in surprise. But she could feel, beneath the soft, expensive wool of his trousers another kind of stiffening as his cock swelled instantly under the pressure. She could feel it growing under her fingers, hardening, straining against the fabric, and it filled her with a sudden, keen exultancy. Under Gabrielle's hand she let her own drift down, scratch against the metal zip, explore the thickening shaft through the cloth, and felt him quiver in response.

Leo made a muffled sound, and Gabrielle plucked the snifter from his hand. 'Perhaps you would prefer this instead?' she whispered.

She began to caress the side of Leo's body closest to hers, running her hands along his chest, fingering his nipple, then dropping to his groin, his thigh. Unthinkingly Gemma imitated her, let her hands follow the same path, finding the blunt male nipple that hardened ever so slightly in response under the fine silk of his shirt, returning to his groin, finding the blunt rod of his arousal, the hard, muscled thigh.

'Yes?' asked Gabrielle softly, capturing Gemma's hand in her own, and curling their entwined fingers around his shaft.

'Yes,' said Leo thickly. 'Yes.'

Together, in unspoken accord, their movements perfectly synchronised, Gemma and Gabrielle removed his trousers, his shirt, the silk boxer shorts and socks and shoes. He had, she saw, a truly beautiful body, powerful shoulders tapering to an elegant waist, penis jutting proudly from the dark bush of his pubic hair, long well-muscled legs.

Gemma let her hand stray to his cock, wondering if her hand would recognise him, if some carnal alchemy would flare at the touch, but Gabrielle drew her away.

'Let me,' she said, hands moving to the zipper of the white dress.

Gemma stood passive under her hands as Gabrielle undid her dress and let it fall to the floor in a white, rippling wave. She was facing Leo, and she saw the heat in his eyes as he took in her naked breasts, the small white triangle of her panties enclosing her mound. She felt at once proud and shy, excited, faintly alarmed and utterly aroused. She felt

Gabrielle's hands move to her panties, slide under the delicate elastic.

'No,' said Leo hoarsely. 'Not yet.' His voice was roughened by arousal, almost unrecognisable as the suave, cultured tones of the Comte Marais, and Gemma felt a shiver down her spine. But it was not the same harsh voice of her dreams, she was sure, almost sure.

Naked, he rose from the settee and came to stand between them. With one skilled movement he stripped Gabrielle's dress from her body, until she too was clad only in a pair of tiny black silk panties. 'Beautiful,' he murmured thickly, his eyes flickering rapidly between them. 'Beautiful.'

He slipped one hand between Gemma's thighs, the other between Gabrielle's. 'A most exciting dilemma,' he ground out. 'As I have two hands, but alas, only one cock.'

Through the thin silk of her panties she could feel him tracing the fleshy petals of her labia, looking for her clitoris, cupping her, exploring her, and knew she was dampening, growing wet. She could feel the brush of Gabrielle's bare arm against her own, hear her breathing coming faster, feel the faint, tantalising touch of Leo's cock against her belly.

Her lower lips were swelling against the damp silk, becoming engorged, ripe and slick, palpitating under the leisured play of his fingers. If only, she thought dazedly, he would bend his mouth to her there, give her that kiss, that annihilating, unforgettable, lascivious kiss that would reveal himself to her, or take her quickly, now, plunge the hard shaft into her, let her inner body recognise his shape, his length.

But Leo Marais was not so inclined. Briefly startled, instantly aroused by the erotic prospect of taking Gabrielle and Gemma together, his connoisseur's imagination was now caught, intrigued. Gabrielle, in manipulating this unlikely trio, had surpassed his expectations; Gemma, in agreeing, had rather surprised him. He had disobliged Alexei the other night, for reasons he didn't even understand himself, knowing that Alexei wanted him to take her, make love to her . . . and now she had found her way to him. With Gabrielle.

But if there were to be some scheme, some subtle manipulation, it would be his, he decided. He could feel both women under his hands, hot and trembling, opening to his fingers, clinging against the damp silk. His admiration for Gabrielle was sincere; he would never have thought she would have dared so much, on her own initiative. And he would express his appreciation . . . in his own fashion.

Reluctantly he withdew his hands from the damp silk and turned to Gabrielle, kissing her softly on the mouth.

'Such a lovely gift you have brought me,' he murmured against her lips, taking her hand in his. 'Come, let us unwrap it together.'

He guided her hands to Gemma's breasts and, her fingers beneath his, clasped the swollen mounds, clasped and unclasped until the pink, untouched nipples were aching points, turned rosy with blood and want.

Gemma, eyes closed, waiting for his touch, felt it by proxy, Leo's large hands guiding Gabrielle's smaller ones, setting the rhythm, making her follow his movements. But Gemma could sense the strong, guiding force, the overlapping strength of his hands and fingers. Her senses began to swim, dissolve in the repeated clasping and unclasping of the sensitive mounds of her breasts.

She was caught, snared in a delicate, sensual web, trapped and transfixed by rhythmic caress of their hands on her breasts. There was an echoing throb deep in the pit of her belly, a pulse conjured by their fingers, a melting heat. Her nipples were rock hard, straining for suction, begging for the hard, pulling pressure that would unleash the pooling heat. The scrap of silk encasing her mound was becoming tight, unbearably tight, and wet with the liquid arousal flowing from her. She heard herself moan aloud, and then the sound of Leo's voice coming from far away.

'Show me, then, Gabrielle, what you want from me.'

Gabrielle's mouth closed on her breast. Gemma arched toward her mindlessly, any hidden motives or secret desires dissolving in the sweet warm wash of Gabrielle's tongue tracing the nimbus of her areola, flirting with her nipple, just grazing the distended point with her teeth.

It was a woman's mouth, soft and beguiling, gentle and coaxing, teasing, promising. She felt her breasts swelling, growing fuller, rounder, round as the plump leaves of her inner lips, now straining against the white silk.

With innate, intimate skill Gabrielle moved her mouth to Gemma's other breast, lavishing the same sweet torture, gently rolling the hard peak between her teeth, finding the tingling friction that arced to the groin, then moved back and forth between the rosy points, always leaving one before it was fully stimulated. Gemma felt her whole body flush, on the brink, craving a hard, hungry suckling yet still revelling in the delicious, gentle stimulation.

Eyes closed, she sensed Leo's presence, knew he was watching with avid eyes. In some strange way it increased her excitement, deepened her arousal.

'And then, Gabrielle? And then?'

Hands and mouth left her breast, and she felt a warm path of kisses along her ribs, the swell of her hips, a teasing tongue flirt with her navel before descending to the delta between her thighs. Through the silk of her panties she felt a questing tongue probe her clitoris, lick the furrow between her thighs.

The muscles in her legs began to tremble and she was feeling faint, lightheaded. Swiftly Leo moved behind her, supporting her, holding her fast to his body. She felt the hard rod of his penis between her thighs, the warmth of his breath against her neck.

'And then?'

Gabrielle's hands were at her hips, sliding down the scrap of white silk, leaving it twisted around Gemma's ankles as her mouth brushed against her pubic hair, browsing, nuzzling, circling the bud of her clitoris.

She was lush and full, tumid and engorged. The flickering path of Gabrielle's tongue left fire in its wake, a moist, burning heat that engulfed the delicate tissues, made her blood flow like lava and her cunt an inferno. The first flames of orgasm were glittering under her skin when Leo spoke.

'And then, Gabrielle?'

She felt him drive into her from behind, plunge into the fervent fiery heat as the first spasm took her. Her body convulsed again and again, racked with the intensity of her climax.

Leo held her against him, relishing the savagery of her contractions, letting her body grip his as wave after wave passed through her. Slowly he felt them weaken in intensity as her orgasm faded.

Through the heated, transcendent rush, Gemma felt him inside her.

It was him, yet not him.

He was too long, yet not long enough, enclosing but not engulfing, too thick, yet not thick enough, familiar but strange.

As soon as she was able, she withdrew, kicking away the silken panties tangled around her ankles.

She felt drained yet triumphant, a strange, bewildered joy. Leo was standing stock still, prick thick and hard and unspent, Gabrielle still kneeling before them. Gemma bent down and retrieved the white silk dress. Quickly she slipped it over her head and turned back to face them.

'And then, Gabrielle? And then?' Leo was saying, eyes fixed on her kneeling figure.

Gemma watched as Gabrielle rose to her feet. They both seemed oblivious to her now, enrapt in each other. Silently she slipped from the room.

Chapter Eight

*T*he woman lay on a raised stone dais, her pale, flowing gown falling in waves to the stone floor, her pale, flowing hair almost touching the ground. Mists and shadows haunted the corners of the cavernous room, sly and chilling.

The woman was still and white, her skin the same muted ivory as her flowing robes, her flesh as waxy as the lily clasped between her breasts. Only her lips had colour, a bright, voluptuous red the colour of blood.

The walls were massive stone slabs, impervious to everything but the damp chill that seemed to seep insinuatingly through every crack. Although it was only a trick of the light, a cool glistening on the cold grey surface of the stone, a seeping malevolent spirit seemed to pervade the cavern, something that only showed itself in the lurking mist, the damp sheen of the stone.

Then, gradually, almost imperceptibly, the light changed, and the stone melted into the shadows, dissolving into the ghostly, flickering mist. It swirled, changed shape. Changed form.

In the eerie light three women materialised, their bodies round and voluptuous, eyes bright and hard, teeth white, lips the slick red of fresh blood. They smiled at the still form, ringed the silent figure and called sweetly, 'Come to us, sister! Come to us!'

With a sweet, lewd grace they swayed together, beckoning with plump white arms, baring rounded breasts, parting white thighs.

'Come to us, sister! Come to us!'

Their hips moved in the rhythm of sex, swaying, arching, rocking. So vividly, so voluptuously did they move that the air seemed suddenly heavy with the musky incense of arousal.

They swayed ever closer to the pale figure lying still on the dais, bending low as if to inhale the scent of the white lily lying on her breast, darting, flickering, yet reluctantly drawing away. One, bolder than the rest, more cunning, had almost touched her lips to the pale, white throat when the mist pooled, darkened, surged and elongated into the black, menacing form of the Count.

His face as pale as death, eyes blazing with red wrath, he swept the three away with one fierce gesture. They fell against the shadows, shattered, scattered insubstantial into the mist.

He stood beside the pale, still figure, drinking in her presence, absorbing her, feeding on the sight of her. The pallor of his face diminished, grew less, as if feeding on the sight of her pale body warmed his blood.

His eyes were hooded, deep hollows that betrayed nothing, his features sharp, almost predatory. And when at last he smiled, a slow, voluptuary's smile, his white canines were pointed.

The air stirred, thickened and deepened.

Watching, it was impossible not to be drawn into the shadowy, murky eroticism as those hot eyes devoured the still figure before him, the motionless blood-red lips, the long, pale throat, the high thrust of breast, nipple faintly shadowed under the thin white robe.

It was an aching moment, thick and potent. Perhaps it was the feel of the air, still thick with the musk of excitement, or the palpable scent, the perfume of aroused female flesh. Perhaps it was the still, dark, enveloping hedonism of the cool assessment of imminent deathly pleasure that captured the senses, made pulses beat more quickly, quickened breathing as he moved closer.

Watching, Gemma herself was caught, physically transfixed. Like the woman on the dais, she felt suspended, in thrall, waiting for the demon lover's touch, the hot, rapacious, demonic possession. All will, all desire, every heartbeat seemed now governed by the enveloping black desire of the vampire lover whose beautiful blood red lips hovered above the pale, exposed throat of the woman on the stone dais.

The woman's body seemed to awaken under his gaze, her utter stillness dissolving, the pallor of her skin warming ever so slightly.

When finally he moved his mouth to her throat, her body arched to meet him, a fluid, graceful, irrevocable movement. He penetrated her with his teeth, sinking them deep into the pale flesh.

And then it was over.

'*Magnifique!*' breathed Gabrielle, who had been standing quietly beside Gemma. '*Magnifique!*'

Gemma turned to her with a smile. Several days had passed since the night in Gabrielle's suite and she had seen little of either Leo or Gabrielle since. They had taken to dining alone in Leo's private apartments and rarely emerged. When they did, it was together, and on the odd occasion Gemma encountered them they treated her with a warm affection, like a favourite sister.

It seemed as though Gabrielle's plot had worked: Leo was never far from her side now and, for the first time, was openly demonstrative, even affectionate, his arm never far from her shoulders or possessively encircling her waist. And Gabrielle herself looked sleeker, more rounded, even rather smug, as if she would be more comfortable purring than speaking.

And while Gemma was pleased for her, their absence had rather changed things. Jay Stone had left for Paris, called away suddenly by some urgent business, and she and Racine had spent the evenings alone together, the two of them dining in the massive hall that could have comfortably held a hundred, then watching the rushes in the small private screening room Leo had set aside for their use.

He was absorbed in the film, so absorbed that he spoke of little else. And if her mind wandered sometimes, straying back to her dream lover, to the physical memory of Leo and Gabrielle, he never seemed to notice.

Certain that Leo was not her mysterious lover, she found herself reluctant to explore further. Her sleep was troubled with dark, carnal dreams of a demon lover that left her feeling hollow and unfulfilled. Sometimes it seemed to her that the film was becoming reality, or reality was becoming the film.

Two nights ago, waking hot and unbearably aroused from yet another dream, she had actually left the chateau and walked around the old keep, replayed herself the graveyard scene from 'Tales of the Vampire', irrationally convinced that he would come for her there. Eventually, exhausted and chilled to the bone, she had crept into bed alone and slept soundlessly, dreamlessly.

'A dark genius,' murmured Gabrielle beside her. 'Very dark.'

Alexei Racine, had he heard the comment, would have admired Gabrielle's perspicacity. For that was exactly how he saw himself. A dark genius. And every night confirmed his opinion, as he inspected the rushes of the day's filming. As he observed Gemma.

The change in her was subtle, yet unmistakable. She moved now with a natural, rhythmic elegance, a physical grace, the fluid ease of a body sensually aware. That it was largely unconscious on her part, he had no doubt, and it pleased him more than any deliberate provocation ever could.

He was getting to know the far-away look in her deep blue eyes, the look that softened navy to azure and warmed her cheeks, ever so slightly quickened her breathing. And he knew what she was thinking. In those moments, believing herself unobserved, she had the warm, voluptuous aura of a woman remembering her lover.

Leo had, of course, referred rather eliptically to the sex play that Gabrielle had initiated, and Alexei had been amused to hear him speak with such unconvincing *savoir faire*, the charged emotion evident in every casual, apparently lazily amused word or gesture.

Naturally it was a stroke of carnal genius, erotically understated yet sensually inspired . . . after all, it was he who had suggested it to Gabrielle in the first place.

He had had no need, indeed, no desire to watch them. They were already perfectly etched in his mind, Gabrielle's dark, sleek beauty, Gemma's long, silvery blonde hair, Leo – the essential male counterpoint – blunt and hard where they were soft and yielding. It was enough – indeed, infinitely more satisfying – to have created the scene.

But he was beginning to tire just a little of the role of erotic impresario. He had watched the other night as Gemma had prowled the graveyard, her hair silver, almost luminous in the moonlight, and had to quell the urge to go to her, take her there in the graveyard, lay her back on the cold marble slabs and open her to him.

Only the French, he mused, truly understood the relation between sex and death, only the French appreciated *la petite mort*, the fatal, annihilating ecstasy of the perfect orgasm. Yes, one day he would take her in a graveyard, meet and vanquish the shades of the dead with the haunting, deathless fury of their mating. Perhaps in Père Lachaise, the most erotically evocative of all Paris's cemeteries, beside the bluntly sexual funeral monument sculpted by Epstein for Oscar Wilde's grave . . . no. Some cretin had wrenched away the stone penis of the winged guardian, a desecration that appalled and disgusted him.

Perhaps near the lovers Heloise and Abelard, where their stone effigies lay together, reunited in the grave. Racine smiled a little at the thought. He had never understood the cloying sweet sentimentality attached to the story. Peter Abelard had, in fact, been a cold-hearted, calculating lover, who had insinuated himself into Canon Fulbert's house with no other aim than the seduction of the lovely Heloise, a lover prepared to bend her to his will with threats and blows if he failed with caresses. A man to be admired, he privately considered.

And sometimes there were blows, Abelard had written, the marks of a tenderness surpassing the most fragrant balm in sweetness, no degree in love's progress left untried by their passion. Their sad end

– Heloise bundled off to a nunnery and Abelard castrated – could only add a piquant flavour to the act, a piquancy that only a Frenchman could truly appreciate.

Was it not after all a Frenchman, de Rougement, who had described passion as the longing for what sears and annihilates us in its triumph?

Soon, he thought, soon but not yet.

In the cool, white silk embrace of the open coffin, Alexei Racine lay back, closed his eyes, and prepared to take a nap before dinner.

Leo, too, was lying down before dinner. His nude body was spreadeagled across the grey silk counterpane, silk scarves by Givenchy trailing from his wrists and ankles to the four posters of the bed. His body was covered with a light sheen of sweat and his cock jutted fiercely red from the curling pubic hair of his groin.

Gabrielle hummed softly to herself as she slowly shed her oyster coloured peignoir, and smiled inwardly as Leo's erection thickened at the sight of her naked body. He had promised not to speak, not to move a muscle unless she commanded it, but he couldn't control the swelling shaft of his erection.

She could feel her excitement rising. Leisurely she walked to the marquetry table intricately worked in ivory that stood beside the bed. For a brief moment she was beyond Leo's line of vision, and she could almost sense his suspense, his excitement as she opened the drawer.

A vibrator, perhaps, that she would run slowly and lovingly over her own body, throat and breasts and belly, stimulating every inch of skin until she was soaking wet inside, while he watched, helplessly aroused, knowing that if he came before she allowed it some deliciously deviant punishment would follow. Mmm. Or perhaps she would take another scarf, cover his eyes, play with his body, stimulate him until he was losing control, then penetrate him with the smooth ivory dildo he had given her. Mmm.

She selected a small jar of salve and moved to the foot of the bed, feeling his eyes on her, hot and hungry. He watched as she began to rouge her nipples, knowing that the rosy ointment, spiked with amyl nitrate and cocaine, created a burning, icy tingling that enhanced every sensation.

The sensitive, delicate skin of her nipples responded immediately, stiffening into hard points, engorged with a fresh flush of blood. She gasped a little as she felt them harden, felt the delicious shivering sensation capture her spine and move to the pit of her belly.

The temptation to move one hand to her sex, annoint her clitoris with the rosy salve, feel it stiffen and surge under the heated sting, was almost irresistible. Her eyes fixed on Leo, she let her hand drop to her mound and felt a rising thrill of excitement as his eyes narrowed and he bit his lip. Her climax, if she so chose, was only moments away, the incandescent, engulfing, brief cataclysm that the ointment promised.

She could create it, summon it, know the twin pleasures of her own orgasm and Leo's helpless response as he ejaculated into emptiness, deprived of her body.

So she tantalised them both a little, let her hand drift ever closer to her mons, knowing, as Leo did not, that she had other pleasures in mind, relishing the power, the sexual high of utter control.

Because Gabrielle de Sevigny, pampered, indolent, aristocratic wife of a prominent government Minister, once obsessed, was learning the complex and infinitely more satisfying rules of domination.

Now inventive, mischievous, cunning, she delighted in applying the carnal lessons Leo had taught her: how to confound expectation, how to prolong the slow burn of anticipation, how to truly savour the cat and mouse of foreplay, please and tease, claw and cajole, torment and dement until the prey was mindless and quivering and aching.

So, for long, breathless, moments she let Leo wonder if she would climax alone in front of his eyes, and then, with the shining malice the cobra shows to a cornered captive, relented. She let her hand drift to her inner thigh, let the salve dissolve in a burning glimmer just where, if her legs were crossed, it might reach the sensitive folds of her outer lips, then moved her hand away, gracefully, languidly.

More salve on her fingertips, she approached his naked body, wearing the abstracted, thoughtful expression of one contemplating a particularly abstruse philosophical problem. She fingered the air above his nipples, making him wonder if she would caress him with it, make his blunt male nipples swell under its spell, then let her fingers drift lower, hover above the hard ridge of his erection.

She knew, and he knew, that one swirling caress on the throbbing, purplish head would trigger his release, one touch of the tingling, icy, consuming heat would make him come despite himself. As she watched, she saw the glistening pearl of his arousal gather at the head of his penis, and smiled.

She let her hand drop lower, contemplate the fecund bulge of his testicles now hard and engorged as his prick, and let him wonder, as she did herself, how it would feel if she stroked the salve there, let it penetrate the fragile, delicate tissues so akin to her own sensitive inner lips.

Leo's eyes were closed and he was breathing hard, his prick shuddering slightly in anticipation. She moved her hand slightly closer, let him savour the anticipation of near release, watched his loins tighten unconsciously, uncontrollably, watched his hips move, his pelvis clench and grind against the silk counterpane, and withdrew her hand, fastidiously wiping her fingers on the grey silk counterpane.

Her body was screaming, her sex heavy and congested, full and ready to burst, but Gabrielle de Sevigny was no dull pupil. She walked across to the neo-modern drinks cabinet, all improbable angles and screaming harsh colours, as she considered her next move.

She was not, she acknowledged, gulping brandy, as adept at this game as Leo. She felt hot and tumid, achingly engorged, her cunt fervent with want, avid with the desire to impale herself on the hard shaft that was waiting for her. And Leo himself was now lost, as lost as she had been. He had succumbed to her carnal rules eagerly and was waiting speechless, motionless, as she had commanded.

The brandy left a fiery trail down her throat. She forced herself to sip slowly, then put down the snifter and returned to the bed. Kneeling beside him, she let her hands drift down his body, fingering the blunt nipples, the hard, muscled torso, sifting through the wiry, dense curls of his pubic hair, then stroking his thighs, his calves. For a long time she contented herself with gentle caresses, avoiding the thick shaft of his penis, and then at last she mounted him.

His penis surged blindly against her soft, damp flesh and her inner muscles rippled and contracted, expecting the hard, assuaging fullness of his shaft. But she kept herself poised above him, only allowing his engorged head to enter her, rocking her hips gently, drawing him inside just a fraction and then releasing him, keeping him at the mouth of her vagina, denying them both the long, sure thrust.

176

Below her, she could feel his hips grinding as he strained for her, but she allowed only a brief, tantalising taste of the sweet, moist nest he craved before rocking away. The muscles of her inner thighs began to tremble and she felt the deep, pulsing throb in the pit of her belly.

For a moment she relented and sank down on his shaft, revelling in the delicious, hollowing sensation as her body stretched to hold him. His hips thrust and she could feel him moving inside her, plunging deeper. She leaned back, forcing his prick to strain against her inner walls, intensifying the pressure so acutely that it was almost painful. She felt a white-hot flickering along her spine as her muscles clenched around him.

Biting her lower lip she suddenly surged away in one swift, slick movement and lay against his chest. His breathing was coming in short, ragged gasps and his skin was hot and damp with sweat. Resting against him, letting her breathing slow, she licked his throat and tasted salt on her tongue. His body was taut with tension and she could feel his muscles straining against her silk scarves.

Raising herself on one elbow, she looked at him. His eyes were screwed tightly shut, his face a mask of concentration, his lips pressed together. Slowly she curved herself towards him until the tip of her nipple brushed his mouth. His tongue darted out to capture it, but she drew back slightly before leaning forward and letting him take her nipple between his lips, gradually allowing him more and more of her breast.

He was sucking hard, using his teeth, abrading her with the desperate friction of tongue and teeth, pulling her nipple into a taut, hard peak. She let him suckle for long moments before offering her other breast, relishing the steady pulling pressure.

Her nipples were achingly distended, almost painfully stimulated, her body readying for orgasm when she moved, knelt above him, legs spread wide above his head.

His tongue was straining for her as she slowly lowered herself to his mouth, darting through her slick outer lips straight to her entrance, then plunging inside.

Her groin was heavy, congested with need. She rocked above him, let him capture the bud of her clitoris and suck it between his lips before pulling back. Again and again she repeated the tiny movement as he lapped frantically at her clitoris, thrust inside her with his tongue.

Her control was loosening a little, dissolving under the hot, heavy need to have him inside her, and she felt flushed with a dangerous, erotic excitement. Now Leo, bound to the bed, helpless, was her plaything, and the hard column between his legs belonged to her. There was time now for all the intriguing variations, all the devious sensual manipulations, anything and everything . . . but she wanted him inside her.

She slipped down the bed and lowered herself to him, taking him in one lyrical, lascivious motion, impaling herself. And Leo, summoning every ounce of control he surely possessed, held himself back and let her set the rhythm, let her move softly and experimentally, rising and falling above him until the imperious avidity of her own need drove her faster and faster. She began to lunge against him furiously, riding him hard and then harder with a wildness alien to what he knew of her, until the heat splintered and orgasm claimed her.

Her body gripped his as spasm after spasm racked her, fusing them together in molten waves, and she collapsed on his chest as the climax flowed through her.

Alone in her suite, Gemma was curled up on a plump *chaise longue* before the window. Beside her was a bottle of Crystal cooling in a silver ice-bucket; before her, spread out on the magnificent Aubusson carpet, lay the pages of the shooting schedule and her own notes. From time to time she paused and sipped from a Baccarat champagne flute as she methodically worked her way through the pile of papers.

Things were going well, almost too well, she thought, superstitiously reaching out to touch the ornately carved wooden scrollwork adorning the edge of the *chaise*. No major disasters, no unforseen catastrophies, no nervous breakdowns . . . or at least not yet. The actor playing Renfield was stubbornly refusing to eat live spiders, which Racine was insisting on; one of the make-up artists had had a flaming row with her boyfriend, a camera man, and had stormed back to England; three minor members of the cast had been arrested for being drunk and disorderly in Carnac and the actress playing Mina had developed an alergic reaction to something resulting in a disfiguring red rash that was going to play havoc with continuity.

All relatively minor, she decided, except perhaps the problem with Renfield. She had no idea of French law as it related to cruelty to animals – cruelty to insects? – but surely Racine could be persuaded to use the horribly real looking plastic spiders that the props department had devised?

Even more astounding was the fact that they were actually more or less on schedule. Racine, the merciless perfectionist who was quite prepared to spend literally hours capturing the perfect moment, had nevertheless managed to stay roughly on schedule.

She stretched and poured herself more champagne, still eyeing her notes. Another two weeks and the location shots should be finished, she realised, crossing her fingers. She jotted down a few reminders in the margin of her day planner, then gathered up the papers.

Glancing down at her watch, she saw that it was already past seven o'clock. Gabrielle had mentioned in passing that Jay Stone was due back from Paris tonight and that she and Leo would be joining them for dinner in the conservatory. Idly she wondered what to wear. Several more of Gabrielle's dresses had found their way into her wardrobe, and she felt that tonight was the night to dress for dinner.

But what to wear, and for whom? Gabrielle, she thought with a swift smile, was certainly proving an unsettling influence in more ways than one. There was the black sequinned tube with spaghetti straps that was dangerously sexy, the saffron yellow silk with the beautifully full, swirling skirt and practically non-existent top, the crimson velvet that hugged from neck to toe, so apparently demure, so utterly revealing.

She opened the *armoire* and let her fingers run over the silks and velvets. The conservatory would be hot. She fingered the white silk dress she had worn the fateful night with Gabrielle and Leo and slipped it from its padded hanger.

Small wonder she sometimes felt she was moving between two worlds, she thought, examining her reflection in the gilded Regency mirror. She left the murky unreal reality of 'Tales of the Vampire' to return to the opulent luxury of the chateau where, it seemed, the slightest whim, any desire, could be gratified with no more than a few words through an intercom.

Yes, the rich were different, she decided, smoothing the white silk across her breasts and feeling her nipples harden. Very different.

She walked down the gilded hall, admiring the soft, honeyed light from the crystal wall sconces. Slowly she was learning her way around the labyrinthine corridors of the chateau, though there were still many unexpected twistings and turnings she had not explored. But she could find her way to the conservatory, and when she opened the doors and entered the humid, leafy salon, she was faintly surprised to find that no-one was there.

She paused beside the gnarled trunk of an immense tree, breathing in the rich, heady scent of warm earth, the sweet green smell of growing things. Bending down to examine an orchid growing in the moss at her feet she had the strange sensation that she was being watched. As she lifted her head she caught a glimpse of unblinking malevolent red eyes.

Sinuously curled around the base of the tree was a snake, its coils gleaming wetly, shimmering black and green. She froze. Its eyes were fixed on her with unnatural intensity, a blank, ruby stare that seemed strangely dead. Rigid, hardly daring to breathe, Gemma stood still. And then she took in the absolute stillness of the coiled form, the hard iridescence of its scales, the glittering red eyes, and realised it was a jewelled replica. The malign ruby eyes were, in fact, rubies, the gleaming scales a mixture of jade and onyx.

A bit shaken, she stepped back and nearly collided with Jay Stone.

'Oh, I'm sorry, I – ' Gemma began, but his eyes had caught the direction of hers.

'Another of Leo's bizarre *objets*,' he observed, leaning closer for a better look. 'Lifelike, isn't it? I'm not surprised you were startled. You don't think he has the real kind slithering around, do you? I hate snakes.'

'I hope not,' said Gemma with a shudder not entirely feigned. 'I don't like them either.'

'But this one's a beauty,' he continued. 'Fabulous workmanship, and look at those eyes.'

Gemma watched him as he studied the bejewelled snake, liking him for the lie that had put her at ease so instantly. 'It just startled me for a moment,' she explained. 'I thought I was being watched.'

'But you were,' he said, turning to her. 'I was watching you.'

She paused, uncertain how to reply, and the brief moment of silence stretched, became significant.

'Shall we join the others?' he said at last, offering his arm.

'Oh, but,' Gemma began, looking around the leafy enclave, 'I thought – '

'Through here,' said Jay, leading her down a small path almost concealed by the fronds of huge ferns that swayed as they passed. The distant sound of running water became closer as they walked down the overgrown path, and when they emerged from the overgrown leafy tunnel she saw a small waterfall emptying into a rock-lined pool.

Gabrielle was sitting at the edge of the pool, dressed in a scarlet sarong that bared most of her body, dangling her feet in the clear blue water and laughing at something Leo had just said. He was beside her, shirtless, trousers rolled up to his knees, both feet entwined with Gabrielle's in the rippling pool. There was a silver ice-bucket between them, and wine glasses in both their hands. Racine was lounging some distance away on a massive rock, fully clothed and sipping a pale amber liquid from a faceted glass.

Their entrance had startled two giant macaws who

fled shrieking in a brilliant blaze of colour to the top of the waterfall.

'It's unreal,' Gemma murmured, taking in the underwater lights that cunningly illuminated the falling water, the flashing play of light and shadow, the luxuriant greenery and exotic flowers. A cold buffet was arranged on a long, low table covered with a white cloth and adorned with hibiscus, camellias and orchids. Rosy lobsters piled on beds of seaweed offered their claws, crabs, *langoustine*, prawns, shrimps and oysters were temptingly arrayed amidst lemons carved into roses. Pyramids of fruit, peaches, apricots, grapes and pineapples towered above blue and white porcelain sauce bowls.

It was an exotic Eden, a dionysiac paradise, lush and sensually inviting. It was as though they had stepped through a secret door into Tahiti, left the pale grey world of winter in Carnac for a tropical paradise.

'Join us, Gemma, Jay,' called Gabrielle, splashing her feet in the water and raising her glass. 'Join us!'

She said something to Leo, then handed him her glass and slipped into the water. Gemma and Jay watched as she swam over to them and slowly walked up the deep steps hewn into the rock. Dripping wet the thin silk of her sarong clung to her body, emphasising the high, pointed breasts, the darker shadow of her nipples. With her black hair trailing wetly across her shoulders and down her back, the wet silk clinging to her hips, outlining the juncture of her thighs, she was unaffectedly sensual, almost exotic.

'Isn't this delightful?' exclaimed Gabrielle, her eyes shining. 'A picnic! And the water is warm. I have been trying to tempt Alexei, but he doesn't put so much as a foot in!'

'It certainly looks inviting,' replied Jay, trying, with

some difficulty, to keep his eyes from drifting down to her astonishing breasts. 'Perhaps later.'

'But of course! Help yourself to a drink, whatever you like. We are informal tonight, very casual.' In the almost tropical heat of the conservatory, her dress was already beginning to dry.

There was an array of bottles chilling on a bed of shaved ice. Gemma selected champagne, and Jay poured several inches of Stolichnaya into a tumbler before moving to join Alexei on the rock seat opposite Leo.

'So, to paradise,' he said, raising his glass to Alexei.

'But what is paradise without a serpent?' said Alexei, returning the toast and sipping his drink.

'I believe I met him on the way in,' said Jay. 'Have you seen it? I never knew Fabergé created pieces so large. Around the trunk of one of the trees –'

'Art Deco,' shrugged Alexei. 'Leo's sense of the symbolic remains sadly obvious. I was only relieved to observe that it was not an apple tree. But what do you make of our two Eves?'

Jay glanced over to Gemma and Gabrielle, now wading in the sparkling shallow water near Leo, both laughing and clutching their glasses. Gabrielle, with her dark colouring and scarlet sarong belonged to Gauguin; Gemma, her amazing silvery blonde hair loose and the white silk dress wrapped around her thighs, looked as though she could have posed for Botticelli.

As they watched, she slipped and fell into the water, emerging seconds later laughing, champagne flute intact and pleated white silk dress clinging wetly to her body.

'A little like Aphrodite on the Ludovisi throne,' mused Alexei. 'But her breasts are better.'

'What?' asked Jay. 'And whose?'

'Gemma's of course. I had forgotten your abysmal

ignorance of classical art. The Ludovisi throne is . . . Oh, never mind?'

'How is the filming?' asked Jay, tactfully changing the subject. He never minded Alexei's casually blistering insults, interpreting them as the natural, verbal abrasion of a frustrated and frustrating creative genius. His own flair with stocks and bonds and mergers he considered much more mundane.

'Brilliant,' said Alexei at last. 'Quite brilliant. You will be pleased that I let you retain some shares. I anticipate a stunning success . . . in many ways. Have you seen the way she moves now? Look at her with Leo and Gabrielle, so natural, so easy in her body. Almost ready. You will enjoy her, I am sure. Tonight, I think.'

Jay gulped his vodka. 'You know, Alexei, I've never really understood – '

'I am sadly aware of that.'

'Look at them,' giggled Gabrielle, pouring more champagne into Gemma's glass. 'So serious, so intense. They must be talking business, so boring of them. Tonight is a revel.'

'And what are we celebrating?' asked Gemma. They were sitting together at the edge of the pool, feet dangling in the water, watching Leo pick his way over to Jay and Alexei.

'Oh, everything! Your vampire, perhaps. My victory.'

'Your victory?' echoed Gemma.

'Ah, yes, I have won, I think,' nodded Gabrielle, her eyes sparkling. 'Leo has fallen victim to his own tactics. Surprise you see, is the essence of attack. It was one of your generals who said this, and he was right.'

'And are you still, mmm, surprising him?' asked Gemma, intrigued.

185

'I contrive,' smiled Gabrielle. 'Look at him now, he's watching us, and wondering. And remembering, too, I am sure.'

Gemma flushed a little.

'Yes,' Gabrielle continued, her voice low and persuasive. 'He is wondering what we are plotting, and how the night will end.' Under the water she tangled her feet with Gemma's and moved one foot slowly and sensuously against her arch. 'And Jay too is watching us, and Alexei. Imagine it, Gemma.' Her voice trailed off suggestively.

'That's not a revel, Gabrielle, that's an orgy!' retorted Gemma lightly. But now that the words had been said, it was impossible not to wonder what it might be like, how it might feel.

'And of course, your mystery lover,' prompted Gabrielle softly. 'Who was not Leo, as we know.'

'No . . . but how did you – '

'You would not have left that night if he was,' replied Gabrielle.

'Oh. Yes, perhaps. I don't know.' Gabrielle's foot was still moving caressingly along her arch, reminding her, arousing her a little.

'Gemma, I've shocked you? It is an idea, no more. Come now, let us eat, and we will speak no more about this if it troubles you.' She rose gracefully and walked over to the buffet, calling to the men to join them.

Gemma sat for a moment, finishing her champagne and watching as Jay and Leo climbed over the rocks. Both men moved with an easy assurance, a natural, athletic grace. Jay was a trifle shorter than Leo, and slightly stockier in build. He had unbuttoned his shirt almost to the navel and rolled up his sleeves, revealing thick, muscular forearms and a bronzed chest. Physically Leo was the more elegant, but Jay had a sort of virile toughness, a rough edge that was sexually appealing.

It was astonishingly easy to picture them both nude, surrounding her, enclosing her, enfolding her in their maleness, Leo behind her, Jay before her, caressing her, searching her body with hard hands and engorged pricks.

A second later, she almost laughed at the fantasy, but looked up to find Alexei's eyes fixed on her. It was a look at once derisive and disdainful, subtly menacing, infinitely mocking, infinitely challenging. It was as though he had lashed her with his eyes. And with that look, something in her crystallised and hardened, some deep-seated certainty.

She met his stare calmly and smiled back, a slow, voluptuous smile, before rising to join Gabrielle.

Deliberately she kept her back to him but she knew, without a shadow of a doubt, when he had left. The very air seemed to lighten.

'One of Alexei's moods,' said Leo lightly. 'No, Gabrielle, let him go.'

They reclined Roman-style around the low table, resting on huge, brightly coloured cushions. Wine and conversation and laughter flowed freely as they prised the succulent white flesh from claws and tails, slowly demolishing the elegantly arranged buffet.

But underneath the laughter ran a thread of sensual awareness, clear and unmistakable. Gemma felt it without discomfiture, acknowledged it without hypocrisy. It was natural, unforced and unthreatening. She had made her decision the moment she had met Alexei Racine's eyes across the rippling blue water of the rock pool; tonight she would have Jay Stone, test her second dream lover. There was little question of seduction. She had felt his eyes on her, a warm, sexual appraisal that lingered on her breasts, flicked to the juncture of her thighs.

Relaxing back on the cushions, nibbling on a prawn, she let her imagination run free, picturing wild and improbable couplings and though she was only half-serious she felt herself growing aroused.

'Bah!' exclaimed Gabrielle, dipping her hand into the finger-bowl at her side. 'Me, I am far too sticky for this little bowl. I shall rinse myself properly, in the pool. Gemma, will you come?'

She hesitated only briefly. 'Yes, of course.'

She could feel Jay and Leo's eyes on them as they walked down to the rock pool and when Gabrielle stripped off her dress she was only momentarily surprised. Unselfconsciously Gabrielle slipped into the water and called to her.

'Come, Gemma, it's lovely!'

She let the white dress fall to her feet, knowing that she was exposed to the pair of male eyes trained on her, now avidly examining her back, her legs, and a little defiantly she peeled off her panties, giving them the taut globes of her buttocks before stepping into the water.

And it was lovely, a warm, liquid embrace. The pool wasn't deep, five feet or so, just deep enough so that she could keep her feet on the bottom while the swirling water lapped at the top of her breasts. Gabrielle was floating on her back, her high, rosy tipped nipples clearing the water, the dark plume of her sex clearly visible.

'They will join us, you know,' said Gabrielle softly, her voice almost lost in the gentle splash of the waterfall.

'Yes, yes, I know,' replied Gemma, just as softly.

'And is it what you want?' asked Gabrielle, closing her eyes.

'I'm not sure,' Gemma said slowly, though her body was already tightening in anticipation. It seemed now that every erotic encounter since the night in the tumulus had led her to this moment. Yet it was the look from Alexei Racine that had goaded her, sealed her intentions, crystallised something inside her.

'It is not of such great import, Gemma. It is a game, no more. You can make the rules up as you go along . . . that's the secret, I think.'

'Yes, perhaps it is,' agreed Gemma.

Alone in the private screening room Alexei Racine watched the rushes, freezing the film at the moment the demon lover bent his head to the woman's white throat. Yes, it was perfect, he decided, chilling yet arousing, deeply, darkly erotic.

He felt at once a great calm and a fierce joy akin to the moment after orgasm, emptied yet exultant. And it was not, he mused, entirely due to the haunting perfection captured on the screen before him.

He let his mind drift, and smiled at the memory of Gemma's smile, voluptuous and defiant, as she stood across from him at the rock pool. He had sensed the certainty in her, felt her dawning understanding, a blind comprehension soon to be replaced with true understanding.

The climax would come soon, he knew, and after that the *dénouement*, the intricate unravelling of the sensual web. Yet he was not entirely satisfied. Some distraction, some misdirection, some twist was necessary, he decided. A carnal red herring.

Floating on her back, eyes closed, Gemma heard the sound of laughter as Jay and Leo splashed into the pool and cried in mock outrage as a hand closed around her ankle, pulling her below the surface. They were boisterous, noisily exuberant, concealing their arousal with the lively antics of playful children, splashing and ducking.

The macaws shrieked and fled in a vibrant blur of wings as the cries of laughter blended with the rhythmic waves of the waterfall. Eventually, panting, half-blinded by her hair, Gemma collapsed against the side of the pool, only to feel the warm, supporting length of a hard male body behind her.

'It's fun, isn't it?' said Jay against her ear. He, too, was out of breath and she could feel the rise and fall of his chest against her back.

She relaxed against him as their breathing slowed and their naked bodies became aware of each other. She could feel his shaft stirring, growing hard against her buttocks, and he shifted a little, embarrassed, perhaps, by the evidence of his arousal. She wriggled a little, refusing the distance, letting her buttocks brush against the jutting shaft of his erection.

Perhaps because he was behind her, faceless, familiar yet anonymous, she felt free, utterly free and uninhibited. It was Eden, free from sin or guilt. She closed her eyes.

The warm water lapped at her breasts as she moved against him, taking his rod between her thighs, and she heard him stifle a groan.

'Yes, it is fun,' said Gemma, almost calmly.

He was long and hard, pressed against the crease of her buttocks, covering her anus, pushing through the tender folds of flesh protecting her entrance. His head was almost at her clitoris; she need only rock a little to find the sweet friction that she was beginning to crave.

She stood motionless, waiting as her body responded to the hard promise of his shaft between her thighs, feeling her groin grow heavy and her breasts swell. And for long moments he too was still, his only movement the quivering thickening of his erection.

She leaned back, resting her head against his

shoulder, relieved at the gentle delicacy, the restraint he was showing, allowing her to find the rhythm she wanted. His hands were on her hips, supporting her against him, and at last she reached below the water and, entwining her fingers with his, brought them to her breasts.

Together they cupped the lush mounds, holding the swollen peaks above the water, fingers clasping and unclasping, thumbs moving rhythmically over her nipples. She felt his body shudder against hers.

'God, Gemma,' he breathed against her neck.

'No,' she murmured.

She felt no need for words, wanted the silence, wanted only the repeated thrum of his fingers against her nipples. They were hard now, distended, engorged with blood and the tingling warmth was flowing to the pit of her belly. She could feel herself growing damp and knew that he could feel her slick warmth moistening his shaft.

Opening her eyes, she saw Gabrielle and Leo embracing near the waterfall. His hands were between her legs and, as she watched, Gabrielle dropped to her knees and took him in her mouth. In some strange way, it heightened her own pleasure, watching the elegant arc of Leo's penis disappear and emerge, shining and slickly red.

She looked down at her own breasts, saw the fingers clasping her, her own small hands almost engulfed by Jay's large palms. One of his thumbnails was a little jagged, and it scraped against the swollen pink flesh of her nipple, a tiny, scratching abrasion that intensified the liquid warmth flowing to her groin.

She remembered with sudden, perfect clarity, how her dream lover had driven her to climax the night in the tomb by the simple touch of his mouth and hands on her breasts, pinching and sucking and biting.

Instinctively she increased the pressure of their hands, rolling her nipples between their thumbs and index fingers, pinching them harder and harder until the pleasure became pain and the pain became a red, rosy glow that engulfed her body.

Her climax glimmered then glittered, arced through her like a wave and she could feel the pulsing throb of her inner walls as they convulsed blindly, contracting and searching for the absent shaft.

He must have felt her tremors, must have been aware of the solitary splendour as she came alone, because his breathing quickened, but he remained motionless, kept the hard rod still against her trembling flesh.

She felt a fierce triumph mingling with the rosy aftershocks of her orgasm, a glowing elation that stayed with her even as her body began to relax.

Impulsively she rocked her hips, felt him nudge against her entrance and then surge inside. He was large, so large that she felt herself stretching to take him, straining with the sudden, numbing thrust. For a moment she rested, let her body realise what her unconscious had already accepted. It wasn't him.

He began to thrust, forcing her to take more of him into her body, and she gasped as she felt him move, plunging deeply. She waited, quiescent and passive as he thrust again and again, pounding the strength of his body against hers. She felt her body begin to quicken, succumb to the driving rhythm, and when he withdrew, poising himself at her entrance, preparing to lunge again, she surged away from him and dive beneath the surface of the water.

She emerged laughing a few feet away, shaking her head. Swiftly he plunged after her, diving down and capturing one slim ankle. Almost roughly, he hauled her against him until they were face to face.

The expression on her face, teasing, wide-eyed and mock innocent, disarmed him completely and he too burst into laughter.

'Not yet, or not like that?' he said, giving her a swift, hard kiss.

Her breasts were crushed against his chest and his erection was hard against her belly. 'We'll see,' she promised, letting her hand drop to grasp him. He shuddered at the touch of her fingers and she tightened her grip, loving the elastic, tensile strength that surged under her hand.

The glowing elation of her climax, of her discovery, was still strong. 'Surprise me,' she said, arching against him before drawing away.

He followed her as she swam towards the massive rock where Leo and Gabrielle were lying, partly submerged in the water. She came to rest at Gabrielle's side.

'So, Gemma, it's a good game, is it not?' asked Gabrielle softly.

'Very good,' replied Gemma, feeling Jay behind her.

'It is, as I said, the element of surprise,' murmured Gabrielle.

Chapter Nine

*I*t was only later, much later, that she truly appreciated the carnal madness that seized her that night, the bacchic fury that led to every wild sensual tangle, every perverse coupling.

She discovered the engulfing, crushing envelope of two male bodies penetrating her, Jay from in front, Leo from behind, one thrusting as the other withdrew, hollowing and filling her at the same time, annihilating her, forcing a climax that seemed to last forever.

She found herself kneeling between Gabrielle's thighs, exploring the soft pink flesh of her inner lips with her mouth as Jay tongued her anus and Leo sucked her nipples.

She lay in Gabrielle's arms as they kissed, sharing their mouths, nipping delicately at swollen lips as their lovers opened their legs and kissed the tender folds.

She laughed as Jay laid her on the cushions beside the table and created a second feast, fixing the rosy pincer claws of a lobster to her nipples, squeezing lemon over her body and then licking her clean.

Some of it trickled between her legs, and the acid sting on her clitoris triggered an orgasm so violent that she screamed aloud.

They all seemed caught, entangled in an erotic vortex that stemmed that night from Gemma herself. She was driven that night, swept away by an uncontrollable frenzy, an extravagant, wanton, shameless need. The revelation that Racine was her lover had sparked something savagely unpredictable, something wild and insatiable within her. Her body was aflame, greedy and thirsty for every new sensation, open and avid, and Jay and Leo and Gabrielle fed the fever, slaking her with climax then tantalising her anew.

It needed only one of them to climax, shaking and spent, to say aloud, 'Oh, no more, I can't,' to rouse the other three to new heights of devious inventiveness, re-stimulating aching flesh to new arousal.

But finally the fury flagged and caresses slowed, raw passion replaced by a warm, sweet, complicit awed awareness. They lay together in a warm tangle of entwined limbs and slick flesh, letting the heat dissolve into a shared warmth.

Gemma felt drowsy, drugged with pleasure, body sweetly, achingly sated, and she barely stirred when Jay finally rose on unsteady feet and scooped her into his arms.

'I'll take her to bed,' he said rather thickly to Leo over his shoulder.

Leo nodded a little reluctantly. 'Yes. And I'll see to Gabrielle.'

Winding her arms around his neck, Gemma nestled into the crook of his shoulder and slept, only awakening when he laid her on the vast Empire bed in her room.

'Shall I stay?' he asked as he smoothed the covers around her.

She looked into his eyes. They were brown with amber flecks, and he had tiny lines at the corners of his eyes. He wanted to stay; she could read the wish in his eyes.

'No,' she said softly. 'But thank you.'

He leaned forward and kissed her on the mouth. It was a soft and gentle kiss, warm and infinitely tender. 'Gemma, I – '

She stopped him with a finger to his lips. 'Good night, Jay.'

'Good night, Gemma.'

She snuggled beneath the covers, trying to recapture the languorous, drowsy warmth, the soft bliss that had enfolded her but it wafted away, dispelled, perhaps by the kiss he had given her, the look in his eyes.

She twisted to her side, then lay flat on her back. The pillows were too hard. The pillows were too soft. She pummelled them into shape and lay back. The covers were too heavy. She pushed them to the foot of the bed and then shivered and drew them back up. Her right ankle began to itch and her eyes felt gritty.

She turned over on her side, forcing herself to close her eyes and breathe deeply. Fragmented images kept flashing before her eyes. The thick, engorged length of Jay's shaft, glistening with her own saliva and a pearl of semen at the tip as he placed it between her lips. The fleshy pink folds of Gabrielle's inner lips as she spread her legs wide. The taut, smooth line of Leo's body as he drove into her, muscles bunching along his back. The glittering, sightless, ruby eyes of the bejewelled snake coiled around the tree.

The look in Alexei Racine's cold grey eyes as he faced her across the rock pool.

She had known that look, recognised it, seen it

before . . . suddenly she remembered. It was the dream she had in London, now so long ago, when he had raised his head from between her thighs, lips stained with her blood, eyes shining in silvery triumph as the nightmare orgasm surged and claimed her.

Grimacing, she sat up in bed, twisting the pillows behind her and tried to distract herself. She could order some hot milk with a few words through the intercom. She could pour a brandy from the decanter thoughtfully placed on the marquetried bedside table. She could take a bath, watch the hot water gush from gold faucets shaped like dolphins and wash away the traces of the night.

Sighing, she reached over to turn on the gilt and crystal lamp at her side, but her hand stilled as she remembered another night when she had reached for the light, the fury and frenzy as he had forced her down, the ravaging heat, the raging climax. The brief aftermath when he had sensed her impulse to bite him, scar him, and he had warned her. Had called her Psyche.

Was there, she wondered irritably, supposed to be some sort of deep meaning, some profound psychological truth in the myth, some Jungian archetype?

She lit the lamp and looked at the ormulu clock. Four o'clock in the morning was no time to decide. There was an elaborately enamelled cigarette case on the table with a pastoral scene of bewigged and beruffled ladies sitting beside a stream. She took out a cigarette and lit it with the matching table lighter.

Perhaps it was the only thing to do in the dead chill hours before dawn, the lifeless truce between day and night, when sleep was impossible. Smoke. And pace. And brood.

For a moment she regretted not asking Jay to stay with her, and wondered why she hadn't. And then she knew. It was the warmth of his kiss, the tiny lines around his eyes. For a fleeting moment he had become a person to her, not just a body.

And so she sat and smoked, and confronted for the first time the fundamental truth that women have always known and men have never learned. There is no such thing as casual sex.

All of her lovers had shaped her, changed her. The clumsy, selfish men of her youth who had left her indifferent, made her into the woman who gave herself to a stranger on the hard packed earth floor of the tumulus. The lighthearted playfulness of Nicholas Frere, who had made her laugh and come at the same time, who had let her learn to savour sex as a need as fundamental as food. The carnal sophistication of Gabrielle and Leo, which had led to the dionysiac, orgiastic revels of the night, and made her . . . what?

And at the centre of this sensual web, like some malign spider, was Alexei Racine, spinning the erotic silken thread that wove them all together.

She stubbed out her cigarette and then driven by some perverse, utterly inexplicable impulse, put on her robe, walked to the door of the adjoining room, and lay down in the coffin where she slept immediately, deeply, dreamlessly.

She woke suddenly several hours later. Disoriented for a moment, she raised herself on an elbow, then smiled faintly as she took in her surroundings. Levering herself out of the coffin she wondered at the impulse that had taken her there, and hoped to God she wasn't developing a sense of irony.

She showered quickly, dressed in fawn coloured jeans and a white shirt, and made her way to the conservatory for breakfast. Briefly she had considered a tray in her room, but after the insomnia of the night before she felt faintly claustrophobic.

Surprisingly, Gabrielle was already there, sipping coffee and toying with a croissant. She was wearing a tailored ivory suit that warmed her skin and flattered the faint, blue hollows beneath her eyes. She smiled at Gemma, a warm friendly smile without the slightest tinge of awkwardness.

'So, Gemma, you are well?' she began, as the maid entered with fresh coffee.

'Fine, yes . . . oh, Marie? I'd like something different this morning. Waffles, and syrup and sausages, please, and some bacon as well, Gabrielle, can you translate?'

'You have an appetite this morning!' exclaimed Gabrielle with a laugh. 'No ill effects, then, from last night?'

Gemma sipped coffee and considered her answer. There was a dull, sweet ache between her thighs, a legacy of the night's excess, but all things considered she felt extraordinarily well, physically at least. 'No. And you?'

'Oh, I am well, very well. One effect, perhaps, but it is not ill. Not at all,' she said decisively.

'And what is that?' asked Gemma as her waffles arrived.

'I am going back to Paris, to my husband.'

'What!' exclaimed Gemma, completely taken aback.

'Yes. It is what you call a strategic retreat, I think, although can one retreat in victory, I wonder? Nevertheless, I will leave for Paris this morning.'

'But why? And does Leo know?' asked Gemma.

'Well, last night, it was magnificent, no? A triumph, a *tour de force*, unforgettable.'

'Unforgettable, certainly,' replied Gemma a little drily.

'And so, you see, I have him. The memory will linger and he will remember. And now, if sometime I wish to enjoy him again, he will come to me. It is rather cunning of me, don't you think?' explained Gabrielle complacently.

'Very cunning,' echoed Gemma in surprise. 'But does Leo know?'

'Yes, well, as I told you, it is an affair of the bodies only,' said Gabrielle. 'I have left him a note.'

'Is there such a thing? Truly? Only an affair of the bodies?' asked Gemma, drenching her waffles in syrup and taking a bite.

'For me, yes,' Gabrielle answered her bluntly. 'But then I am French and therefore very practical. It is maybe not the same for you?'

Gemma was silent.

'But then, yours is a different affair,' Gabrielle added gently.

'Mine?' asked Gemma, spearing a sausage.

'You and Alexei.'

Gemma's heart turned over. 'But perhaps it isn't him,' she said in an unconvincing voice.

Gabrielle lifted an eyebrow. 'But of course it must be! And me, I find it all very interesting. Because it is not just an affair of the bodies. He plays with your mind as well. A strange game indeed.

In his private apartments in the east wing of the chateau, Leo Marais was taking breakfast. Before him was a Bloody Mary, with which he hoped to cure his hangover, and a plate of oysters, with which he hoped to replenish his libido. Beside him, Jay Stone was demolishing bacon and eggs with what Leo privately considered almost indecent gusto.

Lounging near the Rodin of a man and woman embracing, Alexei Racine idly caressed the flowing white marble locks of the woman's hair and eyed them ironically.

'The wages of sin, my friends,' he mocked gently.

Leo disdained a reply.

'I thought you didn't believe in sin, Alexei,' said Jay, smothering his eggs in ketchup.

Leo averted his eyes.

'How absurd, of course I believe in sin,' replied Racine. 'Life would be unutterably dull without it. And sex even duller.'

'Sex and sin have nothing to do with each other,' objected Jay, sopping up the yolk of his egg with a piece of toast.

Leo took a long drink of his Bloody Mary.

'How very American! Of course they do,' corrected Racine. Then apparently tiring of the topic, he left the Rodin with one final caress on the gentle under-swell of the woman's breast, and joined them at the table. 'It is a shame that urgent business recalls you to Paris.'

'What?' asked Jay, perplexed. 'I finished my business in Paris.'

'I am, of course, desolated to have to contradict you, my friend, but you most certainly have pressing business elsewhere,' remarked Alexei imperturbably.

'Elsewhere,' repeated Jay, narrowing his eyes.

'It was to be a cameo appearance, no more,' Alexei reminded him gently.

Jay's face became blank, almost expressionless. It was a look corporate adversaries knew and dreaded. He pushed his plate aside. 'You know, Alexei, when you first mentioned this convoluted, crazy idea – '

'You agreed unhesitatingly. It would be ungenerous of me to remind you of the circumstances that put you in my debt, would it not?' Racine's eyes were stunningly cold.

Jay looked away first.

'So I shall not,' Alexei added softly.

'It's just I rather liked her,' Jay remarked inconsequentially, looking down at his coffee cup.

'Indeed.'

Leo, who had finally picked up the thread of the conversation, turned to Alexei. 'Because of last night? You are inviting my guest to leave my home? And am I too to discover pressing business in Paris?' asked the Comte Marais with awful irony.

'Do you know, Leo,' said Alexei with the ghost of a smile, 'It wouldn't at all surprise me.'

Leo rang for another Bloody Mary.

As it was Sunday, no work was scheduled for the film crew. Gemma, rather envying Gabrielle's escape to Paris, found the ubiquitous Henri and enquired rather hesitantly about local buses to Carnac. She was rewarded with the alternatives of a chauffeur and limousine or any of the seventeen cars Leo kept at the chateau, and gratefully accepted the offer of a Jaguar.

The opulent luxury of the chateau felt oppressive this morning. She was neither anxious nor unwilling to see Jay or Leo again, but she dreaded the prospect of meeting Racine. To wander around Carnac, lose herself in rich, mystical atmosphere of the prehistoric remains or drive further, perhaps as far as Quiberon, seemed infintely more appealing than staying in her suite and working.

Gabrielle had already left, kissed her farewell and made her a parting present of the white silk dress. Gemma smiled a little ruefully at the thought as one of the servants swung a silver grey Jaguar around the sweep of the driveway. She was beginning to acquire a rather bizarre collection of erotic memorabilia; first the black leather costume Pascaline had lent her for the New Year's masquerade, and now the pleated white silk dress she had worn with Gabrielle and Leo . . . and with Jay.

She could visit her cottage, she thought, but discarded the idea almost immediately. That was a part of her that she wanted kept secret, inviolate, a refuge that her present mood did not permit.

'*Mademoiselle*?' The young man was waiting for her with the door of the Jaguar open.

'Yes, thank you,' said Gemma abstractedly. 'I mean, *merci*.'

The car was a delight, powerful, responsive and smooth as silk on the gravel roads. She resisted the temptation to test the engine and drove sedately, aware of how easily she could lose herself in the winding, unmarked roads around the Chateau Marais.

The morning was still and cool, a pale watery sun shedding light but no warmth on the bare earth. After several misturnings she found the road that led to the Menec Lines, the serried row of more than a thousand menhirs, upright stones that stretched for a seemingly endless expanse along the fields, and parked the car in the adjacent lot.

The last time she had been here it was summer, hot and sunny, with crowds of tourists flocking around the menhirs, posing for photographs, chattering, small children running underfoot and eating ice-creams provided by a dilapidated looking truck that also offered small, gaudily painted rocks as souvenirs.

Now it was deserted. An air of calm, frozen serenity seemed to seep from the stones themselves that was faintly forbidding. By their very form they were overtly phallic and she knew that standing stones were supposed to have masculine connotations related to fertility. They reminded her, inevitably, of the carved hunter in the tomb, the massive spear or penis jutting from his torso, and the night Racine had found her there.

But she knew too that the reason the stones were erected some six thousand years ago was shrouded in mystery, their purpose obscure. As obscure as Alexei Racine's motives in taking her that night in the tomb.

She got out of the car, crossed the road, passed through the ugly, blue-painted and absolutely ineffective turnstile and wandered around the menhirs deep in thought. She could, she supposed, try to construct some fanciful theory, much like the archaeologists and ethnologists had applied to the standing stones; but the stones remained standing, obdurate and impervious to interpretation, as, she suspected, was Alexei Racine.

The one inescapable fact, like the very stones themselves, was that he had seared her body with his, wrung climax after climax from her with his mouth, his lips, his hands, his teeth, his hard shaft, had flayed her with the lash of his body against hers.

And she had revelled in it.

Exulted in it.

Craved it.

And craved it still.

Chilled, she returned to the car and drove away.

Alexei Racine settled himself in the open coffin and inhaled the faint scent of Gemma clinging to the white satin pillow. Undoubtedly, he thought, trailing a hand over the black hardwood surface, he was becoming fond of the thing. Perhaps Leo would sell it to him, or he could commission one himself.

It had the sweet lure of perversity, of decadence untainted by morbidity, a warped voluptuousness that appealed to him. Besides which, it was astonishingly comfortable.

He pictured Gemma lying where his body was lying now, the luxuriant, silver-gilt hair spread across the white silk pillow where his head was resting, and felt the first, faint stirrings of arousal. He knew, perhaps better than she, what had driven her here last night, and relished the thought of her slim body, spent and exhausted by passion, resting on white silk as coolly sensuous as the dress she had been wearing.

He felt himself thickening a little at the memory of her breasts, so formed for his hand, so clearly revealed under the wet silk of her dress after she had slipped in the rock pool. For a moment he could almost feel her nipples hardening under his mouth, clenching and puckering into taut peaks, hear the soft moans she made as he used his tongue and teeth on her breasts.

He marked her that first night deliberately, wanting her to see the imprint of his teeth on her pale skin, wanting her to remember the consuming heat. Later he had wondered how she looked when she first saw the red crescent of his teeth on her flesh, the expression of her face, in her eyes, and regretted a little that he would never know.

Disbelief, he imagined; awe, perhaps. But he knew she had felt no guilt. She was too controlled, too logical, too intelligent to scar pleasure with guilt, mar passion with shame. If she had learned now to lust, as surely she had, she knew it for the pure and vital driving force that it was, and wouldn't seek to demean it.

Endlessly symbolic, he always sought images for abstracts. Lust for him was yellow, the pure, brilliant yellow of the sun, hot and life-giving. Gemma was like her name, cold and hard, her icy control the clear, brilliant refraction of a diamond as it struck the light.

He had amused himself once by looking up her name in the dictionary and discovered that a gemma was a small bud that separates from the mother plant to seed, an assexual spore. In a sense, it had been true of her once.

And now the sun had struck the diamond.

After Gemma left Carnac, she drove mindlessly for hours, stopping once for petrol and once to stretch her legs by the sea. The winter Atlantic seemed as cold and grey and empty as Alexei Racine's eyes, so she turned inland, following the signs to Vannes with absolutely no intention of going there, content merely to drive.

For the first time she recognised her love of driving was somehow akin to the purely physical sensation of sex. There were the obvious, trite parallels, of course; the bulbous shaft of the gear shift under her hand, as phallic as the standing stones; the faint vibration from the engine that almost subliminally stimulated the body.

But it was infinitely more than that. There was the sense of freedom, of power. The buzzing excitement of speeding far too fast, so close to the highs of arousal, losing oneself in the cat and mouse foreplay of heavy traffic, darting and retreating, relying solely on instinctive, physical reflexes, every sense alert and attuned to the movements of the other drivers, one's own reactions.

A little like having sex with a stranger, she thought, her mind drifting inevitably back to Alexei Racine. Was that *why* it had been so good? Because he was a stranger, faceless, anonymous? The act therefore untainted by any responsibility, any emotion?

No. that, at least, was untrue. There was emotion,

there was feeling, powerful, inescapable . . . undescribable.

She stopped at last at a rather bizarre fast food joint, where the plasticised, pre-packaged aura of McDonald's met and insulted classic French bistro. The tables were small, scarred and rickety with small, battered metal ashtrays and inadequate paper napkins; the huge illuminated posters above the zinc bar depicted gaudy, grotesquely enlarged hamburgers, hot dogs and seafood platters.

With a certain amount of trepidation she ordered a half bottle of Muscadet and *moules frites* and found a table in the corner. The Muscadet, which arrived immediately, was cold and refreshing; the mussels and chips, which came a little later, were a revelation. The mussels were plump and juicy, in a thin, peppery lemon broth that simply cried out for the crisp potato slivers and she ate hungrily until nothing was left but a scrap heap of shiny black shells.

She leaned back and lit a cigarette as she sipped a second glass of wine, watching the teenagers swarm around the juke box that had sprung to raucous life. One boy, taller than the rest, caught her eye. He was standing close to a girl much shorter than he, fingering, almost absentmindedly, the pert curve of her buttock. Their backs were to the room, their attention focused on the juke box, oblivious to anyone who might be watching as he ran his fingers over her, following the tight crease of the jeans dividing her buttocks, kneading the denim covering her anus. The girl was thrusting back against his hand with tiny, almost unnoticeable movements.

Gemma looked away, aware of a tightening in her groin. Beside her was an elderly, hard-faced Breton couple eating together silently, the peculiar silence of a man and woman long married with nothing left to say. Yet their movements were synchronised, an ingrained awareness of the other that made words unnecessary as, unbidden, she passed him the salt and he sprinkled it over his chips, as he reached for the carafe of red wine they were sharing and filled her glass as soon as she had emptied it.

Suddenly, every trivial action, every commonplace gesture, from the way the waitress leaned over her table to collect her tray, heavy breasts swinging, to the friendly cuff the short-order cook dealt the girl at the cash register, seemed loaded, swollen with meaning, and inescapably sexual.

She stubbed out her cigarette and left without finishing her wine.

'She's gone,' announced Leo without preamble, striding into the screening room where Alexei was watching the rushes over and over again. 'She's gone.' His voice was disbelieving. 'Back to Paris.'

Alexei yawned and froze the projector, taking in the crumpled piece of paper in Leo's hand. 'Who?' he asked.

'Gabrielle, of course,' replied Leo.

'Left a note, did she?' observed Racine with a rather weary cynicism. 'Whatever woman did not?'

'You knew,' accused Leo, his eyes hard. 'You said as much this morning.'

'I suspected as much this morning,' corrected Alexei, rising and turning on the lights. 'Calm yourself, my friend. It's only a woman, after all.'

'She was my woman,' said Leo flatly. 'And I wasn't finished with her.'

'Well, my friend, if she left you a note, one can only presume she is not finished with you as well,' commented Alexei. 'This is unlike you, Leo.'

'I am . . . annoyed,' pronounced Leo, very much the *Comte* as he lifted his eyebrows and his chin. 'It is not, after all, at all *comme il faut* for one's mistress

208

to depart without tears and recriminations, leaving merely a note. To go back to her husband!' the last was said with understandable outrage.

'Perhaps,' suggested Alexei, gently leading him from the room, 'you should acquire a mistress without a husband. They do tend to be troublesome things. Husbands, I mean, not mistresses . . . although, to be fair, the same could be said of both.'

'It is extremely . . . inconvenient,' protested Leo as they entered the gold salon where aperitifs were waiting.

Alexei's eyes were ironic but his voice was kind as he asked, 'Why? There are other women, readily, easily available.'

'Of course,' shrugged Leo, 'But that's not the point. Gabrielle was . . . becoming interesting.'

Racine smiled a hidden, wry smile, and poured Ne Plus Ultra scotch into two glasses, adding ice and water to one in deference to Leo's hangover. That he was prepared to thus desecrate a single malt was a true expression of sympathy.

'It's a classic ploy, my friend,' Alexei pointed out, handing Leo his drink. 'Always leave the audience wanting more. The slogan stems, I'm sure, from American vaudeville, but the concept is purely Greek, death in a moment of glory, Kleobis and Biton . . .' With rare sensitivity he abandoned the analogy, aware of Leo's uncomprehending disinterest.

A classic ploy, as he himself had pointed out to Gabrielle, and one that seldom failed. He felt a faint regret that Leo seemed to be distressed – or was it merely unnerved – but it had been necessary that Gabrielle leave the chateau before the last act.

It was not a reasoned ploy or plot, merely a sensitive response to the unfolding drama. A clearing of the stage, if you like, for the final acts. In a play of

Shakespeare's she would have gone mad or died; Racine had simply removed her from the stage.

'Incomprehensible,' pronounced Leo into his scotch.

'Not entirely,' said Racine.

In her luxurious white and gold bedroom in Paris' exclusive 16th *arrondissement* Gabrielle de Sevigny watched her husband getting ready for bed. Her gaze was fond, although she couldn't help comparing Pierre's stocky swarthiness with Leo's finely muscled elegance.

Pierre had been delighted to see her and relieved that dear old Tante Marthe was so much better. She felt a little guilty at the lie, but only a little.

Dear old Tante Marthe, elderly, eccentric, of uncertain health, who lived in a tiny village near Nantes and was so old-fashioned she refused to have a telephone, was such a useful creature.

Pierre had fussed over her, concerned that she looked so tired, and insisted that next time the old lady took one of her turns they would hire a private nurse. Gabrielle was rather touched. It was a pity that Tante Marthe was so stubborn and so suspicious of strangers, truly it was.

They dined at a bistro not far away that specialised in the peasant cookery Pierre was so fond of. As she expected, he ordered home-made pâté with cornichons, cassoulet, and apple tart. In a gesture of marital companionship, Gabrielle ordered the same and was rather surprised at how much she enjoyed the robust flavours. They drank a rough and flinty *vin ordinaire* and several glasses of marc with their coffee, so that she was feeling quite relaxed by the end of the meal.

Pierre, now in shorts, socks and shirt, was carefully and precisely aligning the crease of his trousers for the press. Gabrielle closed her eyes and waited. In a moment or two she would hear the drawer open as he discarded his cuff-links – yes, there was the creak of the wood. And now he was unbuttoning his shirt, first the right cuff, then the left, then starting at the bottom to the collar. This he would fold and place in the laundry basket before removing his shorts; they too would be folded away in the basket. Then, clad only in his socks, he would go into the *en suite* bathroom and clean his teeth.

She had once remarked that there was no more ridiculous sight than a man clad only in his socks. He had placidly replied that the tiles in the bathroom were rather chilly and he preferred to keep his feet warm.

His lovemaking, soon to follow – ah, yes, there was the click as he shut the lid of the laundry basket – was as predictable as any other of his routines. He was a considerate lover, conscientious rather than inventive, diligent rather than daring, but still considerate.

As if following some internal clock, he would kiss her on the mouth for two minutes or so, then move to her breasts and suck her nipples for three, and then move between her legs and find her clitoris. He would suck her clitoris steadily until she came, three or four minutes perhaps, and then enter her. Then he would thrust until he came, five minutes or sometimes longer if there was something on his mind, some government scandal or political crisis. And then he would withdraw, kiss her gently on the lips, roll over and go to sleep.

He never deviated from this routine, she mused, never, and never had he failed to make her climax. Curious, really, she decided.

The tap in the bathroom was turned off. She heard the click of the laundry basket, signalling the disposal of the offending socks, and then he switched off the light.

His breath was fresh and minty as he kissed her, his tongue moving with the familiar ease of a long-standing lover, taking his welcome for granted. And it was welcome, thought Gabrielle, soothing and rather reassuring, the well known wash of his tongue. No wild tangling, no plunging, no nipping, just the comfortable warm stroke of tongues. Her nipples were already reflexively hard when he bent to them, taking first the right breast and then the left in his mouth.

Her clitoris hardened in response, expecting the customary, pulling pressure of his lips, and she felt herself grow wet. She moved one hand down his back in a long caress that she knew he enjoyed as her body resumed its normal rhythms, knowing that climax was drawing closer.

It was a little like watching a favourite film or play, knowing all the lines in advance, she decided, but still enjoying the dialogue, the action, while confidently aware of the ending. There was no true suspense, no swollen uncertainty, no heart stopping, palpitating tension, only the sure and certain knowledge of the outcome.

Her breasts were swollen when he left them and eased his way down her body, parting her pubic hair and exposing her clitoris with the deftness of long practice. He sucked her into his mouth at once.

Perhaps because it was all so familiar, all so predictable, the scrupulous attention paid to her most erogenous zones, the diligent sucking of her nipples, the meticulous stimulation of her clitoris, the climax that claimed her was all consuming, more powerful than any she had ever had with Leo.

She lay back, stunned, as he drew himself up and thrust inside her.

Chapter Ten

The next day at the Chateau Marais, any underlying tension, any charged undercurrents, any awkwardness, any pressing desire for confrontation was swept away by the blistering, annihilating, terrifying force of Alexei Racine in a rage.

Gemma, who had lain awake half the night tossing, turning, thinking and plotting, overslept and was hurrying through the graveyard to the old keep when she heard his voice carry from the cavernous interior of the tower. It was a sound so menacing, so chilling, so coldly malignant that she stopped dead in her tracks beside a listing gravestone.

'You dare!' It was the familiar, harshly beautiful tones of his voice, but distorted by an anger so fierce, vitriolic, so powerful it seemed to fill the air. Heart thudding, she knew she should hurry forward, but she remained immobile, transfixed by the metallic echo of his voice. It was the voice of her lover from the tomb, a voice now insanely, murderously venomous.

She caught only a low sound that seemed to be appealing to his temper, deliberately measured and reasonable, before the fierce, molten torrent of Racine's wrath smothered it.

Move! she commanded her legs, hearing the echoes of the tirade, knowing that something dreadful was happening only yards away, unable to make herself lift a foot from the ground.

When she finally forced herself to enter the keep, the scene that met her eyes nearly horrified her. Racine was holding the actor playing Dracula against one of the heavy stone walls, his hands at his throat, the cast and crew standing still, paralysed with shock and terror.

His anger seemed to charge the keep, a searing, potent force so strong she felt it envelop her. In the midst of her panic, her mind worked furiously. They were shooting the last major scene, Dracula confronted by Jonathan Harker bearing a cross and a wooden stake. Dracula was to portray the furious, desperate life force of an immortal confronting death, the desperately maniacal, anguished fury of a cornered predator.

A fury that Racine himself seemed to embody.

The actor playing Count Dracula was as pale as one of his mythical victims, and he was cowering back against the wall. At that moment, it seemed as though Racine had taken on the legendary mantle of the vampire demon lover, acquired his prodigious strength, his inexhaustible energy, his fatal, overwhelming force.

She coughed, a small, deliberate sound almost like a snort, the throat-clearing, ingratiating, wanting-to-be-noticed sound more often heard around hardwood tables where men wear three piece suits and nervous expressions.

Their eyes met.

His were blazing. For a moment, with almost photographic precision, she saw the back of the book

Racine had been reading on the drive from Paris, dark type emblazoned on a white background, Stoker's description of Dracula.

'Never did I imagine such wrath and fury, even in the demons of the pit. His eyes were positively blazing. The red light in them was lurid, as if the flames of hell-fire blazed behind them. His face was deathly pale, and the lines of it were hard like drawn wires; the thick eyebrows that now met over the nose seemed like a heaving bar of white-hot metal.'

It was the face of Alexei Racine.

For a moment they looked at each other. She had always thought of his eyes as cold. Now they burned like dry ice.

With a swift, violent movement, Racine let loose his hold on the man, who dropped to his knees.

'Deal with it,' he snarled at Gemma, and stalked from the room.

They all remained frozen, too shaken to even breathe a sigh of relief. It was the eerie silence of the eye of the storm, the false calm of the heart of the vortex. At last, Gemma broke it.

'What happened?' she asked, slumping down on the flagstones of the floor.

Jane, her production assistant, detached herself from Racine's black leather coterie and gave a nervous giggle.

'Um, well, you know, George?' she began in a thin, high voice.

'George,' repeated Gemma blankly.

'George, umm, Vlad, Count Dracula,' she explained, gesturing nervously to the actor who was still cowering against the wall and tentatively massaging his throat.

'Right,' said Gemma briskly.

'Yes, well, you see, George is a Communist,' Jane said with a shaky laugh.

'Yes? So?' Irritation was beginning to etch Gemma's voice.

Jane made an effort to pull herself together. 'So . . . he came up with this new interpretation, right? A sort of Marxist thing, okay? Like, when the vampire sees the cross, he kind of reacts against organised religion and the opium of the masses, right?'

'Opiate,' corrected Gemma automatically, beginning to gain some vague appreciation of the problem.

'Whatever. And André – '

'André?' queried Gemma, determined to have every detail.

'Jonathan Harker,' said Jane. 'The guy who kills the Count, right?'

'Right.'

'And so George, I mean Dracula, felt that André – no, I mean Jonathan – was actually a sort of symbol of capitalist oppression, okay?'

'Capitalist oppression?' echoed Gemma faintly.

'Yeah. And so he had this great idea last night, you know? Like, instead of this animal fury, he should debate with André, I mean Jonathan, kind of negotiate, you know what I mean? Dispell the old myths and – '

'And you knew about this?' asked Gemma calmly.

'Umm, well . . .' Jane hung her head, shamefaced. 'George had this really good mezcal, you know? From Mexico, and we all drank some and it seemed like a good idea . . .'

'At the time,' Gemma finished, nodding. Her mind was now moving with crystalline precision. Ludicrous to even consider salvaging anything from today: Racine was in a fury too fierce to even consider a re-take, too fierce to even consider approaching him; Dracula, or George or André, or whatever his name was, too shaken to imitate anything but a cowering victim.

In fact everyone seemed pale, and they were huddling together almost unconsciously in the chilly, cavernous chamber of the tower. 'Right,' she announced loudly, her voice echoing unnaturally. 'That's it for today. An unofficial holiday, and no over-time when we run over union hours, agreed?'

There was a soft, subdued murmur of agreement. If nothing else, it showed Gemma the annihilating effect of Racine's anger; union hours were holy writ to the camera crew and they would as soon waive time and a half as slit their wrists.

There wasn't a murmur of dissent. They moved slowly, gathering up equipment, exchanging the odd remark. For a moment, she hesitated, watching them. There was no force on earth that could make her confront Racine in this mood; dream lover or director from hell, she knew when to leave things lie.

'Jane,' she said rather sharply to the pale figure by her side, 'I take it you were all drinking this stuff, all decided it was a great idea, am I right?'

'Umm, well, yes, kind of,' admitted Jane in a small voice, shrivelling inside her black leather.

'Powerful stuff,' commented Gemma.

'Yes,' said Jane woefully.

'Is there any left?' asked Gemma.

She followed them back to Carnac in the silver grey Jaguar, feeling numb, as if Racine's rage had anaesthetised her. She drove behind the studio van mindlessly, for once insensible to the pleasures of the road, the powerful engine of the car.

It was a subdued group that eventually gathered in Jane's room, drinking beer and chatting desultorily. There was a pale camaraderie, an unspoken bond between them, as if together they had survived some tempestuous natural disaster, an earthquake, a tidal wave, and were slowly re-awakening to the aftermath. Someone turned on a radio and the melancholy strains of a mournful ballad sung in French filled the room. A window was opened to clear the smoke from countless cigarettes.

Sitting cross-legged, propped against a wall and sipping beer from a can, Gemma looked around the room and felt faintly guilty. It boasted a double bed with an old-fashioned tufted coverlet, two overstuffed plum armchairs, a scarred work table and a small and rather muddy watercolour of the Pont du Gard over the bed. It was a striking contrast to the opulent luxury of her own suite at the Chateau Marais, yet there was a comfortable, homely feel to it that the chateau lacked.

Jane was curled up in an armchair with one of Racine's androgynous black leather acolytes draped beside her. Four of the camera men had claimed the bed, another of Racine's creatures was sprawled in the second armchair, and the rest, like Gemma herself, were lounging on the floor. None of the cast were present: presumably they had preferred to lick their wounds in private.

Gradually a hazy calm, a smoky tranquillity descended. More beer was opened and the room grew hot. She watched as the slim figure next to Jane rose and stripped off its shirt. It was male, she was relieved to see, his chest pale and hairless and almost painfully thin. His ribs were unnaturally prominent, straining against his white skin. There was something compelling about his gauntness, something intensely physical in the skeletal definition of his torso.

Her eyes drifted down to his hips, to the angular jut of his pelvic bones clearly defined by the skin tight black leather trousers. Idly she imagined him nude, the bony frame of his body clearly articulated beneath the skin, making love to a woman, the hard points of his bones digging into her flesh.

Someone arrived with more beer and a Chinese take-away. She devoured a spring roll and some spare-ribs, wiping greasy fingers on thin paper napkins. There was little conversation.

The black leather figure on the second armchair got up to leave, and Gemma took his place, curling up on the overstuffed floral cushions still warm from his body.

She felt blissfully drained, lethargic and too weary to move again. Her eyelids were heavy and slowly she succumbed to the slumbrous, smoky warmth of the room and slept.

She woke to the rhythmic stroke of two bodies joining. Opening sleepy eyes she focused on the scene before her. The skeletal figure of a man, now totally nude, hid the body lying beneath his own on the bed. He was moving slowly, rocking his hips gently. She could see the play of his muscles along the gaunt lines of his back, the tensing of his buttocks as he thrust, the gathering, coiling tension.

She felt an answering warmth in her own body, an instinctive, natural response to the life-giving act before her.

She watched as he moved, felt herself floating with him, sharing each masculine thrust, the sheathing and unsheathing, the warm red pulse, the fluttering, thudding slam as he buried himself in the body beneath his.

She could almost feel the questing surge of his penis, the blind force that drove the hard column of flesh to the yielding moist nest, the gathering heat. Her groin grew soft and heavy as she watched him move, as he increased the momentum of his thrusts, driving harder, driving faster.

His body began to shudder, racked by spasms,

and still he thrust. She could feel the liquid tension gathering and pooling, the tumid explosion beginning to build.

Quietly Gemma rose from the chair, moving softly, knowing instinctively that it would be wrong to stay.

She drove back to the chateau in a strange mood, dreamily aroused yet peripherally anxious. Anxiety lent an edge to her physical awareness, made her more conscious of her body, the simmering arousal that was stirring beneath her skin.

Leaving the keys in the Jaguar, she walked up the massive stone steps of the Chateau Marais. The doors were opened for her not, she was surprised to find, by the imperturbable Henri, but by Leo himself.

'Oh, Gemma, it's you,' he said, obviously disconcerted.

'Yes, I went to Carnac with the crew and – '

'I was thinking it was Alexei,' he interrupted, unheeding. 'He stormed out hours ago . . . I've never seen him in such a temper. What happened?' he asked, leading her across the massive hall to the gold salon.

'A problem of interpretation with one of the cast,' Gemma began, taking a seat on the brocaded settee he waved her to. As concisely as she could, she explained the scene in the tower that morning.

'All that because of a Marxist vampire?' queried Leo, hovering distractedly over the drinks trolley. 'It defies belief . . . what would you like?'

'Nothing, thank you, oh, some water perhaps,' Gemma corrected herself, feeling a little thirsty and dry-mouthed from the Chinese food.

'Champagne, then,' said Leo absentmindedly, plucking a bottle of Cristal from a waiting ice-bucket. 'Quenches the thirst and much better for you. A Marxist vampire, ' he repeated, shaking his head. 'I've never seen him in such a rage.'

The champagne was delicious, a refreshing, icy kiss at the back of her throat. 'Well, he has a reputation for it,' she remarked as Leo came to sit beside her.

'His reputation is one thing,' shrugged Leo. 'But this . . . he took the Maserati. You could almost see the sparks flying from the gravel.'

They were silent for a moment, sipping champagne.

'Like some strange migration,' said Leo a little later. 'Alexei raging off . . . Jay left this morning for Paris. And Gabrielle.' His voice sounded a little forlorn as he spoke her name.

'Oh,' said Gemma blankly. So Jay had gone. She felt curiously relieved yet slightly saddened. 'I'm sure Alexei will be back soon,' she added. For some reason, the moment she spoke the words she knew it was true.

He would come back soon, and he would come to her, fury undimmed, to slake his anger on her body. He would take her in darkness and in silence, in ravening rage and furious lust. She knew it with every bone in her body.

A small, unconscious smile curved her lips.

'Don't worry, Leo,' she said calmly. 'I'm sure everything will work out.'

'As to that, I'm not worried,' he said with a touch of his customary hauteur. 'Simply discombobulated.'

He pronounced the silly word with such cool arrogance that she had to laugh. After a moment he politely chuckled.

'All is not lost,' he said philosophically. 'And tomorrow they are delivering my Degas,' he added, brightening perceptibly.

Something in the quality of his look changed then. She felt it as clearly as she felt the rim of the crystal flute against her lips, the heavy brocade against her body.

'Do you like Degas?' he asked, eyes moving to her legs, caressing, or perhaps assessing the fluid curve of her thighs.

'Yes, very much,' said Gemma, rising from the settee, a little unsettled.

'Perhaps, over dinner,' he began, also rising.

'I'm actually rather tired,' she prevaricated, stepping back and setting down her glass. 'Perhaps I could have a tray sent to my room?'

'Of course,' he replied courteously. 'I shall inform Henri.'

His eyes were fixed on her legs as she left the room.

Alone in her suite Gemma undressed thoughtfully, tossing her clothes into the elegant gold and white hamper and turning on the gold dolphin taps of the bath. The smell of smoke clung to her clothes and her hair, and she was eager to replace it with the fragrant perfume of the oils and unguents arrayed on the marble ledge.

She sniffed appreciatively at the bottles. The fresh, citrus tang of lemon, the subtle smoke of sandalwood, the heady perfume of roses, the lushly exotic scent of white musk . . . none of them seemed quite right. Finally she found one, delicate and evocative that seemed to whisper of spring rain on green grass, and poured it into the water.

She relaxed in the hot, scented water for a long time, savouring her anticipation, savouring the sure certainty that soon he would come for her, driven by the potent force of his rage. She didn't question her knowledge, simply knew that it was true.

She shaved her legs carefully, relishing the fresh sensitivity of her skin under the razor and washed her hair twice, showering away the soapy stream of bubbles. She emerged feeling the special glow that only a long soak in a perfumed hot tub can give, and briskly towelled herself dry.

The rough towel made a pleasant friction against her skin, and she felt a tingling awareness stealing through her, the natural well-being of a body scrubbed clean enhanced by sensual anticipation. She found a jar of body lotion in the same delicate scent that she had used in the bath, and massaged it into her skin.

There was, she mused, rubbing cream between her toes, a rather different edge to the natural pleasure of bathing and moisturising, knowing that soon her body would be under his, a sort of delectable expectancy that made her actions a sort of pre-foreplay. She smoothed cream between her thighs knowing that his mouth, his hard male prick would move where her fingers were, and found herself dampening at the thought.

Her nipples hardened under the silky caress of the cream and in the mirror she saw a rosy flush mantling the tops of her breasts. She put the cream aside and reached for the white towelling robe hanging from the door. No make-up, she decided, combing out her hair and letting it tumble in loose waves down her back.

He would find her as he needed to find her; alone, asleep, her only artifice the beautifully subtle scent of her body, the shining cascade of her hair. Satisfied at last, she went into the bedroom.

In her absence a table had been arranged by the red velvet settee, draped in a white linen cloth and set with heavy silverware and gold plate. She had been vaguely expecting a plate of sandwiches, she realised, taking in the three crystal wineglasses, the silver-domed dishes, the silver ice-bucket.

223

She shook her head and smiled. Simply to prolong the pleasure of anticipation she poured a glass of the white wine chilling in the ice-bucket and inspected the covered dishes. There were artichoke hearts swimming in lemon butter, the delicate green globes pale and glistening, medallions of veal in a creamy mushroom sauce, an array of fresh vegetables and finally a white mousse decorated with swirls of dark shaved chocolate.

The wine was dry and astringent, almost flinty, a perfect companion to the buttery richness of the artichokes, and Gemma ate slowly, enjoying every mouthful.

Her mind was still, calm and untroubled. She felt encapsulated in a shining bubble of anticipation, suspended and weightless. But if her mind was still, her senses were sharpened, more acute. She relished every mouthful of the artichokes, savoured the delicate, creamy veal that seemed to melt in her mouth, the sinfully rich white chocolate mousse.

It was almost eleven before she finished and asked for the table to be removed. When the servants had come and gone, she poured a small brandy, removed her robe and snuggled into bed, turning out the lights.

She lay still, feeling the thud of her heart against her breast, waiting, letting the dark anticipation of the night wash around her, immersed in the cool, impersonal caress of fine cotton sheets on her freshly bathed, freshly scented body.

It was past midnight when he came. She was awake, ears tuned to the silence, waiting for the sound of an opening door. She heard him move across the room, a soft rustle as something fell to the floor and then he was beside her.

He turned her body to his and entered her immediately in one swift, numbing thrust, uncaring whether she was awake or asleep.

There was no pain. Her body, already slick with anticipation, stretched to take him, gloried in the sudden, swamping sensation of penetration.

He moved fast and furiously, as she had known he would, driving into her full length, burying his shaft deep inside her, almost touching the mouth of her womb before withdrawing completely only to thrust again. His hands were beneath her buttocks, opening her to him, forcing her to take him. His rage, his lust, powerful, indissoluble, fired her, drenched her.

She wanted to move, thrust her hips against his, share the frenzy that drove him into her, but he was holding her lower body immobile, almost crushing her beneath his weight, pounding into her with ravaging intensity. The mouth of her vagina grew tender as he pulled back then thrust again, a tenderness that gradually swelled to a burning, molten ache.

It seemed that he would never stop, never come, simply continue the endless, hollowing thrusts that were hurling her to orgasm, driving the breath from her body and searing her senses. She lost all sense of time as the world narrowed to the driving surge of his body against hers.

Her groin was heavy, achingly congested, lower lips slick and swollen. She felt the first flutterings deep in the pit of her belly, the faint, convulsive tremors of her inner muscles as they readied for climax. He stopped then, buried deep inside her.

She could feel the hot rasp of his breath against her cheek, the silky roughness of his chest against her breasts.

Some strange tenderness led her to touch a hand to his face.

With startling fierceness he surged out of her and

forced her face down on the bed, catching both her hands in one of his and forcing them above her head. She felt his penis enter her from behind then withdraw to push against her anus.

He moved himself between the two entrances to her body, fast and furious, imprinting his length on the supple, delicate skin that began to burn in response, confining his thrusts to that tender strip of flesh. Her vagina began to throb and there was an echoing pulse deep in her bowels as her muscles began to clench and spasm.

She moaned aloud as the head of his penis grazed her anus, a dark coil of excitement swirling through her. He was hot and hard, slickly lubricated by the musk of her body, and when he pushed inside the taut channel of her rectum she lay still, poised between pleasure and pain.

He stopped with the head of his shaft inside her. Dimly she realised he was waiting, forcing her to make the choice. She knew he would hurt her, was too thick, far too thick for the tight forbidden tunnel, but the searing, raw wildness claimed her and she thrust her buttocks against him, urging him further.

Silvery shocks of sensation flowed through her as he thrust, a piercing pleasure-pain that flowed seamlessly in an unbroken wave. Now he moved slowly, sliding in and out of her with a controlled deliberation so unlike his initial frenzy that she felt slightly dazed.

Slowly as he moved, his weight rocked her lower body against the cool white sheets, rubbing her clitoris against the soft cotton, a gentle, abrading friction that enhanced the aching fullness of his penetration. She felt the arcing, tingling excitement envelop her, the shivering delirium of impending climax.

Again he withdrew and she gave a small cry at the

loss, the sudden, aching emptiness of her body almost intolerable. And then she felt his mouth move down her spine, hot and fierce, tonguing her, moving lower, plunging between the soft globes of her buttocks, flicking against her tender anus. His hands were almost rough as he opened her to him, as his mouth repeated the path his penis had seared onto her skin, darting furiously between the two entrances to her body.

He kept her body simmering, never ceasing the relentless stimulation, never allowing the pleasure to peak, changing rhythm when he felt the tell-tale trembling of her thighs, stopping whenever her hips began to rock, alternating savagery with gentleness, using every cruel, carnal tender torture that existed to torment them both.

Her body flowed with his, swelling, rising, peaking, then slowing, trapped in the encompassing, flooding, overwhelming demands of his body that enveloped hers. She could feel the anger that still seized him as he moved her body, arranging her on her side, her back, her front, the furious, convoluted rage that drove him to lose himself in the writhing, complicit battle of their bodies, denying them both the cleansing purge of orgasm.

He was insatiable, ravenous, even as she felt his hot fury diminish into a more calculated, coolly contained provocation. He turned her onto her back and loomed over her, guiding his penis to her mouth, allowing her the first taste of himself between her lips, trembling and avid.

She wanted to suck him deep and hard, feel the hard, iron, tensile rippling silk of his organ inside her mouth, learn him with her tongue, her teeth, her lips, imprint his rampant, raging hardness on the soft, plush cavern of her mouth, but he was swiftly

227

impatient, withdrawing to trace the curve of her lips, the arc of her eyebrows.

He used the hot, pulsing head of his shaft like a second mouth, kissing her with the tip of his penis, brushing her eyelashes, the peaks of her cheek-bones, the lines of her jaw with the implacable, burning wand of his flesh.

The pearling moisture at the head of his shaft dewed her lips, moved to the shell of her ear, traced the column of her throat. It was as if he was learning her with his rod, imprinting himself on every inch of her skin. He surged against her breasts, anointed her nipples with his milky fluid, traced her ribcage, pushed against her naval as if he would come into her there, slipped through the curls between her thighs and moved against the swollen folds of her mound.

He rocked against her, blunt, hard strokes that began at the mouth of her vagina, parted the folds of her labia and thrust against her clitoris, drenching himself in the musk of her body. She was burningly distended, raw and achingly engorged, wild for the final, filling thrust inside her when he moved down her body, smoothing himself along the inside of her thighs, thrusting against the sensitive skin behind her knees, following the curve of her calves to her feet.

She felt his mouth fasten hungrily on her foot, sucking one toe into his mouth, laving and lapping with the same assiduous attention another lover might have lavished on her clitoris, rimming the nail with his teeth, nipping at her gently, then pulling her deep into his mouth.

A rosy flesh suffused her groin, her breasts, as if he had confused the pleasure centres of her body, as if the rhythmic wash of his tongue against her toes was actually stimulating her clitoris, her nipples.

Suddenly her toes were as achingly sensitive as her clitoris, as erogenously responsive as her nipples, the pleasure multiplied tenfold as he moved slowly from one to the next. His hands were massaging the sensitive soles of her feet, the high arches, clasping and unclasping in the relentless pressure that her swollen breasts craved.

The gentle tugging of his mouth, the insistent pressure, tightened nipples already hard, engorged her labia already tumid and swollen, stiffened the pulsing stem of her clitoris with a phantom stimulation as arousing, no, more arousing than touch itself.

She throbbed to the rhythm of his mouth, her body singing to the carnal music of his tongue and teeth. Senses swimming, her last coherent thought was that she could never have endured this sensual onslaught had her body not learned from other lovers. She would have drowned in climax, burned, been consumed in the conflagration of her senses . . . and then all thought fled.

His hands were on her waist, raising her, lifting her, positioning her at the tip of his shaft, holding her just above the hard column of his penis. She responded immediately, sinking to her knees, clasping the hard, muscled length of his hips and thighs with her calves, seeking the hot organ already impressed on her body, wet and rippling with desire.

He held her above him for a long moment, then pressed her down, impaling her on his shaft.

He penetrated her more deeply, more utterly than she had ever known, as if he was not only filling her vagina but her entire body. When he moved, she could feel him in her belly, her breasts, sculpting and hollowing her body with his iron length.

Instinctively she tried to ride him, to find the pace, fuse the motion of his body to hers, but he was too powerful, the thrust of his hips too strong. It was he who moved her with his hands, his hips, moved her back and forth, from side to side. And with each thrust her swollen clitoris brushed against the wiry tangle of his pubic hair, an abrasive friction that electrified every nerve.

With each thrust she felt as if the breath was being driven from her body. The air seemed hot and thick and dense as velvet, and their bodies were slippery and slick with sweat. It was an insatiable, carnal madness, voracious and unending.

When the first faint contractions of her orgasm began, the tiny rippling of inner muscles readying to wring the life-giving fluid from his body, he moved swiftly, plucking her from him and turning her to his mouth, so that she lay full-length across his body, her lips close to his massive rod.

She swallowed hard as she inhaled his scent, deep and male and pungent, felt his tongue plunging inside her. She wanted to nuzzle his hair, learn him, lick him, taste the sweet, tender skin of his testicles, imprint herself on his sex as he had imprinted himself on hers, but the thrust of his tongue inside her, slipping from her entrance to coil around her clitoris with slick ease, goaded her climax, urged it, increased the intensity of her internal spasms.

She closed her lips around the head of his penis and found the tiny slit with her tongue just as his tongue thrummed against the achingly electrifyingly sensitive spot inside her.

And in that moment she ceased to exist. There was red mist, a throbbing heartbeat pulse as the cleansing, annihilating storm of her orgasm exploded, tossing her, lifting her, racking her body with spasm after spasm.

She soared as she moaned against his penis, writhed and died against his mouth as the vortex claimed her, sucking her deep into the blinding maelstrom of a thousand suns exploding inside her. Her body convulsed, riven and splintered, and she floated above it all, enveloped in the red mist.

Time slowed to the ebbing waves of her climax, became nothing more than the tides of her body as it slowly, inevitably calmed, as the white heat faded to a warm, suffusing glow.

Dazed, almost insensible with pleasure, she lay boneless, hardly breathing, hardly noticing as he unfused their bodies, calmed and becalmed in languorous erotic bliss.

Something recalled her. A subtle shift in the shaft of moonlight playing across the room as he moved, perhaps. The faint rustle of discarded silk reclaimed.

She opened her eyes and for a moment saw him highlighted in the thin sliver of light issuing from the window, the cold moon playing against his pale skin, the darkness of his body hair. He was so male, so beautiful, so animal, that had he suddenly lengthened, shifted, changed, transmuted himself to the vulpine form of a lean and elegant wolf, canines dripping, to the menacing, enveloping, enfolding wings of a bat she would not have been at all surprised.

He was drawing the folds of a black silk robe around him as she spoke.

'Well met or ill met by moonlight, Alexei?' she asked, and felt him stiffen, even across the room. The words had come from nowhere, misquoting and quoting Oberon to Titania, but there was nothing more she could say, nothing that more perfectly expressed the dreamlike, unreality of the moment. Perhaps she was developing a sense of irony, after all.

He was still, an unnatural stillness, and she realised it was the first time she had said his name in his presence. And it was that that had shocked him.

'And why always in the dark, without words?'

Her voice was a clarion, clear and pure. The question could not, would not, have been asked had she not found the haven of utter release that allows such questions as idle conversation.

'It was the film, perhaps,' she said aloud, testing the fibres of her understanding with an inquisitive, detached curiosity. 'You became the demon lover to understand him, to feel him?'

He had risen from the bed believing her asleep; the sound of her voice, hearing his name on her lips, shocked him to the depths of his soul.

'Very Stanislavsky,' she mocked, the cool, arrogant tone of her voice issuing from some part of her she had never known.

He bent to retrieve the black silk robe that had slipped between his fingers to the floor. And when he spoke, his voice was the harsh, metallic whipcrack she had learned to loathe.

'I have given you something you never knew you wanted, Gemma de la Mare,' he said quietly.

He turned, drawing his robe around him, and the playful shaft of moonlight illuminated his body for an instant, played on his penis, hard and jutting, unspent.

'Take it for the gift it is.'

Their faces were shrouded by the dark, and perhaps neither knew themselves. If Gemma had seen her eyes, cold and colder, navy deadened to the blank lapis lazuli stare of hard stone, she would not have recognised herself. If she had seen Racine's eyes, the pale, grey, lifeless colour of old stones under running water now silvered with some indefinable emotion, she would not have recognised him.

'But why?' she said at last.

He was silent for so long that she began to wonder if he would reply. Finally he spoke.

'Once I offered you a voyage to the heart of the vampire,' he said slowly. 'I told you then you had no choice. And it has nothing, or very little, to do with the film. When life imitates art, the results are inevitable, predictable, disappointing. Yet the end is always the beginning, like Hesiod's snake.'

He spoke with a slow, cold contempt. So, she thought, understanding only the sound of his voice, the anger hadn't left him yet.

Cocooned in her rosy afterglow, Gemma found herself rising from the bed and walking towards him. And then she did something she would never have dreamed of doing.

She slipped her arms around his shoulders and kissed him on the mouth.

He gave a stifled sound that might have been a groan, might have been a curse. Parting his robe, he guided himself between her legs. She stood motionless as he filled her, stood motionless as she felt him throb within her.

And then, as she had expected, he left.

Chapter Eleven

*T*wo weeks later, filming at the chateau was almost finished. The actor playing Vlad, Count Dracula, had abandoned his Marxist principles and summoned a magnificent and terrifying rage, inspired, perhaps, by Racine himself; Renfield, while still actually refusing to eat spiders, had let a few choice, furry specimens crawl across his lips, a compromise that seemed to satisfy Racine; Mina's rash had cleared up.

The old keep had been captured at its listing, eerie best, awash in the cold grey winter light that was now changing and warming in the dawn of an early spring. A few boldly venturesome pale green buds were forming on the stark branches of the trees overhanging the tombstones, and now sleepy birdsong heralded the morning. Slowly the earth was awakening and stirring into green life, a change Alexei Racine seemed to view with cold disdain.

He was aloof, wrapped in an ice-cold, impenetrable distance that was somehow more terrifying than his rage. He was courteous to the crew, which alarmed them; considerate with the actors, which frightened them; and he treated Gemma with a freezing civility that might, under other circumstances, have completely mystified her.

Always remote, he was not utterly unreachable. His androgynous acolytes had mysteriously closed ranks and hovered nervously, protectively around him, like a black leather shield, so that he was never alone. Gradually Gemma began to perceive how perversely isolating that bodyguard was.

In fact, Racine was furious, furious with himself, an all consuming fury that knew no bounds. He, and he alone, had ruined the painstakingly careful seduction he had planned and contrived; he and he alone had allowed the ending to take him by surprise.

She had spoken his name.

Kissed his mouth.

Made him come into her body.

Before he was ready.

He had been unprepared for the sound of his name on her lips, unprepared for the warm, weakening touch of her mouth on his, shocked at the unexpected, unanticipated explosion of his orgasm as he came inside her.

It was astonishing.

Unplanned.

Unscripted.

It rent the careful fabric of the seduction he had so patiently, so painstakingly been weaving since the night he had first seen her, so long ago, as she had wandered around the outskirts of the Chateau Marais.

It defied the labyrinthine, Machiavellian complexity which he had plotted and contrived so meticulously, so dextrously.

Very Stanislavsky, she had mocked, in a voice that could have been his.

A voice that was cool, mocking, ironic, betrayed no emotion, no feeling.

A voice that was a void.

A voice that could have been his.

She had learned too quickly, too well.

He wasn't sure, but he rather thought that he hated her for it.

Gemma, aware of undercurrents too deep to be fathomed, continued to work with the automatic, professional precision of a robot created specifically for the task, checking and re-checking, harassing the crew and technicians, prompting, chivvying, praising and goading, ensuring that every necessary shot had been taken, every detail captured before they broke the set.

And all the while, every waking moment, every conscious thought was devoted to untangling the bewildering, mystifying tangle of Racine's motives and her own emotions.

'I have given you something you never knew you wanted.'

The words he had spoken in that harshly beautiful voice she detested had stayed with her, became a strange code that etched her soul. He had driven her – no, she corrected herself with a smile – directed her through this strange erotic odyssey, piloted this sensual voyage she would never have charted on her own.

She felt free now, free to decide, free to assess, to evaluate, and she found her thoughts lingering on Gabrielle and Leo, on Jay Stone, flowing back to Nicholas Frere, back further still to Pascaline and Jean-Paul, but returning always, inevitably, to Alexei Racine.

Because of him she had discovered a side of herself she might not have known. It wasn't as though she had changed: she had not. She had simply learned another Gemma, a sensual, sexual, uninhibited and erotically daring Gemma who could immerse herself in the myriad pleasures of the flesh while still preserving the necessary, ingrained, rigid self-control that allowed her to work, and work well, in the neurotically frenzied and male-dominated world of film.

She considered the problem dispassionately.

It was unlikely she would know what had prompted Racine to script this bizarre and improbable scenario; perhaps he didn't even know himself.

And yet it was not simply an affair of the flesh, as Gabrielle had pointed out, an affair such as Gabrielle and Leo shared.

Idly she imagined herself as Gabrielle, physically enthralled but intellectually removed, an emotional isolation that allowed her to manipulate her own obsession and Leo's twisted sensuality to such a strange yet satisfactory conclusion, and found it rather appealing.

She thought of Jean-Paul and Pascaline, sharing together the erotic, wayward ways of the flesh that had led them to that moment beside the Greek kouros in the Chateau Marais, where Pascaline had climaxed with a stranger at her breasts and her husband at her back, and found it even more appealing.

Without the abrasive goad of Alexei Racine, she would never have begun the affair with Nicholas Frere, never have experienced his light-hearted, erotic artistry, the playful carnival of his love-making. She tried to picture herself and Nicholas together with another woman, another man, and failed.

Jay, perhaps: yes, Jay, certainly; but there was something too fundamentally solid about Jay, something too . . . respectable? Too . . . American? He could be drawn into a situation, respond if the scene was set for him, but he would never deliberately experiment for the sake of it, never consciously decide to play with carnal matches knowing he might be burned.

And that, too, in its own way, was appealing.

Yet nothing compared with the dark, indefinable allure of Racine. He had, indeed, given her something she had not known she wanted. With a sudden shock of suprise she remembered how she had felt the morning after he had taken her in the tomb, the morning when, believing it was all a dream, she had giggled to herself about the ultimate zipless fuck.

The ultimate female fantasy: no words, no guilt, no smothering, cloying emotion, simply fabulous, fabulous, sex.

So why, then, had she challenged him, taunted him with Stanislavsky, mocked him with Shakespeare, sought to draw into the speaking daylight something that belonged to the wordless dark?

Like some silly Psyche she had been unable, at the last moment, to resist lighting the candle that illuminated the sleeping god.

She had done it with a word.

A kiss.

Still dispassionate, she considered the future. Now that he controlled Horror, Inc., an association with Racine could nothing but further her career.

She had always been too innately proud, too aware of her own self-worth to succumb to the temptation of sleeping her way to the top; she was too honest not to admit that the affair, if it could be called an affair, offered some rather unique opportunities.

And the man himself intrigued her. Arrogant, abrasive, enigmatic, perhaps even unknowable, she had only to watch the rushes to recognise the dark genius that was Alexei Racine, the twisted brilliance that had conjured a Dracula as compelling as any Hamlet, any Lear.

And she thought long and hard about Hesiod's snake, coiled around the world, devouring its own tail.

And the night before they were due to leave Brittany she went to the tomb.

She waited until midnight. It was cold, far too cold to walk so far clad in nothing but white silk, but she scarcely felt the chill air that iced her skin.

And he was there before her, as she had known he would be.

A match flared.

Racine had been waiting for her. The fury that had claimed him at his own weakness had hardened, added another layer to the icy shell that enclosed him. Since she needed words, she would have them. Words that he had never meant to say, words that he would never have said had she not come to the tomb at midnight.

She saw the red glow of the tip of a cigarette.

He held the match between his fingers, letting the yellow, sulphuric light illuminate his features.

She looked at his eyes, deep-set, dark and corrupt, the sharp cheek-bones, the aquiline nose, the predatory curve of his mouth, lower lip full and sensual, upper lip thin and cruel.

She leaned closer and blew out the match.

NO LADY
Saskia Hope

30-year-old Kate dumps her boyfriend, walks out of her job and sets off in search of sexual adventure. Set against the rugged terrain of the Pyrenees, the love-making is as rough as the landscape.

ISBN 0 352 32857 6

WEB OF DESIRE
Sophie Danson

High-flying executive Marcie is gradually drawn away from the normality of her married life. Strange messages begin to appear on her computer, summoning her to sinister and fetishistic sexual liaisons.

ISBN 0 352 32856 8

BLUE HOTEL
Cherri Pickford

Hotelier Ramon can't understand why best-selling author Floy Pennington has come to stay at his quiet hotel. Her exhibitionist tendencies are driving him crazy, as are her increasingly wanton encounters with the hotel's other guests.

ISBN 0 352 32858 4

CASSANDRA'S CONFLICT
Fredrica Alleyn

Behind the respectable facade of a house in present-day Hampstead lies a world of decadent indulgence and darkly bizarre eroticism. A sternly attractive Baron and his beautiful but cruel wife are playing games with the young Cassandra.

ISBN 0 352 32859 2

THE CAPTIVE FLESH
Cleo Cordell

Marietta and Claudine, French aristocrats saved from pirates, learn their invitation to stay at the opulent Algerian mansion of their rescuer, Kasim, requires something in return; their complete surrender to the ecstasy of pleasure in pain.

ISBN 0 352 32872 X

PLEASURE HUNT
Sophie Danson

Sexual adventurer Olympia Deschamps is determined to become a member of the Légion D'Amour – the most exclusive society of French libertines.

ISBN 0 352 32880 0

BLACK ORCHID
Roxanne Carr

The Black Orchid is a women's health club which provides a specialised service for its high-powered clients; women who don't have the time to spend building complex relationships, but who enjoy the pleasures of the flesh.

ISBN 0 352 32888 6

ODALISQUE
Fleur Reynolds

A tale of family intrigue and depravity set against the glittering backdrop of the designer set. This facade of respectability conceals a reality of bitter rivalry and unnatural love.

ISBN 0 352 32887 8

OUTLAW LOVER
Saskia Hope

Fee Cambridge lives in an upper level deluxe pleasuredome of technologically advanced comfort. Bored with her predictable husband and pampered lifestyle, Fee ventures into the wild side of town, finding an an outlaw who becomes her lover.

ISBN 0 352 32909 2

THE SENSES BEJEWELLED
Cleo Cordell

Willing captives Marietta and Claudine are settling into life at Kasim's harem. But 18th century Algeria can be a hostile place. When the women are kidnapped by Kasim's sworn enemy, they face indignities that will test the boundaries of erotic experience. This is the sequel to *The Captive Flesh*.

ISBN 0 352 32904 1

GEMINI HEAT
Portia Da Costa

As the metropolis sizzles in freak early summer temperatures, twin sisters Deana and Delia find themselves cooking up a heatwave of their own. Jackson de Guile, master of power dynamics and wealthy connoisseur of fine things, draws them both into a web of luxuriously decadent debauchery.

ISBN 0 352 32912 2

VIRTUOSO
Katrina Vincenzi

Mika and Serena, darlings of classical music's jet-set, inhabit a world of secluded passion. The reason? Since Mika's tragic accident which put a stop to his meteoric rise to fame as a solo violinist, he cannot face the world, and together they lead a decadent, reclusive existence.

ISBN 0 352 32907 6

MOON OF DESIRE
Sophie Danson

When Soraya Chilton is posted to the ancient and mysterious city of Ragzburg on a mission for the Foreign Office, strange things begin to happen to her. Wild, sexual urges overwhelm her at the coming of each full moon.

ISBN 0 352 32911 4

FIONA'S FATE
Fredrica Alleyn

When Fiona Sheldon is kidnapped by the infamous Trimarchi brothers, along with her friend Bethany, she finds herself acting in ways her husband Duncan would be shocked by. Alessandro Trimarchi makes full use of this opportunity to discover the true extent of Fiona's suppressed, but powerful, sexuality.

ISBN 0 352 32913 0

HANDMAIDEN OF PALMYRA
Fleur Reynolds

3rd century Palmyra: a lush oasis in the Syrian desert. The beautiful and fiercely independent Samoya takes her place in the temple of Antioch as an apprentice priestess. Decadent bachelor Prince Alif has other plans for her and sends his scheming sister to bring her to his Bacchanalian wedding feast.

ISBN 0 352 32919 X

OUTLAW FANTASY
Saskia Hope

On the outer reaches of the 21st century metropolis the Amazenes are on the prowl; fierce warrior women who have some unfinished business with Fee Cambridge's pirate lover. This is the sequel to *Outlaw Lover*.

ISBN 0 352 32920 3

THE SILKEN CAGE
Sophie Danson

When University lecturer Maria Treharne inherits her aunt's mansion in Cornwall, she finds herself the subject of strange and unexpected attention. Using the craft of goddess worship and sexual magnetism, Maria finds allies and foes in this savage and beautiful landscape.

ISBN 0 352 32928 9

RIVER OF SECRETS
Saskia Hope & Georgia Angelis

Intrepid female reporter Sydney Johnson takes over someone else's assignment up the Amazon river. Sydney soon realises this mission to find a lost Inca city has a hidden agenda. Everyone is behaving so strangely, so sexually, and the tropical humidity is reaching fever pitch.

ISBN 0 352 32925 4

VELVET CLAWS
Cleo Cordell

It's the 19th century; a time of exploration and discovery and young, spirited Gwendoline Farnshawe is determined not to be left behind in the parlour when the handsome and celebrated anthropologist, Jonathan Kimberton, is planning his latest expedition to Africa.

ISBN 0 352 32926 2

THE GIFT OF SHAME
Sarah Hope-Walker

Helen is a woman with extreme fantasies. When she meets Jeffrey – a cultured wealthy stranger – at a party, they soon become partners in obsession. Now nothing is impossible for her, no fantasy beyond his imagination or their mutual exploration.

ISBN 0 352 32935 1

SUMMER OF ENLIGHTENMENT
Cheryl Mildenhall

Karin's new-found freedom is getting her into all sorts of trouble. The enigmatic Nicolai has been showing interest in her since their chance meeting in a cafe. But he's the husband of a valued friend and is trying to embroil her in the sexual tension he thrives on.

ISBN 0 352 32937 8

A BOUQUET OF BLACK ORCHIDS
Roxanne Carr

The exclusive Black Orchid health spa has provided Maggie with a new social life and a new career, where giving and receiving pleasure of the most sophisticated nature takes top priority. But her loyalty to the club is being tested by the presence of Tourell; a powerful man who makes her an offer she finds difficult to refuse.

ISBN 0 352 32939 4

JULIET RISING
Cleo Cordell

At Madame Nicol's exclusive but strict 18th-century academy for young ladies, the bright and wilful Juliet is learning the art of courting the affections of young noblemen.

ISBN 0 352 32938 6

DEBORAH'S DISCOVERY
Fredrica Alleyn

Deborah Woods is trying to change her life. Having just ended her long-term relationship and handed in her notice at work, she is ready for a little adventure. Meeting American oil magnate John Pavin III throws her world into even more confusion as he invites her to stay at his luxurious renovated castle in Scotland. But what looked like being a romantic holiday soon turns into a test of sexual bravery.

ISBN 0 352 32945 9

THE TUTOR
Portia Da Costa

Like minded libertines reap the rewards of their desire in this story of the sexual initiation of a beautiful young man. Rosalind Howard takes a post as personal librarian to a husband and wife, both unashamed sensualists keen to engage her into their decadent scenarios.

ISBN 0 352 32946 7

THE HOUSE IN NEW ORLEANS
Fleur Reynolds

When she inherits her family home in the fashionable Garden district of New Orleans, Ottilie Duvier discovers it has been leased to the notorious Helmut von Straffen; a debauched German Count famous for his decadent Mardi Gras parties. Determined to oust him from the property, she soon realises that not all dangerous animals live in the swamp!

ISBN 0 352 32951 3

ELENA'S CONQUEST
Lisette Allen

It's summer – 1070AD – and the gentle Elena is gathering herbs in the garden of the convent where she leads a peaceful, but uneventful, life. When Norman soldiers besiege the convent, they take Elena captive and present her to the dark and masterful Lord Aimery to satisfy his savage desire for Saxon women.

ISBN 0 352 32950 5

CASSANDRA'S CHATEAU
Fredrica Alleyn

Cassandra has been living with the dominant and perverse Baron von Ritter for eighteen months when their already bizarre relationship takes an unexpected turn. The arrival of a naive female visitor at the chateau provides the Baron with a new opportunity to indulge his fancy for playing darkly erotic games with strangers.

ISBN 0 352 32955 6

WICKED WORK
Pamela Kyle

At twenty-eight, Suzie Carlton is at the height of her journalistic career. She has status, money and power. What she doesn't have is a masterful partner who will allow her to realise the true extent of her fantasies. How will she reconcile the demands of her job with her sexual needs?

ISBN 0 352 32958 0

To be published in December . . .

DREAM LOVER
Katrina Vincenzi

Icily controlled Gemma is a dedicated film producer, immersed in her latest production – a darkly Gothic vampire movie. But after a visit to Brittany, where she encounters a mystery lover, a disquieting feeling continues to haunt her. Compelled to discover the identity of the man who ravished her, she becomes entangled in a mystifying erotic odyssey.

ISBN 0 352 32956 4

PATH OF THE TIGER
Cleo Cordell

India, in the early days of the Raj. Amy Spencer is looking for an excuse to rebel against the stuffy mores of the British army wives. Luckily, a new friend introduces her to places where other women dare not venture – where Tantric mysteries and the Kama Sutra come alive. Soon she becomes besotted by Ravinder, the exquisitely handsome son of the Maharaja, and finds the pathway to absolute pleasure.

ISBN 0 352 32959 9

WE NEED YOUR HELP . . .
to plan the future of women's erotic fiction –

– and no stamp required!

Yours are the only opinions that matter.

Black Lace is the first series of books devoted to erotic fiction by women for women.

We intend to keep providing the best-written, sexiest books you can buy. And we'd appreciate your help and valued opinion of the books so far. Tell us what you want to read.

THE BLACK LACE QUESTIONNAIRE

SECTION ONE: ABOUT YOU

1.1 Sex (*we presume you are female, but so as not to discriminate*)
Are you?
Male ☐
Female ☐

1.2 Age
under 21 ☐   21–30 ☐
31–40 ☐   41–50 ☐
51–60 ☐   over 60 ☐

1.3 At what age did you leave full-time education?
still in education ☐   16 or younger ☐
17–19 ☐   20 or older ☐

1.4 Occupation _____

1.5 Annual household income
    under £10,000 ☐ £10–£20,000 ☐
    £20–£30,000 ☐ £30–£40,000 ☐
    over £40,000 ☐

1.6 We are perfectly happy for you to remain anonymous;
    but if you would like to receive information on other
    publications available, please insert your name and
    address

    _____

    _____

    _____

    _____

SECTION TWO: ABOUT BUYING BLACK LACE BOOKS

2.1 How did you acquire this copy of *Dream Lover*?
    I bought it myself ☐ My partner bought it ☐
    I borrowed/found it ☐

2.2 How did you find out about Black Lace books?
    I saw them in a shop ☐
    I saw them advertised in a magazine ☐
    I saw the London Underground posters ☐
    I read about them in _____
    Other _____

2.3 Please tick the following statements you agree with:
    I would be less embarrassed about buying Black
    Lace books if the cover pictures were less explicit ☐
    I think that in general the pictures on Black
    Lace books are about right ☐
    I think Black Lace cover pictures should be as
    explicit as possible ☐

2.4 Would you read a Black Lace book in a public place – on
    a train for instance?
    Yes ☐ No ☐

SECTION THREE: ABOUT THIS BLACK LACE BOOK

3.1 Do you think the sex content in this book is:
   Too much ☐ About right ☐
   Not enough ☐

3.2 Do you think the writing style in this book is:
   Too unreal/escapist ☐ About right ☐
   Too down to earth ☐

3.3 Do you think the story in this book is:
   Too complicated ☐ About right ☐
   Too boring/simple ☐

3.4 Do you think the cover of this book is:
   Too explicit ☐ About right ☐
   Not explicit enough ☐

Here's a space for any other comments:

SECTION FOUR: ABOUT OTHER BLACK LACE BOOKS

4.1 How many Black Lace books have you read? ☐

4.2 If more than one, which one did you prefer?

4.3 Why?

SECTION FIVE: ABOUT YOUR IDEAL EROTIC NOVEL

We want to publish the books you want to read – so this is your chance to tell us exactly what your ideal erotic novel would be like.

5.1 Using a scale of 1 to 5 (1 = no interest at all, 5 = your ideal), please rate the following possible settings for an erotic novel:

Medieval/barbarian/sword 'n' sorcery ☐
Renaissance/Elizabethan/Restoration ☐
Victorian/Edwardian ☐
1920s & 1930s – the Jazz Age ☐
Present day ☐
Future/Science Fiction ☐

5.2 Using the same scale of 1 to 5, please rate the following themes you may find in an erotic novel:

Submissive male/dominant female ☐
Submissive female/dominant male ☐
Lesbianism ☐
Bondage/fetishism ☐
Romantic love ☐
Experimental sex e.g. anal/watersports/sex toys ☐
Gay male sex ☐
Group sex ☐

Using the same scale of 1 to 5, please rate the following styles in which an erotic novel could be written:

Realistic, down to earth, set in real life ☐
Escapist fantasy, but just about believable ☐
Completely unreal, impressionistic, dreamlike ☐

5.3 Would you prefer your ideal erotic novel to be written from the viewpoint of the main male characters or the main female characters?

Male ☐ Female ☐
Both ☐

5.4 What would your ideal Black Lace heroine be like? Tick as many as you like:

Dominant ☐   Glamorous ☐
Extroverted ☐   Contemporary ☐
Independent ☐   Bisexual ☐
Adventurous ☐   Naive ☐
Intellectual ☐   Introverted ☐
Professional ☐   Kinky ☐
Submissive ☐   Anything else? ☐
Ordinary ☐   _____

5.5 What would your ideal male lead character be like? Again, tick as many as you like:

Rugged ☐
Athletic ☐   Caring ☐
Sophisticated ☐   Cruel ☐
Retiring ☐   Debonair ☐
Outdoor-type ☐   Naive ☐
Executive-type ☐   Intellectual ☐
Ordinary ☐   Professional ☐
Kinky ☐   Romantic ☐
Hunky ☐
Sexually dominant ☐   Anything else? ☐
Sexually submissive ☐   _____

5.6 Is there one particular setting or subject matter that your ideal erotic novel would contain?

_____

SECTION SIX: LAST WORDS

6.1 What do you like best about Black Lace books?

_____

6.2 What do you most dislike about Black Lace books?

_____

6.3 In what way, if any, would you like to change Black Lace covers?

_____

6.4 Here's a space for any other comments:

_____
_____
_____
_____

_____

Thank you for completing this questionnaire. Now tear it out of the book – carefully! – put it in an envelope and send it to:

Black Lace
FREEPOST
London
W10 5BR

No stamp is required if you are resident in the U.K.